Play

LUKE PALMER

First published in 2023
by Firefly Press
25 Gabalfa Road, Llandaff North, Cardiff, CF14 2JJ
www.fireflypress.co.uk

A CIP catalogue record of this book is available from
the British Library.

ISBN 978-1-915444-31-8

This book has been published with the support of
the Welsh Books Council.

Typeset by Elaine Sharples

Printed and bound by
CPI Group (UK) Ltd, Croydon, Surrey, CR0 4YY

For A, E and I
O U Everything

Play

LUKE PALMER

Firefly

Everyone's setting their socks on fire.

We're up on the school playing fields, the moon a hard gash in a darkening sky, and everywhere little orange flares are glowing around people's feet. From where I'm lying they look like stars, or fireworks. Puffs of light coloured by laughter.

Sometimes the laughter tightens into a scream, or opens to a shout, or floats off into the night.

The grass under my palms has been warm all summer. I can hear it growing between my fingers.

Orange pulses register on the inside of my eyelids. There's a smell of deodorant and burning. And green, of course. You can always smell the green on nights like this, thick and sweet. And the laughter has a smell too – a kind of welcoming, warm smell, like dinner on the table when you get home. But maybe not so wet.

I smile. The lights inside my eyelids are dancing.

I can hear Mark's voice, or I remember hearing Mark's voice. He's probably gone by now, called away to some more important something, his phone pulling on him and taking his wares elsewhere. I laugh at that one. Wares elsewhere.

I like words like that. Words that play together. My favourite one is the difference between 'nowhere' and 'now here'. That little gap. Amazing what changes when you add some space. Some air. Such a small difference, but it makes all the difference.

I worry about Mark, though. Wonder if a little gap will open inside him, let in the air and light. Before it's too late.

I worry for Luc, too. But I worry differently. I can hear him as well, his voice mapping his body, coming out of the night like a growl. It's funny how people's bodies can be a perfect map of themselves. Every ounce of Luc's body and how he carries it is seeping through that voice. It'll be the death of him, one day, all that tone and muscle.

And Matt, sitting behind me. It's his hand on my back, rubbing gently. It always is, poor Matt. But he's storing these things away for later. That's what he does.

The fires are flowering inside my eyes, and I feel somehow like all the moments that have ever happened in the whole world have led to this one. And how there's a balance in that, because all the moments that could ever happen now will come from here, with me lying on the school field, my friends around me, setting their socks on fire.

But then the moment passes. Into a new one.

Could you ever work out the different ways each moment could go? Draw a map that would tell you the paths to follow, the ones that might go somewhere?

Or which would lead to a cliff edge?

MARK

1

This was the game.

You build a den, or a camp, or whatever you want to call it. As high as you can build it. It's best if it has more than one level.

To make good dens, you need to really think about it before you start. It's hard finding old pallets in skips or taking them from building sites. And dragging them up to the heath on your own takes ages, so you want to make the best of what you've already got. Sometimes, doing a drawing helps.

And then, when you've planned it, you make it as well as you can, tie all the knots properly, pull the ropes and wait for the smell, like burning or skidding on carpet. It's the smell that tells you they're as tight as they can go. You get all the joins right so it will last for ages, or until you want to change it. And you put shelves in there with jars or pots full of all the stuff you've found and collected – the complete football sticker collection that will definitely be worth money one day, the little toy gun you nicked from a shop last year because Mum had said 'no, not this time' again and again, and the biscuit tin containing the complete wing of a seagull, still with bits of blood on it.

And that was it.

When you got bored of one den, you'd just take it down, piece by precious piece, and make another one. And it was fine to spend all summer after Year 7 finished, and the one before, playing that game because Mum was always at work, and Brendon was always Brendon so didn't care what you did, even though he was left in charge.

The best den I ever made was the 'L' den. It took two days to build, and I used all of the wooden pallets I'd collected and dragged deep into the copse, which is a little group of trees maybe the size of a centre circle on a football pitch. It's surrounded by heather, and then there's the rest of the heath with its sandy paths and gorse bushes all around. I chose the copse because the birch trees and the cedars were tight against each other, and to make the 'L' den I found a place between two trees that was the exact same width as one of the pallets. I tied one of the pallets into the gap, up on one end, then I put another pallet on top of the first, with sticks through the middle of them like my uncle said you do when building real walls in massive buildings.

It was called the 'L' den because, when I was finished, it looked like a capital 'L', like you'd draw on square paper in a Maths book. It had a tunnel you had to crawl through to get in, then the main space at the end that you could stand up in, like a tower. It was three pallets high on each side, and I made little seats all the way up the tower, all facing different ways so you could always see who was coming, from any direction.

But the main reason it was the best den was that I put the top roof on a slope, which meant there was a little window on one side. From that height you could see out of the copse and across the heath, all the way to where the trees had grown bent over in the wind. Some days, if it was early, a misty morning, or if it was summer and the heat was coming off the ground in waves, making everything wobbly, the tree's branches looked a bit like arms. Matt once said all the trees were like that because they bowed down to worship the devil at midnight on Halloween, and he'd seen it. He couldn't persuade anyone – not even Luc – to go out and see if that was true, though. Matt had drawn a picture of it in the last year of primary school that was actually pretty good. He didn't win the drawing prize though because his pictures were a bit weird.

I was sitting in the den, the summer before year eight started, the sun throwing thick bars of dusty light between the trees, the inside of the den warm and earthy, when I saw an armchair floating across the heath towards me.

It was upside down, its ripped lining flapping. Every now and then, the armchair would lurch into a little gorse bush, and have to back up, then it would go on again, floating slowly towards me like a clumsy ghost.

There was a steep slope on that side of the copse, so the chair had to go around. I watched through a gap in the pallet, expecting this strange floating chair to go on past me and trundle off to wherever it was going.

But it didn't trundle off.

It stopped.

The armchair flipped over then, revealing the boy who was under it. He squinted into the thicket of trees. The weirdest thing was that he stood with his hands on his hips. No one I knew stood like that. It was an old man way to stand. If you wanted to stand still, you put your hands in your pockets, or folded them on your chest. Putting your hands on your hips was almost as bad as putting them behind your back. But the boy stood there with his hands on his hips, peering at the trees. He bobbed his head around as he looked, and crouched down a bit sometimes, like a weird chicken.

He was trying to spot a way in.

I dropped right down to the bottom of the den and eased backwards into the darkest corner, pleased that I'd pulled the tarpaulin door shut behind me when I'd arrived that morning.

The boy had got the armchair past the trees and was moving it over the uneven ground, rocking it from side to side on its back legs like it was walking. The chair was pretty manky and you could see the bare material where most of the soft stuff had worn away. There were a couple of bits of tassley ribbon attached to the ends of the arms. The boy got the chair almost right in front of the den, then he stopped. Now I was certain that he was going to try to steal the den from me, and I grabbed my Swiss army knife from its special shelf, deciding that the saw blade looked scariest, and gently prised it open. He must be after my football cards, or some of my other valuable stuff, and he wasn't going to get them without a fight.

The boy rearranged the cushion on the armchair, dusted off a few pine needles, hit it a few times to get rid of some dust.

'Hello,' he said.

I didn't answer.

'My mum said we could use this chair if we wanted. So I brought it.'

We? Who was we?

'It's a bit shit, but it's still pretty comfy.' A pause. 'I've got some other stuff, too.' The boy pulled off his backpack, emptied it onto the chair. Out came a couple of candles, a box of matches, a screwed up old tarpaulin, a few scraggy ends of rope, and what looked like a collection of small, square saucepans that clattered on to the floor. 'I took Giles' old tranny stove. Mum doesn't know but she won't mind. And Giles doesn't need it any more. So...' He trailed off. 'Giles is my stepdad, not my real dad,' he added, quieter.

I sat as still as I could. He didn't know I was here. He'd leave in a minute.

The boy flopped down on the ground, next to the chair.

'It's OK if you don't let me in for a bit,' he said. 'I can sit out here.'

A pinecone dropped from the trees above and landed by the entrance of the den.

The boy looked up. 'You ever catch a squirrel?' he asked. 'I got one once. Hit it with a stone.'

'Squirrels are too fast to get like that. You need to set a snare,' I replied. Then, for some reason, I added, 'I had one but then I sold it.'

'My uncle had an air rifle he used to shoot them with. They kept coming into his garden and taking the bird seed.' The boy drew his bare arm across his nose, sniffed.

'My uncle's got an air rifle, too,' I said, even though I hadn't seen either of my uncles since I was tiny. 'It cost him loads because it's got a night scope on it. He says I can have it when he gets a new one at Christmas.' I eased the saw blade closed against my thigh.

The boy nodded, impressed. He tapped the arms of the chair, tugged at one of the tassly bits.

I leant over to the other side of the den and picked up the biscuit tin with the seagull's wing in. It was the best thing I'd found, and if someone else was going to come into my den I didn't want them seeing it straight away.

'Are you coming in then? Careful of the nails on the door. They're holding the tarp in place.'

The boy stood up, scuffed around on the floor in

front of him for a bit, then walked – almost sideways – towards the door.

I climbed up to the second level.

'Wow,' he said, coming through the door on hands and knees. 'Pretty good job.'

He ran his hands along the pallets, plucking at the ropes that tied them together, craning his neck around to look at the ceiling. He clocked the hazel spears I'd slotted into it – I'd been sharpening the ends of them that morning, so they looked really clean. He touched one, smelt his fingers.

'Can I come through to that bit?' the boy asked.

I moved right to the top, and the boy crawled further in and stood up in the tower. He was about the same size as me. He was wearing a red t-shirt, which wasn't ideal as you could see that from miles away. I preferred greens and blacks.

'Nice boots,' he said, pulling at the laces on one of them. 'Army surplus?'

'Yeah.' It wasn't a complete lie. They had been army surplus once, but they'd been my brother's before I'd been given them at the start of the summer. 'They do the best stuff.'

'I know.' The boy pulled himself up onto the second level seat, and we sat like that for about a minute. He kept looking around, touching the shelves, occasionally giving things a probing wobble, checking to see how I'd lashed the pallets to the trees.

'So how do you bring it down?' he asked.

'What?'

'How do you bring it down? That's the best bit, bringing them down.'

'I don't know. I haven't planned that bit yet.' I didn't know what else to say. I'd spent the last week getting this den perfect, adding the shelves and the footrests. I wasn't ready to turn it into another one yet. Everything was where it needed to be.

'Want me to do it for you?' the boy asked. He was eager, excited.

'Yeah, whatever.' I kicked my feet around a bit, trying to put them too close to his face, show him that he shouldn't do whatever it was he was talking about.

But he was already wiggling back down the tower and out of the den. 'Can I use this?' he called back, waving my penknife under my feet. I must have left it on the bottom shelf when I climbed up.

'Yeah, but don't break it. It's the really expensive model and I just had the saw sharpened. I've got a sharpener for it in the shed at home.'

But he was gone.

I stayed where I was, using my ears to keep track of him. The boy circled the den a few times, doing things to the ropes, sawing at things, and he kept running back to his bag.

After a few minutes, he crawled back in. Bunched in his hand were the ends of different bits of rope, their

10

other ends trailing behind him, tautening. Some of them were mine, some of them were new – must have been the ones he'd brought. I thought for a second of a set of demolition expert's fuses. He passed the bundle to me.

'You do it. It's your den.' He spoke in an odd, grand way. Like we were going to launch a ship or something. 'Just give them a pull.'

I gave a half-hearted tug. Nothing happened except a kind of popping sound.

'Wait a minute. Let me get up there with you.' The boy hauled himself up to where I was sitting and crouched down, the toes of his boot just on the edge of my seat, his hands braced against the walls. 'Go!' he shouted.

I tugged again, harder this time, and with a dull kind of ping and a horrible lurch that shot through my stomach, the tower swayed. I put my arm out instinctively, tried to grab the pallet next to me, but it was tipping, tipping out and away. Next to me, the boy was laughing like a mad animal, using his feet to push at the pallet my seat was attached to. Everything was slipping backwards and I was swinging my legs out to balance myself when I felt a sharp crack on top of my head – the roof pallet, robbed of its walls, had fallen in. With a snap, the little periscope window disappeared. The boy gave a half-moan-half-guffaw noise and I saw him put a hand to his own head as the pallet slid over his scalp. It fell forward, onto my knee, and then I got an eyeful of sky for a second as the pallet I was sitting on finally toppled, me flailing helplessly on top of it.

The fall seemed to last for ages. Inside the collapsing tower, I heard the boy cry out.

Then, with a thud that rattled my whole body, my back met something solid – the pallet over the entrance. For the briefest of moments it held me, then a creak and squeal and a skewed tumble, wood screeching against wood, and I rolled over my own back and found myself lying face down in pine needles, my feet on the seat of the boy's chair, as the last of the 'L' den came down with a series of tinny clacks and loud thunks.

I could taste something like blood in my mouth, and my armpits were cold and itchy. My forehead tingled where the pallet had hit it, and for a few seconds I wasn't sure which way was up or down. I slowly got up onto all fours.

The two pallets I'd tied in the perfect gap between the trees were the only things left upright. All around were pallets and bits of rope, splintered wood, smashed sticks. Up against the still-standing section, another pallet was leaning at a funny angle. There was a leg sticking out from under it, and a strange noise like some kind of animal.

It was the boy.

I scrambled over and pulled the wood off him, my heart beating in my ears. I still felt a bit woozy and staggered back as I picked up the last pallet. There he was, eyes closed, his arms clasped across his stomach, and shaking uncontrollably. I picked up his limp arms, searching for whatever splinter of wood or stick had clearly stabbed him.

But I couldn't see anything.

Then I got it. The boy was laughing. Helplessly, unstoppably laughing. Laughing so much he was unable to open his eyes.

I stepped backwards, caught the heel of my boot in the tangle of pallets and went over, sending another shotgun blast of sound around the thicket.

Then I started laughing, too. What with the giddiness, the slowly subsiding wave of nausea, the tingling feeling not just on my forehead, but down my back, along one of my arms where, looking between blinked-away tears, I must have scraped it along a rough edge or the head of a nail because it was bleeding gently in three or four places, my whole body felt like it was vibrating. My heart was pounding in my chest, right down to the bottom of my feet.

And the whole thing was hilarious.

'I'm Johnny, by the way,' the boy said when he'd stopped laughing enough to speak.

'I'm Mark,' I managed to splutter.

Then we both started laughing again and spent the rest of the morning comparing newly forming lumps and the places we were bleeding from.

I'd never felt so alive.

And that was the new game.

2

The new den is huge. There's a tower in one corner where we've nailed planks to a tree to make a 'Y' shape, with one of the pallets on top like a crow's nest. Johnny brought his stepdad's saw; said he wouldn't miss it. He brought a bunch of nails and a proper hammer too. I was making do with a bit of old pipe I'd found. It's quicker with a hammer.

It's quicker with two of us.

It's lucky because Johnny's only just moved here, into one of the big houses on the new estate. I think Johnny might be rich, but we don't talk about that kind of thing. And he doesn't act rich if you know what I mean. And anyway, he's going to the same school as I go to so I can show him around and he can join my friends tomorrow.

Matt and Luc have both been on holiday for the last three weeks. They keep sending pictures of the beaches they've been on. It's been ages since I was on a beach.

Luc sent a video two days ago of him tucking into a huge burger he ordered on their last night, and he said a girl on the other side of the restaurant was really into him for it but he couldn't do anything because she didn't speak English and he wasn't bothered anyway because he'd already hooked up with three girls on the campsite. I didn't believe him, but I couldn't say anything about it.

Matt sent a picture of a museum he went to that actually looked alright because there were loads of things you could do, including an exhibit where you got to build your own thing for lifting water up a hill, called an Archimedes Screw. Luc said Matt could do with a screw, then sent some aubergine emojis. Matt did a crying-laughing face.

They've both been allowed to take their Xboxes with them, and they had wi-fi (obviously), so they've been gaming with each other, although Luc's wi-fi kept dropping out. I've told them my wi-fi's been broken all summer and I was having to use 4G, but actually my brother's decided to move out and taken the Xbox with him, so I can't play it anymore. Mum's not said anything, but seems fine with me looking after myself while she works.

Johnny's got an Xbox, but he doesn't play it often. He says he's tried it a few times and he can't get into it.

'It's like I stop playing a game, and I feel like I've gone to sleep or something – everything in the real world moves too slowly and isn't exciting enough. And I get this feeling, right here,' he points to the middle of his chest, 'like a tight feeling, whenever I play them. I don't like it, so I stopped. Well, started playing them less, anyway.'

Johnny's taking the kettle off the tranny stove, which he said he googled and it's actually called a trangia. We're down to our last hot chocolate, but we decided to have a blow out as we're collapsing the last den today. We both like hot chocolate really strong and thick. I managed to get some money out of Mum this morning and bought as many biscuits as I could on the way here, so we've been munching on those. Johnny's mum wants him home by lunchtime so he can get ready for school tomorrow. I'm not sure my mum knows we're going back yet. She's not said anything.

We both climb up to the crow's nest and look out across the heath, sipping on our hot chocolates, wincing against the scald on our lips. There's a heat shimmer rising off the heather, but it's cool in the thicket. White butterflies are skittering over the long grass and a pair come chasing each other up the side of our tree, fly around our heads for a bit then go back out into the sunshine. There's a beautiful, sweet sap smell from the bulbs of orange goo where we've driven the big nails into the tree trunk. We've taken a couple of branches off, so we've got space to sit, and the fleshy ends of the stumps are gumming up with sap, too. When it dries, it turns white and dusty. Johnny's t-shirt's covered in hardened circles of it. It's the same shirt he's worn all this week, the red one I first saw him in. Bits of dirt and pine needle have stuck to the sappy patches, so he looks like a ladybird, covered in black spots.

'What's school like then?' Johnny asks.

'You know. Like any school, I guess,' I answer. 'It's alright, I suppose. Last year was OK, and we won't be year sevens this time.' A pause while we sip our drinks again. 'What was your last school like?'

'Fine. I didn't spend much time there, to be honest.'

'Do your family move around a lot then?'

'Not really. It's...' Johnny trails off. I've noticed him doing this sometimes. It looks like he's going to carry on talking, but he doesn't.

A magpie shoots across in front us, making its clacking, chirping, warning noise.

'I was taken out of lessons a lot,' Johnny continues. 'I find it quite hard to sit still, you know?'

'You're sitting still now though,' I say. Johnny's back is against the trunk, his leg dangling idly from our platform.

'It's different out here. Normally, I've got too much energy or something. Like I always feel I need to move around or pick things up. School is...' he fades out again.

'I'm the same sometimes.' I speak into the open space in front of us. 'They thought there was something wrong with me at primary. Had my mum in for talks and everything. She said I was just a certain kind of boy, and they should be better at dealing with it.'

'What kind of stuff did you do?'

'I don't know really.' The memories are a little fuzzy. 'I just did stuff and then someone told me I shouldn't have, you know?'

'Yeah, I know what you mean.' Johnny slings the last dregs of his hot chocolate into the view. 'I do the same. Like, if I see a plug in a wall – an electrical plug, I mean – I really want to unplug it. I don't want to turn off whatever's plugged in. I just get this odd feeling that I want to unplug it and plug it back in again, just for something to do.'

'Did you get detentions and stuff?'

'Yeah. A lot. And we had this place where you'd get sent if you were really naughty or got kicked out of lessons or something – the Hub, it was called. On the first day of my second term, my tutor told me I needed to go straight to the Hub at the start of school. That I didn't need to go to tutor time anymore. I tried to stay in tutor, some of my friends were in there, but every morning the head of year and the strict woman who was in charge of the Hub would come and get me.'

'We haven't got anything like that. Just detentions. Or you get sent to the head of year, Mrs Clarke. And there's Miss Amber, who's like her deputy. They're alright really. I've had a few detentions and stuff, for not doing homework. And they're a bit tight on uniform.'

'Sounds alright.' Johnny's picking at one of the sappy clumps on his t-shirt.

'Hey, tell you what,' I say. 'Why don't we go and look at it now?'

'Look at what?'

'The school – the field backs onto the heath. It's that way.' I point somewhere vaguely behind us.

'Maybe. I went around at the end of last year, did a tour and stuff, with my mum.'

'Yeah, they don't show you the important bits, though. Come on,' I say, swinging myself off the edge of the platform and dropping the six feet or so to the floor. 'Just a look. I'll point to where the year eight block is.'

'Alright. Then we'll come back and bring this down, yeah?'

Much as I enjoy bringing down the dens and the way we design each den with a weak spot so they collapse better, Johnny still gets more out of it than I do. 'Definitely. We've got loads of time, I lie. I'm putting off thinking about how I'll fill the day after Johnny goes home.

We push through the branches on the other side of the copse and make our way to one of the sandy paths that criss-cross the heath, follow it downhill through a stand of birch trees on the edge of my housing estate, then back over another hill before it levels off. A few more bends and forks in the path, and we're walking alongside a thick clump of brambles speckled with unripe berries. We stop at a place where their stretching, curling thorns are a bit lower.

'There it is,' I say, trying to sound impressive for some reason.

The bulky grey block of the school hall squats across the field. Clumped around it are smaller, lower blocks, with off-white panels on the sides and bright red doors. There's a green fence around the whole perimeter.

'Looks OK,' Johnny says. He sounds non-plussed. 'So which is your classroom?'

'Last year I was around the other side, in the year seven block. But this year all the year eight tutors are in that block there.' I point to the low set of buildings closest to us, squat bushes clumped around the outside. There are blinds across the windows, but you can just about make out the faded colours of some posters on the inside of the glass. 'I hope you're in mine.'

'Yeah,' Johnny says. His foot is starting to tap.

'Like I said, it's alright really. It's just ... y'know. School.'

'Yeah.'

We stand and look at it for a few minutes. I check the clock on my phone's cracked screen. This time tomorrow will be the start of break. Almost on cue, a group of teachers come out from one set of buildings, some of them still wearing their summer shorts and t-shirts. They're carrying bags over their shoulders and talking to each other in twos and threes. We can't make out what they're saying, but a few notes of laughter drift to us over the fields.

'Must be a training day or something. Look, there's Mrs Clarke.' I point to the blonde-haired lady, walking on her own, a few steps behind the main group. 'She's alright really. There was a rumour that some kids in her last year group got radicalised and made a bomb or something and were going to blow up the school. And this biology teacher was helping them. But he got fired. It was on the news, apparently. Anyway, that all happened the year before we started.'

The teachers file across the corner of the playground before they turn out of sight down the side of the technology block.

Johnny shuffles his feet. 'Yeah, it looks alright. Thanks.'

As we turn back, Johnny plucks a handful of blackberries from the bushes – bright red, but he eats them anyway. His mouth puckers up and he squints his eyes tight.

'Lovely.' He hands me a few.

It's like chewing a battery or something. Like when Brendon used to make me put the two points of those big 'D' batteries on my tongue. I make the same face as Johnny, and then we're both spitting sour, reddish-purple juice onto the sandy path, trying to scrape any traces of the berries from our tongue. Johnny picks a dandelion leaf, and eats that to try and get rid of the taste, then wretches all over again.

Then, five minutes later, we're passing another blackberry bush with its curtain of red globules, and we do it again, laughing all the way back to the copse.

We've already sawn halfway through the den's central pole, and when we've packed up all our stuff, buried the tin with the seagull's wing in it (which Johnny agreed was the best find), and prised half of the supporting planks off the big pine tree, we take the demolition rope up to the platform. We've decided to do this one standing – it's the highest we've fallen from – and we're going to pull the rope together.

I can feel the platform complaining underneath me as I gingerly climb up onto it. Johnny hands me the rope and wobbles up beside me, walking his hands up the trunk of the tree before standing. There must only be two nails holding the whole thing up.

Standing either side of the tree, I catch Johnny's eyes. They're gleaming playfully behind his shock of hair, which is probably just as full of sap as his t-shirt. For me, these are the best bits. The knowing you're about to do something completely stupid. That you might hurt yourself, or worse.

But also knowing that you're about to feel completely, utterly, powerlessly free.

We do the countdown together.

LUC

3

So this is the game.

Basically, you've got to get someone to look at the clock. It's as simple as that. But the problem is that the people who're playing *know* you're trying to get them to look at the clock, and they *know* they'll lose if they do. So you have to trick them.

We've played a game like this for ages, all through year eight. I guess we've played it since Johnny joined our school last year. He said you had to get someone to look at a circle you were making with your thumb and forefinger, but it had to be below the waist. That was easy. I'd start by feigning a punch to someone's stomach, so they'd bend over to get out of the way, then I'd grab their head and hold it downwards. I was the master. And when Matt and Mark started saying they had their eyes closed, I switched it up. I'd ask if I could borrow a pen in a lesson, and when they turned round to give it to me, there it was – the little circle, under the desk, winking at them. Or I'd slow down in the corridor, pretend like I was getting something out of my pocket and when they all turned around to look, POW – there it was again! Sometimes I'd walk around school with my shirt untucked, and whenever a teacher caught me, whoever I was with would always watch me tuck it in, just like the teacher did. And guess what came out when I tucked the last bit in? That's right. The little circle.

I've decided we need to raise the bar a bit this year, throw in a bit more challenge now we're in year nine. And I worked out that there's one thing you're guaranteed to find in every classroom in the school: a clock. So the game this year is to get someone else to look at the clock.

But that's not it. It gets better. If you get them to look at the clock, they've got to put their arms into whatever position the clock's hands are showing. So if it's midday, for example, that's both hands over their heads. If it's half six, both hands straight down. Not that we'd be in school then, obviously. I've worked out that the best time to get someone to look at the clock is quarter to three, or quarter past nine, especially if they're sitting in the middle of a row.

The boys don't know this is the new game yet. I'm going to tell them today.

They'll all come in late to tutor. Well, later than me anyway. Dad says being early is a good habit to get into, so here I am. He also has this thing about making sure you're well presented, and that first impressions count. It's not really a first impression today, I've been here two years now and I know everyone, but Mrs Clarke came in at the end of term and said we'd have a new tutor from the start of year nine and brought in this guy called Mr Cook or Crook or something, so that's who we've got from today. So best to make a good impression. Just like Dad says.

But the new teacher's not here yet either. I'm the first. And I've had a shower, done my hair and the uniform's all new and looking tidy, so he'll come in and see me sitting here and that'll be his first good impression of me. I had a protein shake for breakfast too, and a can of Comeup on the way to school, so I'm feeling energised and properly hydrated and sharp.

I look up at the clock. Twenty past eight. I put my arms out like wings, or like Iron Man or something, and I have a bit of a giggle to myself.

It's going to be a good game.

At twenty-five past, our new teacher comes through the door looking a bit flustered and annoyed. He's with Johnny, so it's not surprising. Johnny's spent the summer obsessing about how Mr Cook or Crook or whatever is a Geography teacher and how Johnny's always loved maps and how excited he is. Barely a day's gone by without Johnny bringing up our new tutor.

We've spent most of the summer messing around up on the heath, Mark, Johnny, Matt and me. We used to make these little den things up there, all through last autumn. It was funny to make them fall down. But it was kids' stuff and I got bored of that and didn't want to do it this year. It was Mark and Johnny's game, really. So, this year, we just made the one den at the start of the summer – a really big one where we could all sit around. I'd always sit in the armchair. It's crusty and pretty old, but it's better than the floor, or the car tyres we thought would make good stools.

I'd invite the girls up there – Alice and Amy and whoever else was around – but they didn't want to come up after the first few times. Can't say I blame them. Johnny's got an older sister so knows girls a bit more I guess, but he just wanted to show Amy the maps he'd been drawing of the heath – how he'd colour-coded them and all the different ways he'd done the contours and the heights and getting the trees in the right places. We'd taken a few tins of Comeup with us – my dad gets the best brand and lets me have however many I want – and we'd downed them before the girls arrived. Dad says it's called Comeup because it makes you get harder quicker. Maybe it was too much for Johnny. He gets this wired look sometimes and needs to keep his hands doing something or he goes a bit left. I've seen it loads through year eight. And he got it bad that day, going on about his maps. He ended up dragging Amy off on some stupid mission to show her this dried-up stream he'd been drawing a map of. I think Amy was a bit freaked out, to be honest, like Johnny might do something to her or something. But Johnny's not like that.

So Mr Cook or Crook comes in and Johnny's already chewing his ear off about something, and he sees me sitting in the middle of the room.

'Boys, would you mind waiting outside please,' he says to both of us. 'Just give me a few minutes to get plugged in,' and waves his laptop at us.

'Can I leave my stuff here, Sir?' I ask.

Mr Cook or Crook wobbles a bit. 'No, take it with you please. I want to put you in a seating plan straight away, so it'll be less faff if you've got it with you.'

I already knew that the first few hours this morning would be in tutor groups, doing timetables and that sort of thing, so I've got my stuff out – new pencil case, new pens – on the desk I sat at for all of last year. I try to keep calm and breathe easily as I pack it all away again, as neatly as I can. Try to see the teacher's side of the argument. But Johnny's wandered over and has picked up a pen, twirling it in his fingers, rolling it along his knuckles in that way he does.

'Bit of space, please, boys?' says Crook or Cook or whatever. His voice is starting to annoy me now. Can't he see I'm going?

I stuff the last few things in my bag, snatch the pen off Johnny and he follows me outside.

When we're in the corridor, I do some of the breaths that Dad taught me. I'm calm by the time Matt arrives, looking neat and smart, but not as neat as me. Mark turns up a few minutes later, looking the opposite. I wonder if Mark's mum actually buys his shirts in that washed-out grey colour.

'Right, lads. New year, new game,' I announce. Their heads drop into a little circle, and I tell them the rules.

By the time I'm done, and everyone's grinning, I'm completely over our new tutor, who couldn't even be bothered to see that I was doing everything right before he had a go at me and told me to get out. I don't like him, and his smarmy face comes out of the door all smiley.

'Good morning, year nine. Welcome back. I've put a seating plan on the board so please find your seats.'

I give him a little smile on the way in, but I don't think he notices. Anyway, I'm sat at the back, right under the clock. Which is perfect.

I leave it a while before I start – long enough for the others to forget that we're playing a new game – and I colour-code my timetable using my new highlighters.

At five to nine, I can't wait anymore.

'Johnny,' I hiss. He's sitting two rows in front of me, talking to Amy about how timetables are like a map. She's pretending to be interested. 'John.' I flick a ball of paper at him.

Johnny turns around. I point at the ceiling with my pencil. 'What's the time?'

Johnny looks up, realises what he's done straight away, and turns back around in his seat. Without missing a beat, his right arm shoots straight out from his shoulder, barely missing Amy, bent over her timetable. His left arm goes straight up and over to his right a bit. Five minutes to nine. He's got it spot on.

Amy tries to sit up and clunks into Johnny's arm, which is unflinching. You've got to admire his commitment. You'd never get that from Mark, and definitely not from Matt.

'Oi!' says Amy, her head trapped a few inches from the desk. 'Let me go!'

Mr Cook, who's written his name on the board in spikey handwriting so we all know it, is on the other side of the room talking to Matt's table about something.

'Excuse me, what is going on?' he exclaims.

'He won't let me up, Sir!' Amy's voice is muffled by Johnny's arm. She's giggling.

I'm giggling too, rocking back on my chair, holding my stomach. Mark turns around, realises what's happening, and he creases up. Even Matt looks across, lets out a bark of laughter. Then everyone's laughing.

'Johnny? It is Johnny, isn't it? What on earth is going on?'

'It's five to nine, Sir.'

'Put your arms down, now. Let the poor girl up.'

Johnny's left arm ticks round to nine o' clock. He lets out a loud 'bong' and crashes his arms back on the desk, making Mr Cook step back. I can't take anymore and throw my head back in a laugh so loud my chair tips over. People in the front row stand up to watch me collapse on the carpet, tears streaming down my face. Johnny vaults over the table in between us, barely missing Greg Hunter's head, shouting 'Luc, I'll save you!' and the whole class are on their feet. The nervous energy of the summer that has been bubbling just below the surface all morning is unleashed, and Mr Cook doesn't know what to do.

When Johnny and I are on our feet again, he points to the door. 'A word, gentlemen, please.'

We wait outside for him to settle the class down. Johnny re-enacts my fall down the wall. He's wired. It'll be a while until he calms down.

We hear Cook's raised voice fall slowly back to quiet again, then the door opens. 'Boys. Would you please explain to me what just happened? Johnny, we'll start with you.'

'It was five to nine, Sir.'

'And that's the time you act like an arse, is it?'

The swear-word from a teacher, mild though it is, is enough to catch us both off our guard. We're stunned for the half second that Mr Cook needs.

'If I *ever*,' he shouts – we both spring instantly to attention – 'have to interrupt my tutor time again, for whatever ridiculousness you two have concocted, there will be phone calls home. Do I make myself *abundantly clear*?'

We nod. There are no noises from inside the

classroom; everyone must have heard Cook shout at us.

His voice drops again. 'That is not, I hope, the first impression you wanted to make today. Now, back in, pipe down, and not another noise. *Do you understand*?' He stares at me.

I stare back for a full five seconds before I have to look down. 'Yes, Sir,' I mutter in unison with Johnny, then we file back into the room. I walk straight back to my seat, pick up the chair, throw myself into it.

My pens and pencils are still laid out in neat rows on my desk.

One by one, I snap each of them in half.

4

Dad says that if you want to really beat people, it's not enough just to get what *you* want. You have to take away what *they* want. That means you've got to show it to them first, whatever 'it' might be. You don't just win; they lose. That's what competition is all about.

Like with rugby, for example. Here I am lining up behind the scrum at inside centre. When the ball comes out, and it comes to me, my job is to show the other team what they really want – the ball.

If he's quick, their second row will peel off the side of the scrum and be the first man to get to me. But he doesn't look quick. It looks like their coach has just chosen the biggest guys on the team to be the forwards, and left the skinny, quick guys to be the backs. Which suits me fine.

So the first defender to get to me will be one of those little whip-thin kids, probably that one there, who's all knees and elbows.

I flash my gum shield at him, show him some hate-face. He looks terrified.

When I get the ball, I'll run straight at him. What he wants (or should want, if he's any good, which he probably isn't) is the ball. So I'll show it to him. I'll carry it right out in front of me like a baby.

Then, when his eyes have locked onto that, I'll tuck the ball in tight, drop my shoulder and drive straight through him.

Dad calls it 'visualisation'. It's something all winners do.

I'm on top of Elbows before he's ready, and he puts his skinny little hands out towards the ball, like I'm just going to give it to him, like I've gift wrapped it for his birthday or something. That's exactly when I tuck the ball under my right arm, drop my left shoulder and charge at his chest. I lift him a few inches off the floor and keep moving forward.

That's another thing that Dad says. Keep. Moving. Forward.

Elbows is on his arse, and I've stepped through the gap between their centres. Their fly half has shot across though. He's pretty good actually. He plays for Grange at the weekends so we've met before. A proper rugby player – none of this school-boy league pussy crap where most of the team don't know what they're doing. He shoots in with a decent tackle. I manage to push one of his arms away, but he slips down and takes me around the knees. I twist as I go down, and Johnny's right behind me.

Johnny's useless, technically. But he's got more energy than the whole team put together, and he's so unpredictable that other teams just back away from him. Tackling him always means catching a stud somewhere, or getting one of his bony joints in your face. And he must be coated in eel skin or something because I've never seen a guy slip so many tackles. Not even the guys that play on the team Dad coaches. The team he says I'm almost ready to join. Just a few years to get my weight and muscle tone up.

So I offload to Johnny, and he just about manages to gather the ball before he gets caught on the back of the collar by one of their guys. But Johnny puts his head down and keeps sprinting, the collar rips clean off his shirt and he's away again, giving a big laugh as he goes, and turning to me with one of his massive idiot grins.

He doesn't see their full-back coming, and the ball pings straight out of his hands, bobbling over the uneven ground.

He takes the penalty for the knock on, and hands off to their winger. He's pretty quick, almost as quick as me, and he's spotted that the flank to his left is almost completely open. He's got about twenty yards on me, and about half the length of the pitch to run. But the blood's pumping in my ears and I just know I'm going to catch him. I'm visualising it already. I know the rest of the team have stopped. Our full-back, Andy, is puffing away behind me, but he soon gives up and shouts a half-arsed 'go on, Luc!'.

The winger knows I'm coming, and his chin drops to his chest as he tries to squeeze a bit more speed from his legs. Big mistake. If he put his chin up, opened his lungs a bit more, he'd have a better chance.

His eyes never leave our try-line. Fair play to the guy. He doesn't look over his shoulder once, commits himself completely to the thing he wants. Which I'm about to take away from him.

We're just inside our 22-yard line when I catch up. I launch off my right foot, gauge his speed perfectly, and bring my right shoulder straight into his waist, hard. My arms go round his middle and my momentum lifts him off his feet as we both sail across the touchline. I land on top of him and don't let him go as we skid to a stop on the wet grass. Through his back, I can feel his heart kicking like a little horse.

He tries to push himself up, but I keep holding on, my weight keeping him down. Not yet, mate. Not 'til *I'm* ready. I push up off his back, give him a friendly little pat on the cheek, then pull the ball out from under his chest. He doesn't resist, just gets slowly to his feet then hobbles back towards his team.

I place the ball on the touchline ready for the line-out. There are few pats on the back, and one from Andy who's trying to say thanks for doing his job for him. I shrug him off, take my place in the back row again.

From the opposite touch line, I can hear our PE teacher and coach, Hughsie, shouting my name. He gives me a massive thumbs up. I spit through my gum shield, and it takes me a few more seconds to still myself, draw up all that fire in my gut, the delicious ache of the contact, let it course through my hot blood, feeling the win.

Their coach is refereeing, and he gives the winger a rub on the head as he walks past him. Says 'well done', and 'any other day and you'd have made that, lad.'

I smile at that. 'Any other day.' There's no one like me.

I stare at Elbows lining up opposite me again.

He looks away.

In the changing rooms after, Mark asks if I'm coming out tonight. Johnny's at his back like a puppy or something, jumping around.

'What's the plan?' I ask. I know the answer though.

'Dunno,' says Mark. 'Lanes. Same as always, I guess.'

The Lanes aren't really lanes. It's what we call the bunch of interconnecting paths behind all the houses on Mark's estate, joining up all the blocks of garages at the end of all the cul-de-sacs.

'The Lanes, again?'

'Yeah, why not? They're alright.'

We've been out on the Lanes every Friday night for the past few months, since someone decided the heath was for little kids. I think it was Matt. He has some weird theory about the trees up there, why they all grow bent over to one side.

'And there's green,' Johnny adds, bobbing his head like a pogo-stick and making his eyes really wide.

'Yeah,' Mark adds. 'There's green. Brendon said he'd sort us out. Money up front though.'

Mark's brother is a pretty unreliable source, so I'm not convinced. And I'm not that keen in the first place, to be honest. It's not really my thing. It's no different from the cheap vodka that the girls always bring, and I don't feel so bad the next morning if I stick to that, especially if I have a few tins of Comeup along with it.

'I guess we're going up the Lanes then,' I say, kicking my feet back into my school shoes.

'Yes, Luc! Blazer!' Johnny puts his hands on my shoulders and follows me out of the changing room, jumping up and down all the way to the minibus chanting, 'Blazer, blazer, blazer!'

I try to shrug him off.

Hughsie counts us on to the bus. It stinks on there. Feet and BO.

'Right, ladies. Time for Man of the Match. Would our captain care to do the honours?'

I'm the captain. Of course I am. Dad sorted that out with Hughsie at the start of the year. He said it helps me be a team player, and keeps my head from getting too big. Hughsie went along with it. But it means I never get to be Man of the Match. Being captain is accolade enough, Dad says, whatever an 'accolade' is.

'Er... Johnny had a good one.'

37

'Mate!' Johnny exclaims, diving over from his seat into my lap to give me a big hug.

'But I think, this week, Joe put in a pretty decent shift. Two tries himself and lots of hard graft in the scrum, including a couple of turnovers.'

Joe's our Number Eight, and we've played on the same Sunday team for years. We link up pretty well on the pitch, but don't see much of each other off it. We move in different groups, I guess. And when I join the adults' team soon, I suppose we'll lose touch even more.

'A good choice, Luc. Joe, you may claim your reward.' Hughsie starts the engine as Johnny pulls himself out of my lap, bawling some crap about how he never wants to speak to me again.

For away games, the reward for Man of the Match is getting to choose the music for the bus on the way home. Joe's sitting in the front seat of the bus already – like I said, we move in different groups – and plugs his phone into the stereo, hitting play on some grime track and turning the volume way up. I'm not really into music that much. My dad is. His car's got a massive sound system in it. Huge door speakers, a sub-woofer in the boot and couple of tweeters behind the dash. He plays it loud when we wash the car on a Sunday.

The mini-bus' crappy speakers can't really cope, and what comes out is a sloppy, tinny mess. But it's alright, I guess, and I'm as high on the victory as everyone else. Johnny and a couple of the others replay my awesome tackle on each other as the van rocks its slow and noisy way out of the car park and back towards home.

I get my phone out, send Alice a message to ask if she's coming out tonight. I say I'm not sure I can be bothered.

Of course, I already know she'll be there, but it's fun to make her persuade me to go. It's fun to make her show that she wants me. That she *needs* me. That way, it makes it better when I win.

And I always win.

MATT

5

This is my game.

Always do everything you're asked to do, as well as you can. That's it.

And if it sounds pretty simple, that's because it is.

A lot of people don't understand just how simple it is. And as long as you're doing what people want you to do, no one asks you any questions. They just let you get on with stuff.

They never try to find out what's 'up with you' or what's 'going on' or ask 'do you fancy boys or girls'.

Everything's just easier this way.

School is a perfect example. You know those people who stand at the front of the room and talk a lot? The teachers? Well, they're better at things than I am. OK, so there may be exceptions to this rule, but it's a pretty reliable starting point. Their job – their *actual job* – is to help me get better at whatever that subject is, right? And all that stuff they ask me to do? Well, lo and bloody behold, if I do that stuff as well as I can, I get better! So that's my game.

Sometimes, I think I'm the only one playing it.

People think that, because I've always been good at school, I must be naturally gifted or something. That's what the term is, 'gifted'. Like someone turned up on the day I was born with this big box of intelligence, wrapped in sparkly wrapping paper and with a big shiny bow on it. But that's crap. I've just always done what I was asked. My parents haven't really stepped in that much. Mum's normally working late, even when she's home, and Dad's busying himself in the garden with his veg or whatever, or he's up in his studio, painting. They've never really helped me with homework or shown me how to do things – school things, that is. They've shown me heaps of other stuff, but school stuff I just get on with on my own.

And it's going pretty well, I'd say.

Next year we're in year eleven – actual GCSE year. According to the near-constant refrain that every teacher has droned out these last few months, 'things will get serious'.

OK, I'm not saying the people at the front of the room can't be annoying sometimes.

But sitting here in my tutor room and looking at my timetable for next year, I'm not surprised that I got my first choices for options, or that I'm still in top sets for everything. That's like the prize. The reward.

Johnny's trying to use the grid of his timetable like it's the net of some 3D shape, neatly folding along all of the lines in different directions, using some scissors he's borrowed from Emily to put little cuts in. He's doing that thing with his tongue that he always does when he's concentrating.

People don't normally notice it – probably because Johnny's not normally concentrating at school. But in those moments when he's quiet and he's completely absorbed in what's in front of him, Johnny's tongue is always pressed out between his teeth.

It isn't the work that he gets lost in. He's figured out he's not very good at it, and he wants to show that he doesn't want to be good at it.

He's really good at that.

Luc's a few rows behind me. When I turn around to talk to him, he doesn't look happy. He probably has to drop an option or something and pick up extra Maths. Luc's pretty good at most games, but not my one. They're mixing up the tutor groups, too. I don't think Luc's with any of us – not me, not Mark, and not Johnny either.

It'll be odd, not being in a tutor with them all next year. We're not all that similar, I guess, but I can't really imagine what school will be like without the four of us together. Everyone sees us as a group now. A little gang. A posse, if you like. I sometimes wonder how we've managed to rub along so well since year seven.

In a way, maybe the same rules apply. You do what you're asked, and you do it well. Sometimes you're not *actually* asked to do stuff, you just have to figure out what the expectations are, and not go against them. Like that summer we spent on the heath, making dens. It was great. I followed Mark's instructions, tried to follow what Johnny was doing, laughed hard when everything fell down on top of us because that's what you were supposed to do. And I watched Luc, warily sometimes. No one asked anything more of me. And I fitted in.

And this year, every weekend up the Lanes, I was drinking a bit, smoking a bit, doing what everyone else was doing. And no one's ever asked any questions or thought I've been any different from anyone else. And I'm *not* different, to be honest.

There's another boy in our year who's gay and everyone's fine with it. In as much as those people who aren't fine with it just keep their distance. He pretty much only talks to girls, though. I worry that if I came out, all my friends would just assume I didn't want to hang out anymore, or they wouldn't want to hang out with me because they'll think I'll make a move on them or something. Boys are weird like that – all their relationships seem to be about sex, somehow, except with other boys. Or so they say. Luc keeps telling us about the stuff that the men's rugby team get up to when they're 'on tour'. It gives me serious reservations about heterosexual culture.

Anyway, I don't fancy them.

I used to think I fancied Mark. When we were in primary school we'd have sleepovers, always at my house. Sometimes he'd ask if he could come into my bed. Sometimes we practised kissing – that's what Mark said it was: practice. Sometimes he just wanted to cuddle. We'd never talk about it the next morning, though. And it definitely wasn't something we mentioned at school, or to other people.

That might lead to questions.

So, this year, I've tried to do what everyone else has been doing, laughing and being stupid and getting together with girls – just kissing and stuff. I've done as well as I could. And the reward is that I get to fit in.

I know it won't last forever, and I don't want it to, but for now it's good. Like I said, it's easier.

There's one more week until the end of the year. Mr Cook looks exhausted, sat at his desk, pretending to look at his laptop, idly twiddling a pen. As I watch, he heaves himself to his feet. I think he'll be glad to see the back of us.

Johnny's timetable has turned into a weird shape that roughly resembles a pyramid, with lots of jagged bits sticking out of the side of it. He's trying to balance it on its tip, his tongue still poking out through his teeth. The fact that he's pretty much in bottom sets for everything is ridiculous because there's no one else who thinks like he thinks or who can do what he does. It's amazing, the shape he's made. There's not a wonky flap or unintended line in sight. He's written 'nowhere' on the side of it. Or maybe it says 'now here'.

'Johnny, what have you done?' Mr Cook comes over, the slightly concerned smile on his face that he's adopted recently when talking to Johnny. It's like he knows he should do something, but also it's getting close to the end of the year, so...

'It's what a week looks like, Sir. Well, time in general, really. But this is just a week's worth.' Mr Cook holds it up. 'Careful, the glue's not dry yet.'

'Why are you glueing your timetable, Johnny?' Mark calls from the other side of the room.

'Well it's not like I was going to keep it safe over the summer, is it?' Johnny calls back.

'That's true, I suppose.' Mr Cook's voice is resigned, a little deflated.

Mark laughs, goes back to the conversation he was having with Alice.

Johnny's facing Mr Cook again. 'So, I thought I'd make something memorable out of it. Want me to explain it to you?'

'Why not.' Mr Cook turns the shape in his hands.

'The cube at the top is Monday because Mondays are neat and orderly. You can see the edges of Mondays. There's a tube bit in the middle which you can't see and that's like the middle of the week, because all the days are the same and it's like being sucked along, and the spikey bit on the end is Friday.'

'And why is Friday spikey?'

'Because they are, aren't they? You're all tired and itchy and you don't want to get too close to it or you might get a thorn off it or something.' Johnny takes the 'week' back from Mr Cook and stands it on his desk, trying to get it to balance on the very tip of Friday.

'I'm sure you're right, Johnny.' Mr Cook spots something going on at the back of the room. Jess, who sits next to Luc, is shouting something at him. Mr Cook's voice is weary. 'Luc, keep your hands to yourself. Leave the poor girl alone.'

My dad's dubious of Luc. He says Luc goes out of his way to prove himself against 'outdated parameters concerning conquest and overthrow', and that he's 'a proper old alpha-male, just like his dad'. Back when he was still an accountant, my dad used to do Luc's dad's finances. And Luc, he says, is a chip of the old block. But he thinks Johnny's brilliant. Whenever Johnny comes over, Dad asks if he wants to have a look at his latest painting and drags him out to the studio.

Actually, Johnny goes willingly, standing in front of all dad's multi-coloured canvases and gawping. Dad's stuff is what he calls 'abstract'. But he sells a few of them so some people must like what he does. He doesn't get much for them. The biggest ones he sells are a grand, which sounds a lot, but the materials and everything are really expensive. He took me to his art supply shop once – some of the paints are fifty quid a tube. And he goes through loads of them on every painting.

Dad hated being an accountant. Always referred to himself as 'nothing more than a bean counter'. Since I can remember, whenever he had a free evening or weekend, he'd paint. Like he worked all week just to buy himself that time. He was good, too. I thought so anyway. Even as a kid I could see his pictures were more than just pictures of things. But he never seemed happy with them. He'd always complain about not having enough time to finish things properly or try anything more challenging.

Mum spent years telling him to just do what he wanted, and eventually he did. A few years ago he cashed in his pension, put half the money into shares or something and used the rest to overhaul the garden of our pokey old terraced cottage. He put raised beds everywhere and built a little cabin at the end for his painting. The cabin – or 'studio', as he calls it – has got windows all along the north side. North light's better for painting, he said, because it doesn't change as much – it's more consistent because you never get direct sun. But it also means it's bloody freezing up there, even in the summer.

Dad doesn't mind. He's never in the house between eight in the morning and five in the evening, which suits Mum because she works from home a few days a week. She used to drive vans for the council, but now she's in charge of the vans – where they go and what they're carrying. She works in the 'study' upstairs, which is really just a little box room at one end of the hallway, barely bigger than a cupboard. If Dad's not in the studio, he's looking after his garden, which he plants in a chaotic mess rather than everything in neat rows with signs on them. It drives Mum mad because she never knows what, or where, anything is. But it's Dad's domain, and he loves it. I often think the garden looks a bit like his paintings.

Which is what Johnny said when he came over one evening last week. He stayed for dinner, like usual, and asked about what the vegetables were and how long they took to grow. It was beans – a mixture of beans all with different patterns on them, which Johnny was fascinated by.

'No two are the same, are they? Even the ones that are the same aren't the same.' Johnny was turning over three beans on the side of his plate with a fork.

'No,' said Dad, pointing to a big white one with purple swirls on it. 'That one's a Cranberry Bean, the one next to it is a Scarlett Runner, and the little black and white number is a Vaquero. First year I've tried those.'

'They look like cows with no legs.'

Mum laughed. 'I suppose they do. Do you want some to take home, Johnny? We've got armfuls.'

'No, thanks. Mum wouldn't know what to do with them. She only knows beans in tins.'

Mum and Dad shared that weird look that they often do when Johnny's around. Like they think that if Johnny's parents were a bit more 'present' and actually cooked for him rather than leaving a bunch of processed crap for him to heat up in the microwave while they swan off abroad for weeks at a time, then Johnny would be better. But when he's here, I can see how much Johnny's still trying to rein himself in. Like there's tension in him that keeps tugging and tugging. He often says he has to leave really quickly after dinner, and I'm sure he just runs all the way home.

Johnny was talking to Dad about the insides of the bean casings, about how the tiny hairs on the inside of them were like a map for where the bean's colour was going to go. Then he asked Dad if he had a map, too – whether he planned his paintings before he started them.

'Not really. I just let the colour guide me, I suppose. I do what I feel the colour wants me to do.'

Mum and I shared a wry smile, but Johnny was hooked.

'So do you have to learn how to speak colour then, so you can hear it talking to you?'

Dad thought for a while. 'Yes, I suppose I do.'

'Like how your garden speaks green, you mean?'

Dad paused. A different pause. 'You've lost me there, John.'

'Your garden. It speaks green, doesn't it. Even now, when it's getting a bit dark. Or when you can't see it. You can hear it, whispering "green" to you.'

I was getting a bit concerned, sure that Johnny was making some link between the garden and the stuff he'd been smoking pretty regularly all year, more than the rest of us because he said it helped to calm him down. I'm sure my parents wouldn't mind about me doing that. I even smell it in the house sometimes, after they have their friends over. I considered kicking Johnny under the table to make him shut up.

'That's why it's so calm here,' Johnny carried on. 'That garden. It talks to everything in the house and makes it feel OK.'

There was another pause. I put a forkful of multi-coloured beans in my mouth.

'Thank you, Johnny. We're very happy that you like it here.' Mum put her hand on Johnny's arm, which made me die a bit from awkwardness. 'You can come here whenever you like.' She's a good mum – a great one, probably – but still a bit cringe, you know?

After dinner, Dad showed Johnny his latest sold painting before he covered it in bubble-wrap, ready to post the next day. Johnny was appreciative, polite, but I could see the coiled spring inside him starting to tick against his skin. He kept clenching and stretching his fingers.

'So, I'll see you at school tomorrow then?' I asked, giving him his cue.

I stood at the front door to watch him go, his quick footprints slamming into the pavement as he pounded his way home. I listened until I couldn't hear them anymore, then helped with the washing up before going upstairs to my room, flicked through a couple of the art books that Dad's always lending me, then went to sleep.

Back in the classroom, I can see that same spring twitching away now as Johnny runs a finger over the spikey, triangled end of his 'Map of Time'.

He gives me a quick smile, then smashes his flat palm down hard on the model he's taken so long over, thumping the table and bellowing 'FRIDAY' at the top of his voice. It makes the whole room jump.

'OUT!' bellows Mr Cook, his voice having to tower above twenty-eight laughing and shouting students, all desperate for the summer to start.

But Johnny's already heading for the door. He knows the rules.

6

First Sunday of the summer holidays, and I'm waking up groggy. Bright sunlight slants through my blinds, making patterns on the floor of my room. I watch them for a while, then roll over and check the time on my phone. It's just before eleven.

There's a message from Mark, checking I got back alright. I had to take Johnny home after he went left and took a bit too much again. Of everything. Which always happens. Last night was my turn to get him home, hand him over to Anna who thankfully was still awake. We got him inside without his mum and stepdad seeing.

Luc will be out at training by now. 'Rugby, off-season, so it's mostly fitness,' he said last night. He won't be allowed to touch a ball until he hits his hundred-metre target. Luc went a bit heavier than usual last night – celebrating the end of year nine. He told me he's getting away with it because it's easy to hide the hangover vomit as over-exertion vomit. He said his dad even looks at him with a kind of smile when he's bending over, retching it all up on the grass.

Luc's fit. And it's difficult not to look at him all the time. Just as a *specimen*, he's nice to look at, to catch the

52

odd glimpse of his stomach when his shirt rides up a bit, like it does in class when he puts his hand up. But everyone does that. Looking isn't a problem. No one asks questions if you're just looking.

Luc's been bulking up a lot this year. He said that his dad's going to let him join the adults' team if he can get big enough. I'm not sure Luc's an adult yet, but it's like he's a step ahead of everyone else. Like his body is hardening quicker than ours are. I look under the duvet at my squidgy chest, the smooth soft curves of my upper arms. Luc's never been squidgy, but more and more he looks like he's been carved from something.

I send a message back to Mark – *yeah I'm fine. Thx.*

Then I message Johnny.

Johnny won't reply. He probably didn't plug his phone in last night when he passed out, hopefully in his bed, or on the sofa at least.

Slowly, things are filtering back to me. We'd not been to the Lanes last night. Someone had had the idea of going up on the heath, like old times. It always freaks me out a bit at night, that place, but last night was warm and cloudless, so it stayed pretty bright. It's not a long walk from the Lanes, and we were soon kicking along the sandy paths, talking and smiling and passing cans and joints back and forth.

Then I can't remember easily anymore.

It's like my memory is sitting behind a fog. It must have started like every other Saturday; we meet up at

Mark's as we always do. Johnny's sister's no longer with her boyfriend who gave us free weed, so we pool our money and Mark's older brother sorts us out. But recently, Brendon's not been home when we get there, and maybe Mark's been sorting things out himself. I don't know what his deal is, whether he gets a cut from his brother. Whatever, we don't ask questions, just give Mark our money in the week and he magically turns it into other stuff by Friday night. Then we go to the Lanes and meet the girls. Amy can get served at the newsagents, so she brings the vodka, and Luc brings the Comeup from his dad. It's a pretty slick operation.

So that's how last night started. And Mark had a new phone – don't know where he got it – and he was showing it off, playing with the camera, taking pictures of everyone and the flash strobing us all against the darkness. Then someone mentioned the heath and that's where we went, and that's how we ended up at the back of the school field.

Mark had led us there, up and over a few hills. One of the girls, Beth maybe, complaining about the sand then falling over on a slope and laughing, the vodka hitting her pretty early. Then we went along some bramble bushes and suddenly there it was – the grey-brown lump of the school glowing in the moonlight.

We hopped over a bit of fence where the brambles were thinnest and sat around the edge of the long-jump pit, as far from the school as we could get.

It was weird, sitting there, feeling that familiar building looking back at us. Sometimes Johnny gets a bit paranoid, and I wondered if being close to the school might be a problem. Not that Johnny cares much about the place, anyway.

The school was completely deserted. Term had ended a few days ago, and apart from the scrappy ends of posters in a few of the windows, you'd never know anyone had ever used those buildings. They had an abandoned and dusty look to them.

Our bare feet in the sand. Still enough heat in the air not to need a coat. I think I shared a smoke with Luc, then Mark – who wouldn't stop fiddling with his phone – mentioned he had to go in a bit and was bored and wanted a walk. By that time Luc was making out with Amy. Or was it Alice? It's like he has them on a loop. Johnny was making sand-castles using his shoes. So I decided to go with Mark and we skipped back over the fence and went off into the heath. Mark's house isn't far, and he said he had something he wanted to show me anyway. I was a bit giddy by this point, giddy and giggly, so it all felt a bit conspiratorial. Like we were on a secret mission.

I smile remembering it, sunlight on my face, my body just the right temperature under the covers.

We'd gone up to the bowl – a big, sandy crater on the heath – and found a nice soft bank to lie on and watch the stars roll around. Then Mark took this little bag out of his coat pocket with a couple of orange pills in.

'Want one?'

I didn't know what it was that Mark was offering, but I felt all hot suddenly, and a bit like I'd drifted into one of those cringy videos about peer pressure they show in Personal Ed or Citizenship at school. It was a weird feeling.

'What it is?' I said, laughing.

'Something new. It'll blow your mind.' He smiled.

I fell for it. In the video, I'd be 'peer pressure victim #1'. I said, 'OK, but maybe not a whole one, yeah?' as if that was the kind of thing you're meant to say.

'Half each then?'

'Alright.'

Mark bit straight through the pill with a dusty snap, kept his half and passed the other one over.

I put it in my mouth. It had the taste of Mark's breath on it – kind of earthy, a bit sour, warm. I showed Mark the little wedge on the end of my tongue, which had started tingling. He showed me his – his dagger tongue, all pointed and red and dangerous.

Then they went down, and we waited.

Mark opened a can of Comeup – that's why we call it Comeup; it speeds things along, brings on the high from the green quicker – and we took a few slow sips. He started talking about which of Beth's friends he was thinking of making a move on. Ones Luc hadn't already been with. Mark's getting really weird about competition, with Luc, with Johnny, with anyone. I was doing a good job of appraising, making all the right noises, doing what I needed to do, following the rules.

Then Mark asked, 'Do you ever think about our sleepovers, when we were in primary school?'

The question caught me completely off guard, and something in my chest shrivelled up. 'Er … what? No.'

My head was reeling, but Mark's hand had landed, at that moment, on my shoulder, grounding me for a second. 'It's alright, mate. Sometimes I do. It's not like it made us gay or anything.'

'Yeah, right.' I shrugged him off, tried to laugh a bit.

'Not that it would be a problem if you *were*, right…?'

There was a sudden ringing in my ears. 'What do you mean? I've had girlfriends.'

Mark looked at me sideways.

'Well, I've *been* with girls…' I stood up, shuddering to my feet, my voice too tight and not feeling like my own. Was this the orange pill, starting to work on me? Or something else?

'Yeah, maybe. Look, sit down, will you? You're making me feel aggy.'

'*You're* aggy? I'm the one accused of being gay.'

'It's not an accusation, it's a question. And if you're

gay, why would that be a problem? It's not a crime, is it? It's not like it's the olden times. I'm fine with it.'

What did he mean 'fine'? What right did he have to say 'fine' like there'd been some kind of vote, that a meeting had been held and I'd been *waved through* with no comment? As if *his* feelings about my sexuality were the most important thing.

I don't know why I was so twitchy. Something about the Comeup, maybe, or some ill effects of Mark's latest batch of green. Or the pill he'd fed me.

'Look, I'm not trying to force you to come out to everyone or whatever,' Mark had continued from his sandy bed. 'I'm just saying that it's not a problem.'

'Fuck off, Mark. Just…' A pause. Had someone just come out *for* me? 'Just give me a minute.'

'Take as long as you like, mate. No problems.' He crossed his arms behind his head, closed his eyes.

Recalling it now, the sunlight on my wall, the duvet warm around me, I get another quick burst of that anger in my chest. It had felt as if something was being taken away from me, in some way. I'd thought about – had *felt* – the possible embarrassment, the awkwardness, of coming out. And that hadn't really materialised. Instead of all that, I got anger.

I slip back into the film-reel of last night, feeling it all again as something weird had started to happen in my stomach, in my chest, in my face. I'd lain back down again, next to Mark.

The night grew around us, the sky's orange and pink fading into purples.

'Alright. Maybe you're right,' I'd said, my voice sounding a bit more like mine but not entirely. I tried to breathe. Stood up. Sat down again.

'So, is it weird, for you? Talking about girls? I've noticed you go a bit quiet when Luc does it.'

'Yeah, but that's a whole other level of "talking about girls", right? Remind me why we still hang around with Luc?'

Mark laughed. 'Oh, come on. Luc's alright. Besides, who else would he play with?' Mark's voice was beginning to slur. Or was it my hearing?

I took another deep breath. 'No,' I said. 'Not weird. I mean, it's not that I don't fancy people, right? It's just that…'

'…that some of them are boys?'

'Yeah.' I smiled.

Mark punched me lightly on the arm. 'Alright, primary school. Who says "fancying" anymore?'

'Clearly not heteronormative people.'

'What? Mate, that's exactly the kind of stuff you keep coming out with that means I'll never fancy you. Heter-nora-*what*?'

'Heteronormative. It means—'

'Whatever,' Mark went on, our eyes fixed on some distant treeline as the sky above started to go milky. 'I know what it means.'

59

And that had been it.

I squirm deeper into my morning bed, vaguely aware that the clock is ticking on towards midday. But the sun on the floor, a few shafts of it creeping over my bed right under the window, warming my face, are holding me in that moment. The memories are sharper now, and I want to bathe in them a little bit more. Besides, I know what comes next.

I'd turned towards Mark, his face swimming in the landscape that shifted around us as if on some kind of delay.

'Have you always known?' His voice was honeyed, the breath catching on itself. A beautiful burr.

'That I was gay? Maybe. Yes.' Something in the Orange was making these words flow easily. I mean, I'm normally pretty good with words, but it was as if some kind of screen had been lifted, a screen that caught the words that would normally be difficult, which was strange because I'm not sure I'd ever noticed that filter was there before last night.

'I wish it could be easier, sometimes,' I'd continued. 'Talking about it, I mean. With people my age, I mean. I told Mum and Dad ages ago that I thought I might be. And they were really supportive. I told them over breakfast some time in year eight when we were talking about Uncle Pat and his husband. Just said "I think I might be gay." Mum gave me a hug and Dad went and got some books about an artist called Francis Bacon.'

I swallowed, the words making my spit thick in my mouth. 'His pictures looked really weird, you know? But Mum said I probably wasn't old enough for that kind of thing yet so he took it back and gave me a David Hockney book instead. Presented me with it like I'd done some kind of achievement.' I mimed my reverential receipt of the book. 'I liked the colours, but I wasn't sure what it had to do with being gay.'

Mark was giggling next to me. 'That's such a your dad thing to do.'

'Tell me about it. Anyway, my parents have always said that love is love is love. Obviously there's Mum's brother, and they've got friends who are gay, too, so I guess... Well, I guess it just *is*, you know? Like it's not something too *involved*.'

'So what's it like then, being gay?'

'That's a fucking stupid question. What's it like being straight?'

He'd laughed loudly then – a peel of notes scattering away into the darkness like birds. I saw them floating up and away as we lay face to face on the sand. 'Maybe I'll try it. See if I can tell the difference. Well, try it *again*, I suppose.' Those sleepover memories are lying on the sand with us, next to us, inside us.

'OK, then. Maybe I'll let you. *Again*.' God, was I *flirting*? With a *mate*?

He looked over at me, his face glowing, just out of focus.

'Where'd these come from anyway?' I pointed to my mouth.

'Oranges? New stock. More on the way. Limited release, I reckon.' His eyes were closed, chin tilted upwards like he was sunbathing. 'They're good though, right?'

'Where are you getting this stuff? You know it's bad, right?' My voice was slowing down, the 'a' of 'bad' drawn out like a sigh. 'There are, no doubt, many b*aaaa*d, b*aaaaaaa*d people involved, M*aaaaaaa*rk.'

'Get you, questioning me after scoring free pills.' Mark's hands dug a little deeper into the sand, easing his fingers into it. I moved my hand towards his. They touched. He didn't move away.

'But Mark,' I drawled. 'Everything is so *important* this year.'

When we laughed it was like a god moved its tongue. I moved my hand again, put it on top of his.

We both watched our hands mingling, not sure whose fingers were whose, whose wrists, whose forearms. I pulled my arm back. His came with it. I bit his arm. Nibbled it, really. He laughed. I pulled harder. His body fell across mine. Playdough on playdough. The salt and sour of it as our mouths touched, opened.

'Tea, Matthew?' Mum's knock at the door explodes into my daydream. I baulk, scramble for something to hold onto, coming back up through the layers of duvet and sunlight and last night's memory.

'No,' I almost shout. 'No thanks, Mum.'

'Are you up, love? It's pushing on for midday. Come on, your father wants a hand with something in the garden.'

'Yeah. Just a minute.' The world is not quite real, yet. I'm half in and half out of the daydream, or memory, or whatever it is. There's warm light on the floor, dryness at the back of my throat, my boxers unceremoniously tented under the duvet.

But I want to sink back down, stop feeling my limbs as real and remember Mark touching them, last night.

Who knows how long we were there, Mark and me, feeling little fireworks of light and heat running through our bodies. That's how it felt to me, anyway. And the way he looked at me – really looked at me, like he *saw* me.

And when he took out his phone – his new phone that he'd spent the evening showing to anyone that would listen – it had seemed so natural, us laughing at blurry selfies, close ups of our faces blinking in the light of the flash while the night ran on like a river around us. And that little camera light had shone as Mark muttered something about how great the image was, how crisp the screen, and I'd laughed.

And my face against the warmth of his stomach, looking up at him with the blue glow of the screen cascading across his face as he watched me, really *seeing* me, pin-sharp in the melting night, the little red light next to the lens showing that it was all being recorded for posterity like some beautiful, undying memory.

I sit bolt upright, cold sweat exploding across my body.

What have I done?

MARK

7

I invented two games this year.

The first one was because of all the cans we had lying around. The Comeup and the other ones too – whatever people were drinking. What you do is hold your empty can a little bit above the base – about a third of the way up, maybe – and you squeeze the opposite sides of the can between your thumb and forefinger. It makes a pair of little creases. Then you turn the can ninety degrees and do that again. If you do it properly, the creases all join up and you've made a perfect square. If you're really good you can use two hands and do all four creases at the same time. You've got to be really careful not to push too hard or you'll make a big crease that you won't be able to bend back again, and the square won't be even.

When you're happy with that bit, you can move on to stage two. Where you've made your first square, you'll see the sides of the can look like diamonds, touching at the corners. So, next, you press against the sides of the can again to make another square at the top of your first set of diamonds and make another set of diamonds.

Then, when that's all looking neat, you do the same again and make a *third* row. What you end up with is a can with a round top and a round bottom, but with 12 perfectly flat, diamond-shaped sides. And you've got four half-diamonds at the top, and four at the bottom.

And then if you're really, really good, like I am, you can put that can on top of another one, and the half-diamonds at the top of one can line up with the half-diamonds at the bottom of the next can, and you can make a whole tower that's just diamonds, all the way up. I tried to sell my biggest tower once. No one wanted it.

When I showed Johnny, he made a tower of ten cans of Comeup, and because those cans are a bit bigger he got four rows of diamonds on each can, and if you count the rows where he'd lined one can up with the next one – which he was pretty good at, even though he'd just started – he had forty nine rows, with four diamonds in each row, which is one hundred and ninety six diamonds.

Johnny being Johnny, he smashed it all up afterwards. But it was pretty impressive while it lasted.

People were even doing it in school for a while, bringing in their own cans even though you weren't allowed to. They were taking the cans home afterwards anyway, adding them to their collections, so no harm done, even though Mrs Clarke had a go at us in assembly for it. She went on and on about people dropping cans on the field and the school lawnmower going over them and kids cutting their legs up when they were doing slide tackles in football practice. Not that anyone listens to assemblies. Not since about year eight, probably.

My collection fills up the whole of my bedroom wall, next to the window. It's a whole wall of diamonds in loads of different colours from all the different drinks cans. Mum gets a bit annoyed, but it's not like she ever goes in there anymore, except to put a pile of washing on my bed whenever she remembers to do it, which is barely ever, so I don't see why she complains.

She never goes into my brother's room. He had to move back in a few months ago and works nightshifts. He sleeps through most of the day. Sometimes I see him eating cereal at four in the afternoon. And sometimes, if Mum's not there, he puts his head around the kitchen door when he gets in from work in the morning. If Mum's there, it normally ends in an argument. Mum worries about Brendon. A lot. But she doesn't always have the best way of showing it. He didn't have an easy ride through school and wasn't really home much because she'd be on his back all the time. He still isn't home much, to be honest. Same reasons, I guess. When he lived here before, there were run-ins with the police. Lots of them. And we don't really know where he went for the eighteen months he wasn't living at home. Now he *is* home though, I'm not sure Mum's any less worried. She tries to ask him about work, or his plans, or stop him going out, but mostly he just ignores her and does what he wants anyway. Same as usual.

Usually, at the weekends or on Friday evenings, his

friends come over before they go out into town, or wherever it is they go, to do whatever it is they do.

That's how I met The Guy.

The Guy taught me the second game.

It was a Saturday evening, and we were waiting for my brother to have a shower, me and The Guy, sitting at the kitchen table. Mum was at work. She'd had a call to say that someone was ill and could she come in. The soles on my school shoes were peeling away. We'd glued them three times already. So this extra shift meant she could replace them. She was going to get me some shoes on the way home.

Anyway, me and The Guy were sitting at the kitchen table. He'd cracked open a beer from the fridge – one of the few things that Brendon *does* buy – and was puffing away on his e-cigarette. I was on my phone, messaging Matt, Luc and Johnny about something. I'd drunk a Comeup and made the can into the diamond thing.

'That's cool,' The Guy said.

I shrugged.

'Your brother teach you that?'

'No. Just worked it out myself.' The Guy's eyebrows went up. He was impressed.

I went back to messaging.

'Is your brother shaving his balls or something? He's taking ages.' The Guy rummaged in his tracksuit pocket, pulled out a handful of coins and put them on the table. 'Want to play a game?'

'Yeah, alright.' I sat up, trying not to look too interested in the heap of money – there must have been well over twenty quid there. The Guy picked out two two-pound coins and one one-pound coin, all shiny, and put the rest away.

'You know coinball?'

I shrugged.

The Guy set his three coins in a triangle at his end of the table, with the back coin – the one-pound – just hanging over the edge. He pointed his chin at the two cans on the tabletop. 'Move those.'

When I'd put the cans on the sideboard, he gave the back coin a little tap with the heel of his hand, and the three coins slid across the table in different directions. The Guy seemed a bit annoyed. 'They don't slide much on this. Your mum ever clean it?' He ran a finger over the surface. 'Greasy.'

I shrugged.

Then The Guy explained. 'So, that's the kick-off, right? Now I've got to go down the pitch and score in your goal. Put your hand on the table. Like this.' He showed me, pointing his first and fourth fingers out like rocker horns and placing them on his end of the table.

I did the same at my end.

'Right. That's your goal. So I've got to move the coins down the pitch until I can shoot. Like this.' He was using his finger to flick one coin – always the back one – and aiming to slide it in between the other two coins.

Sometimes the gap he was aiming for was big, sometimes it was small, but he always got it through. In six flicks, he had one coin on either side of my goal, and his last coin – the back one – lined up perfectly.

'Do I get a keeper?'

The Guy scoffed. 'No.' He hunched down over the table, ready for the shot.

The coin went straight between my fingers, hit my knuckles pretty hard and bounced up onto my chest.

'One nil. Your turn, kid.'

I lined up the coins like he had done, but when I hit them with the heel of my hand it was too hard, and one slid all the way across the table and fell off the side.

'Tough luck. That's your go finished.'

'Don't I get a throw in?'

The Guy rolled his eyes, collected the coins and started again. This time he tried a shot after only four moves and the coin hit the outside of my little finger.

'Fuuuuck. Did you move your hand?'

I shook my head, bent down to pick up the coin from the floor.

On my next turn, I was better. I got most of the way down the table, but it took about nine flicks. I missed the gap on one flick, which meant my turn was over.

Then The Guy scored again. Two-nil.

On my third go, I got it right, and shot my final coin straight between his fingers.

'Nice one. Two-one. You're getting the hang of this, kid.'

I tried not to smile.

The Guy missed his next two goes, and I scored mine, so it was 3-2 to me and The Guy was just lining up for his next go when my brother appeared in the door. I could smell his aftershave from across the room.

He looked at me, then spoke to The Guy. 'Ready?'

'At last. Did you have to go big toilet or something?' The Guy put the coins back in his pocket, picked his beer up from the worktop and drained it.

As he was heading out of the room, he turned around. 'Oi, kid?'

I looked up.

'Got another game for you.' He tossed me a small plastic bag – the kind you put loose change in when you want to put it in the bank. It landed with a little flutter on the table.

It was green. Not loads, but way more that I could smoke in one night.

The Guy was still in the doorway, smiling. 'That's not all for you, yeah? See how much you can make out of that. See if you do better than your brother.'

It rained all the next week, which meant lunchtimes spent in classrooms. I taught everyone how to play coinball and we had a league running by Thursday. People were loving it.

I found some kitchen scales under Mum's sink to divide up the green properly and, on Wednesday, I took everyone's money for their weekend's supplies. I didn't need to go to my brother at all. I got over a hundred quid in notes, and a handful of coins.

I could tell The Guy was pretty impressed, sitting at our kitchen table the next weekend. He pocketed eighty quid from the roll I gave him, leaving me the two cleanest tenners. He pushed the bag of shrapnel back across the table as well. 'Just take notes in the future. Don't accept this lunch-money bullshit. Good for coinball and fuck all else.' Then he gave me another bag. A bit bigger this time.

'Welcome to the game, kid.'

My brother was hanging around, making himself a bowl of cereal. Even he looked pretty impressed at how much I'd made. But I played it cool, nodded at The Guy, pocketed the new gear.

The Guy was pissed off when I beat him at coinball though. Even made my brother wait by the front door while he tried to score an equaliser. 'You've been practising, kid.'

I shrugged.

8

I meet The Guy on the heath, mid-morning on the first Monday of the summer holidays.

I don't know his name, and I can't remember if he told me or not. I could ask my brother, but it's probably too late. It'd be awkward. 'Hey, Bro, what's the name of that guy who's been coming here every week for the last few months?'

Brendon would grunt at me because that's what he does.

'You know,' I'd say. 'The one that gave me a brand-new phone last week.'

He gave me the phone as a prize for how well I'm doing. Came out of his own pocket, he says. I believe him: his socials (username GuyGuy68684, so no clues there) all show how loaded he is. He's an entrepreneur – got loads of businesses. The green is just a side hustle for him. It's not a huge operation or anything. He says he gets the product from his cousin, who grows it himself. This cousin gives anything he's got spare to The Guy, who gives it to me. And I sell it. It saves him the trouble, The Guy says.

I make two hundred quid some weeks. Before expenses, that is. It's like in Business Studies – gross profit and net profit. I guess I am learning something useful at school. The Guy says that his costs fluctuate and I'm not on a fixed percentage or anything – that's just how the game works – but he always gives me at least twenty back, straight away, and always the cleanest notes. And then, after he's sorted his own costs out, The Guy pays me some extra, too, but not in cash.

I haven't got a bank account. Never been any point. Until now. But I don't even know where to get the forms and stuff, and I think I need Mum's signature, too. The Guy says it's best not to bother her so he's holding on to that portion of my earnings for me. Which is fine. For now, I guess. I can sort all that out later.

Anyway, he sends me a screen grab of the balance every week. And every week it goes up, up, up!

And then there's the extras, like the phone. So it's money in my pocket every week, bank balance soaring, and then extra prizes. The orange pills from the weekend just gone – they were extra prizes. It's the best game to be in.

The Guy says I'm doing market research for him with the oranges. And that's the best way to expand any business; I learnt that in Business Studies, too.

So maybe this phone was an 'incentive' rather than a 'reward', but either way it's brand new, fresh out of the box, and a pretty recent model. Everyone was impressed at the weekend. It's got three cameras, and it takes really sharp pictures. I've been scrolling back through the ones I took over the weekend. Loads of inside my bedroom, just playing around. A few selfies that will need filters before I upload them anywhere and loads from Saturday night up the Lanes. There's a few of Beth after she fell over and was giggling on the floor, a couple of Luc and Amy that I delete straight away, and a few towards the end of me and Matt looking a bit spaced out and wonky. I was out of it, to be honest, but I can kind of remember what happened. It was nice. It's a good product, the orange. Blows people's minds.

Brendon'll be jealous of the phone. He keeps buying reconditioned ones off eBay, thinking he's getting a bargain, and they always break. He's a mug, my brother.

Not like me.

You've just got to know the right people. Then you get box-fresh merchandise from a reliable source. Mint condition. I open the photos again, see if there's a usable selfie. Something to start building an online profile, like The Guy.

Like I said, from the looks of the pictures on his socials, he's completely loaded. Maybe not as much as Johnny's stepdad, but he's much more flash with it – pictures and videos of him holding stacks of cash, making it rain in his huge, white lounge with a massive 4K TV. And shots of him driving these cars, too. Loads of cars, all of them tricked out. They're rentals, he told me, to pick up girls. But they cost hundreds a day. Thousands, some of them.

I'd love to have that kind of money, be able to upload pictures like that and leave my shitty house behind me.

And The Guy said he could help with that. Just wait for the call, he said.

So here I am, with my new phone, waiting where he told me to.

I'm not far from the edge of my estate, only took about ten minutes to walk it. Everyone calls it 'the bowl', because that's what it looks like – as if someone chopped the top off a hill and scooped the insides out. I come here with the boys sometimes for a smoke. It's the perfect place to go if you don't want to be seen.

This is where I came the other night. With Matt.

I'm sat in almost the same place. Maybe some of these scuffs in the sand are the ones we made, the memory playing warm and fuzzy over the inside of my head, but not very clearly. Something wriggles in my stomach.

The Guy comes over the hill, a cloud of smoke around his head from his e-cigarette. There's not much wind, so it hangs above him for a bit, giving him a kind of halo before it fades away. He's carrying a backpack and wearing shorts and a tight t-shirt, showing off his pecs. He's built, for sure. All that money must pay for some serious gym memberships. And his trainers are immaculate.

I recross my legs, trying to show off the pair that I bought last week with the money I've been saving.

'How can you be wearing that much stuff, kid? It's *hot* out here.' He throws himself down on the sand next to me, pulls a bottle of water out of the backpack and takes a long swig. 'Trackies? A jumper? What are you playing at?'

Now he's mentioned it, I feel a prickle of sweat on the back of my neck. But I can't take my jumper off straight away. 'I'm fine,' I say.

'Whatever. Look, I need you to do something for me.'

'Yeah? What?'

'I need you to go somewhere for me. Collect something from a friend of mine. I'd go myself but, you know, work stuff.'

I nod.

'Don't worry, I'll pay you. You do me a favour; I'll help you out. That's how it works, right?'

'Yeah, sure.' I swallow, the sweat-prickles spreading across my shoulders.

'Got this for you.' He throws the backpack across to me. It's new. Still got the labels on it. 'Got it for myself but decided I don't want it anymore. It's yours if you want it.' He takes another swig of his water, sounding like he's out of breath.

I turn the backpack over in my hands. Everyone at school's got one of these. Mum said she'd try and get one off the market for me next time she's there. It's the exact colour I'd have chosen. And the logo on this one is stitched, not screen-printed like the cheap versions most people have got. The ones you get off the market.

'Look in the front pocket.'

I unzip it. There's a bank card in there. I turn it between my fingers. At the bottom of the bag, there's a key attached to a little yellow fob. I pull it out. 'What's this for?'

The Guy explains that I need to go to the train station, get on the next train to the city. When I arrive, I've got to go to something called 'left luggage', which is a set of lockers by the toilets. I need to put my backpack in locker number twenty-two, then go and have a coffee for half an hour or go shopping or whatever. Then I pick the bag up again sometime after midday and get back on the train and come home.

'So your friend will meet me there? With your stuff?'

'Do you know what? He's a busy guy as well. I'll just get him to drop off my stuff in that locker. Number twenty-two. He'll put it in your backpack. That saves you having to wait around for him, doesn't it?'

'So he's got a key for the locker as well?' I drop the bank card I've been fiddling with.

'Yeah, sure. Look, that bank card's linked to the account where I've been keeping your money. You don't need to give it back to me afterwards, OK? I don't need that account anymore. It's yours.

'Sure, yeah.' Finally, a bank account! And imagine having so much money you didn't need all your accounts!

The Guy sits up, fixes me with a look over the top of his sunglasses. 'Tell you what I'm going to do. Rather than the faff of sorting your own account out, I'm going to keep that account open for you. It's yours now. And everything you make, I'll just keep putting into that account. You just use it whenever you need to. OK?'

I'm speechless. But I should ask about the PIN. I open my mouth, but The Guy cuts me off.

'You're doing pretty well, huh? New phone, new pack, new kicks.' He nudges my trainers with his foot. He did notice. 'A proper little businessman.'

I shrug, fail to hold back a smile. I'm opening my mouth to ask about the PIN.

'But a businessman needs cash in his pocket, too, right? Makes him feel more like a man, yeah? So this...' The Guy peels four twenties off a roll of cash he's gotten from his pocket. 'This is for your troubles today.' He holds out the cash. I'm stunned, that's four times what I normally get in a week! But before I can reach across for them, he smiles and adds another. 'You drive a hard bargain, my friend.'

I take the hundred, put it in my front pocket, all thoughts of the PIN forgotten.

The Guy pushes himself up off the sand, dusts himself down. 'I'll text you this afternoon with where to bring my stuff.' He pushes the sunglasses back onto his nose. 'Say hi to your brother for me.' And he's over the rim of the bowl in a few quick steps.

I take my jumper off, feeling the sharp sting of sweat under my arms. A hundred quid just for going into town!

My heart's going like a drum. A hundred quid *and* free train tickets. I can ask about the PIN next time. Besides, I don't want to piss The Guy off with questions, do I?

I start making a mental list of the things I'll buy.

I carefully fold my jumper and put it in my new backpack, put the key on my own keyring, and the bank card and the money in my beaten-up old wallet.

Maybe I'll get myself a new one, today.

On the walk to the station, I browse a few clothes websites, brands I've heard the others talking about. A couple of t-shirts from here, maybe a pair of shorts from there. The Guy's right, I do need to sort my summer wardrobe out. My trackies are clinging to my legs.

I use the self-service machine at the station, press the card to the contactless plate, and I get a weird little kick when the lights go green and it starts printing off my tickets. Boop. I've never done that before.

When the train arrives, I jump on, find a seat and put my feet up. There's nothing on the group chat from the boys, but it's still pretty early, I guess. Not even eleven o'clock yet. I think about posting a message – quick shot of my new trainers up on the seat – but then I delete it.

It's hot on the train, so I open the window above me. A little further along the carriage and across the aisle, a group of four girls are sitting, passing their phones around and laughing, probably at that new app that lets you put your face on famous actors' bodies in scenes from films. Beth was showing everyone last night. Maybe

80

I'll download the app, too. It'll run sweet on my new phone.

I don't recognise the girls. One of them sees me when I stand up to do the window, enjoying the wind on my face. When I turn around, three of their heads drop to their screens again and they start laughing. But one of them is still looking. I nod at her, give her a little smile. She smiles back, holds my eye, then I sit down slowly in my seat and put my earbuds in.

With the money in my pocket, I could take her for a coffee or whatever. If I wanted to. Maybe buy her lunch or something, too, like on those dating shows.

The train starts picking up speed, passing the backs of people's gardens with their different coloured trampolines, their sheds, their toys left out on the grass. None of them look like my gravelly garden of pressed dirt and weeds. There're kids on some of the trampolines, enjoying the first day of their holidays, and a few others – younger ones – running around with their parents who aren't bored of them yet.

The gardens break off into open countryside, the kids replaced by cows quietly sweating in their fields. There's a manky old caravan rotting away on the edge of one of them. In another, it's the back of an old lorry with an advert for a campsite painted on it.

It's not long before it changes again. Car parks around glass office buildings glinting in the sunlight. And then even taller buildings, closer together. And then the train tracks branching, the blackened gravel they're laid on widening with the approaching station.

The announcer's voice fills the carriage – *this train terminates here* – and I stand up.

I time it perfectly so that when I step onto the platform, the next track on the playlist kicks in. The song drops with a huge, dirty bass line, horns blaring and the MC spitting fire. I can't pick out the words, they're too quick, but they sound sharp and angular, fresh and raw. It's the perfect soundtrack. I can almost see myself in some kind of film, and I just know that group of girls is behind me, walking along with their arms linked and all wondering who I am.

Minds. Blown.

I pick out the signs overhead for 'left luggage' and find the lockers. Number twenty-two is at the bottom, and looks a bit kicked-in. But the key works. I place the backpack inside, lock it up again, then head for the exit.

Business done. Money earned.

Now let's go spend it.

*

I've always wanted to be one of those kids walking down a high street with a bunch of bags from different shops. And not the little plastic bags for a pair of socks or something. The big, square bags with a huge logo of the shop they come from. The ones that say you've shopped big, bought loads of stuff, spent a tonne of money.

So, heading back to the station with bags like that from three different shops dangling from my fingers, I feel amazing. The bank card is now sitting snug in a new wallet that I picked up at the tills where I was buying t-shirts. I just looked at it, liked it, then casually chucked it on top of the pile of clothes the cashier was putting through the till.

'That one too, please,' I said, like it wasn't even a thing.

The cashier looked up, gave me a really quick smile like they have to do or they get fired or something, and put it through. But when I took out my cash to pay and peeled off crisp notes from a roll of twenties, I swear he did a double take.

'Cheers, mate,' I said, picking up the first of my big shopping bags.

It was in the third shop, looking for shorts, where I'd found my star purchase. The hoody was black – kind of – but made from a material that seemed to shine and shift in the light. There was a huge graphic on the front that looked like fresh spray-paint, and a smaller one on the back, down at the bottom. It was amazing. I looked at it on the hanger for a full minute, holding the arms out, imagining myself in it. Imagining the selfie I could take while wearing it.

I slipped it off the hanger, pulled it on and stood at the mirror in the middle of the shop. I pinched out the little creases on the shoulders, and turned side on so I could see the little logo on the back. As I moved, the material glinted slightly, like I was made of oil. Buying it meant that I'd have to put back the two pairs of shorts that I'd picked up, but I didn't care. My legs aren't made for shorts anyway. But this hoody... This hoody was made for me.

And now it's mine. I put it on as soon as I left the shop.

Back at the station, I open the locker. The backpack doesn't look very different. Am I too early? I pick it up, and it does feel a little heavier. I open the top zip. My old jumper looks up at me like something shameful. I'll bin it later. I put a hand underneath and touch what feels and sounds like a plastic bag that definitely wasn't there before. Job done, then. Mission accomplished. Swinging the bag onto my shoulder, I close the locker, then go and wait for the next train.

On the platform, I'm looking at the new t-shirts in the bags again. The creases where the t-shirts were folded are crisp and straight, and the labels, held on by little miniature safety pins, look like they've never been touched. I stroke the soft material, breathe in that smell. I saw a TV show about a guy once who only wore brand new underwear – put on a new pair of boxers every day and binned the old ones. Didn't bother washing them, not even once. Sounds perfect, right?

To my left, about twenty metres away, a pair of police officers are standing. I clocked them when I sat down. I always notice police officers. I guess that's the point. They've both got their hands tucked into the front of the thick stab-vests, and they're laughing with each other. Then the female officer does a really big belly laugh, and I look up. Without meaning to, the male one catches my eye, and on instinct I look away fast.

I give it a few seconds, then casually look up again, not at the police officers, but in their direction. Or where they used to be. In the time I wasn't looking, they've moved a bit towards me, and when I look up, it's straight at them.

And they're both looking straight back.

I freeze, then look away again. For some reason, my heart's really going now. I get my phone out, put my headphones on and pretend to scroll through some pages, check my messages: there's something from Johnny asking where everyone is. I'll reply in a bit, send a pic from the train – definitely do the one with my feet up on a seat. My finger hovers over one of the videos from last night that I don't remember taking. Maybe I'll see what it is. Casually, like. As if the cops aren't even there.

I hit play on the video and there's a scuffly shot of a head, some hair, quite close. I can hear my own voice, giggling. And someone else. Matt, maybe? It's all pretty badly lit, mostly shadows.

Then I chance a look up again.

The officers are moving closer. They're not looking at me this time, still pretending to scan the rest of the platform, but they're walking very deliberately in my direction.

I can hear the video playing in my headphones. There's laughing: it's definitely Matt's voice saying something about playdoh, and I can hear mine, too, and some heavy breathing, and a noise that sounds like...

I look back at the screen, a flash of skin – mine? Matt's? – on the screen, and me making a low, groaning noise that I definitely recognise. I fumble for the off button, kill it dead and stuff the phone back in my pocket, but not before I catch a glimpse of Matt's eyes looking straight at the camera. Straight at me.

I don't remember filming that at all.

I feel hot, itchy at the back of my neck and behind my knees. First the cops and now this. But I've got to keep my cool. 'Check the time, Mark,' I say to myself as the departures board resets itself, orange letters tumbling across the screen.

Still two minutes until the train arrives.

I get my phone out again, check the time, again. The police officers can't be more than ten metres away from me. My foot starts tapping the floor. I put some music on to accompany it, make it look deliberate.

'What you listening to?'

I nearly jump in the air, pulling my earbud out quickly. But the voice didn't come from the police officers' direction.

'What you listening to?' she asks again.

It's the girl from the train earlier. She's sitting next to me on the bench.

'Er...' I bumble, snatch a quick glance to my left. The two police officers are walking right behind us.

'Nice top, by the way.' She brushes the oil-black arm of my new hoody. 'So, can I get your number then?'

'Er ... sure, yeah.' I scroll through my phone, trying to work out how to find my number. 'Sorry, new phone. New number.'

The girl smiles. 'Looks expensive. Give it here.' She takes it out of my hands, opens the messages with a few flicks of her bright blue fingernails, and keys in what must be her own number. 'What's your name?'

Her voice makes something vibrate in my stomach. 'Mark,' I say.

The announcer's voice calls from the loudspeaker, and the train pulls in.

From the corner of my eye, I watch the police officers moving off. I'm sure I see one of them smirk to the other one. I start to relax. I watch her type 'Hot Station Girl.' She hits send.

'Thanks. Er, I'll text you, yeah?'

'You'd better.' She hands me my phone and is gone, back to her group of friends at the little coffee stand down the platform. The police officers walk past them, doing that lazy stride as if there's nothing to be worried about. Which, of course, there isn't. I watch them walk away as my train grinds into the station.

I smile to myself, wonder how I could let myself get so worked up, then jump on the train just before the whistle blows and the doors shut with a hiss.

I brush a piece of fluff off the front of my new hoody and start looking around for a good place to take that selfie.

LUC

9

Me and Dad are working on the car. We're both sweating, shirts off. It's hot. The car's a 1995 Subaru Impreza GT in quartz blue pearl and we're getting it ready for a tinted clearcoat later in the summer. Dad says you can't spray at the moment because it's too hot and the paint won't take, but his mate at the spray shop is keeping a slot open for him so we've got to keep it clean for when he gets the call.

Dad's tuned the engine himself and it sounds awesome. The big exhaust box I helped him fit last week shudders and growls. I wanted him to take it all out, get rid of the mufflers and everything so that you get more backfires and the exhaust would pop and blare as we drove along, but he said that was trading off engine efficiency for kids' tricks and he didn't need to impress teenage girls anymore so it was a hard no from him, but that's fine.

You have to know when to ask Dad certain things, make sure he's in the right mood first. Especially if it's something to do with the car. He calls it his big blue baby, and teases Mum about how he's having an affair

89

with it, so you have to be careful about asking whether it's OK to clean a certain bit, or where you can put your feet when you go for a drive.

It's got bucket seats and five-point harnesses. Mum says it makes her feel like she's being strapped down in an asylum or something, so she refuses to go out in it. But that's fine because it means I get to sit up front, and it means Dad can gun the engine a bit harder because she's not there to tell him off. Yesterday he kicked the back out going around a roundabout and he pretty much shouted at me when I put my arm up to hold on to the roll bar above us. Said I shouldn't be such a pussy, and he might as well have brought Mum along. Then we went for McDonald's.

It was hilarious because he kept gunning the engine when he was speaking into the drive-thru bit, which meant the girl on the other end couldn't hear what he was saying, just the guts of the Subaru. When we drove round, she gave us this filthy look when she handed the bag over. Dad told her to cheer up and he'd give her a reason to if she wanted. But she didn't even smile.

Dad gunned the Subaru and we flew off.

You're not allowed to eat in the car, which kind of means that going for a drive-thru is a bit pointless, I guess. We drove up to the car park by the heath and leant on the bonnet to eat. After we'd finished, and Dad had checked my hands and got me to wipe down the front of the car, he gave me another quick driving lesson. I went too heavy on the accelerator though, and the back wheels kept spraying car-park gravel as we lurched forward, so it wasn't a long lesson.

Mum had made lunch for us when we got home. I had a bit, but Dad said he'd already eaten and went off to his office to get some work done, telling me he wanted me to help clean his blue baby tomorrow because I'd made it especially dirty with all my wheelspins.

Which is fine. I like cleaning the car.

The blue paint shimmers under the cloth as I work over the bonnet. He wants me to do the rims next, gives me a toothbrush to get right into the boltheads and make sure all the grease comes out. The rims aren't being resprayed, but it's about pride, he says. You wouldn't wear a suit with dirty shoes, so why drive a clean car with dirty rims?

Dad talks a lot about pride. It's his most important thing, I reckon. He says it's the reason he's got to where he's got to. He runs a scaffolding company, worked himself up from a grunt after he left school at 16, and now he's got eight teams and contracts all over town. And it's all about pride, he says. He won't let his workers slack off on the job. No shouting or calling out like everyone thinks scaffolders are meant to do, and definitely no swearing. If anyone on one of his jobs looks like they're not proud to be there, they get their pay and they're out. No questions.

I've seen it happen. Last summer term was work

experience. Mark found a spot in an accountancy firm where he just got to make tea, and Matt worked in a café at his mum's offices. Both pretty pointless, if you ask me. Johnny didn't go anywhere – the school decided it was best. Dad sent me out with one of his crews for a week. So I'm the only one that was doing a *real* job.

Dad's foremen – the guys who are in charge on site – have all been working for him for years. The one I was with, John, is like an uncle to me. Anyway, it was a hot day, like today, and one young guy – must have been about twenty – is up the top of the tower on a four-storey job on a block of flats, and he takes his company polo shirt off, tucks it into his belt. I'm down the bottom with John, talking through all the different structural steels that are bolted in: the angles, the joints, the platforms. My head's reeling a bit, to be honest. But John spots this guy take the polo shirt off and he tenses a bit, stops talking. Up on the platform, one of the other workers nudges the shirtless guy on the arm and mutters something to him. But the guy shrugs him off, and I hear him say 'Fuck that, mate. It's fuckin' boiling up here'. Then he takes the end of his polo shirt in his gloved hand, and he wipes it across his forehead.

'Oi!' calls John. The whole site stops for a few seconds, because in all the years I've known him, since I was tiny, he's never raised his voice once. John beckons the guy down from the tower.

The guy unclips himself and comes all the way

down the ladders with the whole crew watching him. John hands me his clipboard. He talks in this calm, low voice, like I've heard Dad use before.

'Put your shirt back on,' John says.

'What?'

'You heard me. Put it back on. We're professionals here. That's not how we work.'

The guy puts up some resistance, swearing about the 'fuckin' heat'.

'Would you work in a bank dressed like that?' John takes a step forward.

'What?' The guy steps back.

John keeps moving forward, really slowly, as he speaks. 'Or a lawyers' office? You think when the architect turns up on a job like this one, he takes his shirt off if he gets a bit sweaty?'

But the guy's not getting it and starts mouthing off. John's backed him up pretty much out onto the road by now, and the guy's giving him some verbal about where Dad can shove his fuckin' polo shirt.

Then Dad turns up. Completely by surprise. As if it's all planned or something. Anyway, he pulls up behind the truck in the BMW; he never takes the Subaru to site.

'You can tell him that yourself then,' John says, walking towards Dad as his door opens. 'Good luck.'

'What's the issue?' Dad says, stepping out of the car.

'New guy won't wear his polo. Has some feedback

for you, too.' He looks my way, winks. He knows what's coming and so do I. 'Your boy's doing great, by the way. Got a real knack for this. Right, lads, back to it then,' he calls up the tower. Some people move, but most are staying to watch. They know what's coming, too.

Dad steps closer to the new guy, who's starting to look a bit nervy. 'What name does it have on that polo shirt?'

'I dunno.' The new guy looks a little confused.

'Why don't you have a look?' There's a pause while the new guy looks. 'That's my name. Stitched in red. Do you know why it's stitched in red?' Another pause. 'Because my blood is in this business. A little bit of my blood runs through the veins of everyone that works for me. They wear it on their chests because they're proud of it.'

'So?'

'So when you take it off and start showing disrespect, I feel it. I feel it, and I don't like it.'

'What do you mean?'

'Would you use my arm to wipe sweat off your head? Or my chest? My back?' Dad's voice is getting louder and louder, bit by bit. The rest of the crew are still watching from the top rail.

'No. Course not.' The employee looks up, sees the faces looking down at him.

'So why use my name? My name is to be worn with pride, not for wiping the sweat off your head. And my workers understand that. My blood is their blood. Their blood is my blood. Isn't that right, lads?' Dad looks up; he knew they'd be watching.

'Yes, Mr Durel,' the lads shout back together.

'How many hours have you done this week?' Dad's attention pings straight back to the young guy in front of him, who probably feels like the whole site's ganging up on him. Which they are.

'Er... What?'

'Shall we say about eighteen? Eight Monday, eight yesterday, and we'll call it two for this morning? I know it's not ten o'clock yet, but I'm a generous man.' Dad's started counting notes out of his wallet. 'Eighteen hours. And I'm going to pay you to lunchtime today. So, no hard feelings, understand?'

'Er... You're firing me for not wearing a shirt?'

'You're not my kind of person. Not my blood. You have no pride.'

And that was it. Dad paid him pretty much three days' wages, dropped the stack of notes right on the pavement at the guy's feet. He had to scrabble around to pick it up, everyone on the site laughing at him. And that was it. Gone.

So Dad's pretty much the proudest guy I know.

'Oi, stop daydreaming and get those rims done or I'll clean your teeth with that brush.' Dad gives me a friendly cuff round the head, places a can of Comeup on the driveway next to me. 'You can have that when you're done with those. Tell your mum I've gone to site.'

10

Early afternoon, Mark puts a message on the group chat saying we all need to meet at McDonald's in town. I tell Mum I'm off out and put the tin of Comeup in my shorts' pocket. Mark reckons he can get served it in some places, but he's yet to prove it, so it's easier this way.

When I arrive, Matt and Johnny are already there, hanging around on the benches outside, trying to throw little pebbles into a milkshake cup they've stood on a table. Matt invented the game and it's pretty weak to be honest, like all of Matt's games.

'Who wants a burger then?'

We all turn around, and Mark is coming out of the doors, sweating inside a hoody that looks like it's made of rubber. He's carrying a tray loaded with boxes and drinks. From the looks on the others' faces, they didn't know he was in there either.

'You been hanging around the bins in there, Mark?' I ask.

'Nope. All fresh. I got two Chicken Legends and two Big Macs. Who wants what?'

'Chicken for me,' Johnny says.

'Sprite, Coke or Fanta?' Mark asks.

'Ooooh, Sprite please. No, Fanta.' Johnny grabs his

burger and drink, while Mark pulls four large cartons of fries from a bag, handing them round.

'You went large? Must be feeling flush, mate,' I say, pulling a few fries out and starting to chew on them. 'You look a bit hot. What's that hoody made of, leather? Are you a leather-wearer, Mark?'

'Just wanted to enjoy lunch in the sun with my friends to celebrate the summer.' Mark pulls the new top over his head, and actually folds it before putting it on the seat next to him. 'Chicken or Big Mac, Luc?'

I take a Big Mac, clocking the new wallet that's also sitting in the middle of the tray. 'Cheers, mate.'

'No problem. Matt, what do you want?'

'I don't mind. I'll have whatever you don't want.' That's classic Matt. Pushover.

'Honestly, it's your choice. What do you want?'

'Could you two stop acting like you're on a date or something?' I say.

Mark pushes the Big Mac towards Matt and opens his chicken burger. He picks up the wallet, spins it between his thumb and forefinger, then slides it in his back pocket so we all see it. I think I see Matt blush.

We all munch away for a few minutes. Mark's had a bit more money to spend these last few months, since he's been hooking everyone up at weekends, but this is a bit of a step up. His t-shirt looks new, too. You can still see the creases across his chest, even though it must have soaked up a fair bit of sweat under that hoody.

Johnny puts his hand out to touch the garment sitting next to Mark, but Mark clocks him and slaps him down. 'Not with those greasy hands,' he says. This is like a red rag to Johnny, and he goes again at the hoody, feinting and bobbing up and down to get through Mark's defence. He lands a few slaps on it before Mark throws a handful of chips at him, then Johnny throws some back. Matt leans back a bit to avoid getting caught in the crossfire, then Johnny ups things again by slamming his fist on a packet of tomato ketchup in the middle of the table.

It explodes everywhere.

We all groan, 'Fuuuuck, Johnny!'

Mark's got a napkin and is trying to get a few flecks off his new clothes, I get a gob of it out of my lap and flick it back at John, and Matt seems to be relatively untouched. His hand's over his mouth, trying to keep the burger in it while he's laughing. Most of the sauce flew out of Johnny's end of the packet and squirted across his own chest. He does an elaborate show of making out like he's been shot.

'You're a fucking prick,' says Mark, throwing his dirty napkin at Johnny, who's writhing on to the floor in mock agony.

'How can you say that? I've been shot!' Johnny's voice comes up from under the table. 'Hey,' he says, climbing back up, his voice and his whole body changing direction in a moment. 'It's hot. Let's go to the river.'

Just outside town, there's a bit of the river that curves along the edge of an open, flat meadow. There's a footbridge over it, and the water's deep enough that you don't touch the bottom when you jump off. It's perfect on a hot day like today.

We've not been there for ages. It's over an hour's walk or a much quicker bike ride, but Mark's bike got stolen a few years ago – *he* says that his brother sold it, but I don't know – which means getting there takes ages. And there were rumours about how polluted the river was getting. Someone at school knew someone who knew someone who got really ill after swimming there a few summers ago because of it. Their eyes swelled up really big, apparently, and they were sick for weeks.

'What about the cow piss?' I ask.

Johnny lets a bit of Fanta dribble down his chin. 'Mmmm,' he purrs. 'Cow piss.' Then he stops. 'No that's all bollocks, mate. Nothing wrong with that water.'

'Yeah, it's just a load of bullocks,' says Matt.

So we finish our burgers, bin the rubbish and head out of town. The route weaves between a few housing estates before picking up an old railway track. The path is raised up above the fields, and even though there's a few trees the sun is roasting, coming straight down from overhead. We throw stones as we walk, trying to hit the tree trunks, and when we do there's a hollow knock that seems louder because of the heat. We pass a few other people, an elderly couple first and then two mums with a crowd of little kids between them. The mums look at us and go a bit quiet as we walk by. I smile at them and say hello. They're about to smile back at me, but the other boys start laughing, so the mums' faces go hard again.

On the way, Mark shows us the conversation he's been having with some girl he met on the train yesterday. He won't show us a picture though, says she hasn't sent him one.

'No point carrying on then,' I say.

'What do you mean?'

'If she's not sent you a picture yet, it's going nowhere, mate.'

'Yeah, it is. *She* asked for *my* number. She's up for it.'

'Then ask her for a pic then. Get her to show you something to look forward to.'

Johnny can't cope, starts running around us in circles making sex noises and grinding himself against imaginary girls.

'Look,' I say to Mark. 'I've linked more girls than the rest of you together, right?' No one denies it. They can't. 'If you're not getting pics, they're not putting out. End of.'

Mark shows us some selfies from one of her social feeds, but I shake my head. 'Not those kind of pics, mate. You know what I mean.' I take my phone out and flick through some of my gallery. I open the folder of the ones I've downloaded; these guys won't know the difference, and it feels weird to show them the pictures that Alice has sent me.

Johnny recoils in mock horror, then laughs. Matt is characteristically quiet. He always goes quiet when we talk like this. I think there might be something wrong with him. He keeps throwing these weird looks at Mark, too. Like he's worried about something. Desperation's pouring off him. He really needs to get laid.

Mark just looks jealous. 'That's never from a girl you know. You've screen-grabbed that.'

I get him in a head lock, bend him over. 'Say that again,' I whisper into his ear through gritted teeth. I feel Matt's hands on me, trying pathetically to pull me off of Mark. I shrug him off. Mark splutters in my grip. I give him a few more seconds, then I let him up. He's gone bright red. 'And for fuck's sake take that hoody off.'

When we get to the river, we've made up again, and decided not to talk about it. There's a group of four younger kids on the other bank, their bikes laid on the grass around them. It's like looking back in time. They've got backpacks on the grass in front of them, their towels spilling out. Of the four of us, Johnny had the best towel with a huge Iron Man or Hulk face on it. Matt's towel was always a proper mum towel with some ridiculous pattern on it. Mine was blue and black striped, and Mark's – when he remembered it – was a worn-out old orange one that smelt a bit sour.

The dark water glints deep and cool. Johnny's first in, inevitably. He kicks off his shoes and almost trips out of his shorts as he's running for the bank. He enters the water with a huge splash, his socks and t-shirt still on.

Matt's next, getting down to his boxers pretty quick and wincing over the pebbles, lowering himself down the rocky part of the bank and into the water. He swims out to where Johnny's resurfaced. Then Mark's up on the bridge, standing on the top of the handrail and launching himself out into the air. He hangs there for a second before he's plummeting down, the water rushing up to meet him and a massive boom erupting across the fields as he hits it.

I leave my shorts and shoes in a neat pile on the bank, then slip my t-shirt over my head. The bridge's wooden boards are warm under my feet. I climb the handrail, then carefully turn around so my back is facing the water. I've not done this for years. But I know my body will remember how.

My toes are on the very edge. I breathe in.

I launch myself up and out, back arching, head tipping back, eyes taking in the deep blue of the sky then the dark brown of the water as it tilts into view. My legs kick up and over me, finding a still point for a split second before I pull them in to my chest, completing the rotation of the backwards somersault, then push my feet down again, straightening up just before I hit the water.

The chill is breathtaking and all around me. I open my eyes, see the bubbles rising through the green light. My feet rest on the cold stones at the bottom, toes curling into the film of silt that lies on top of them. I hold myself here for a moment, still and weightless, my arms making small circles to keep me under, the breath held in my lungs beginning to ache and stab. Then I push up, up through the water like a bubble, rising towards the light as my head breaks the surface, the boys all cheering for me.

MATT

11

I've been trying to catch Mark's eye all day. The more I think about it, the more I'm wondering if I'm remembering right. Maybe I've blurred all the bits of Saturday night together. Mark's new phone, the camera, what we did. He's not mentioned it, so maybe I've got it wrong and there is no video after all. I've been thinking about it for days. But, here at the river, what I want to say keeps getting stuck in my throat.

No one's brought trunks. We never used to either, just stripped down to our boxers. As I ease myself into the water, and everyone else jumps in loudly, I watch a group of younger kids on the other bank huddle together, whispering, looking furtively at us. Then they pack up their still-dry towels and push their too-big bikes away.

The others don't notice them leave.

There's a place further upstream – a little island that the river forks around. In the spring, swans nest on it but they'll be gone by now. There's a spot where the river's deep enough to swim, and there's a kind of beach on the island that's good for sitting on. It's not obvious, but I hope those kids know it's there.

After a swim, and watching everyone else do jumps off the bridge, I wade back out onto the bank. I jumped off a few times, a few summers ago, but then Beth said her older brother saw someone dump a shopping trolley under the bridge once and I haven't jumped since. So I watch, pick at a few stones in the grass, lever one out of the summer-warm earth with my finger.

Luc's still doing backflips, trying to teach Johnny who keeps bottling out at the last moment and doing a weird turn mid-air to land all spread-eagled and ugly in the water. Mark can just about pull it off, but Johnny's all over the place, like he's got too many elbows and knees. With a massive slap that must have hurt, he goes in chest first once more, then drags himself out of the water and flops next to me on the grass, like a slick otter – if otters had slapped, red bellies. We watch Mark and Luc trying to go higher, faster, deeper than each other, or seeing who can stay underwater the longest.

Luc's body looks like a weapon. Like a spear entering the water, so quick it's as if the river just opens its throat and swallows him with a thick, whooshing sound. Mark keeps pace with him – he always does – but he doesn't quite have the precision, the grace, the beauty of Luc and the body he's in control of. He's like a torpedo. Maybe he's just one, gigantic, phallic symbol. Mark's got something else, though. Something I can't put a finger on, but that definitely grew quite a bit with his lunch treat earlier on. And it's not just the new hoody, either.

'You're drooling,' Johnny says, leaning in a bit, his head closer to mine.

Luc dangles under the bridge, his hands walking along its steel girders, bent at the elbows in a perpetual chin-up. Him and Mark are doing races along the underside.

'Whatever.' I shrug him off, smiling.

Luc straightens into a pendulum, swings three times then releases, tries to do a backflip.

I wind myself up to speak. 'I need to tell you something, Johnny.'

'Yeah, sure. What about?'

'I need to tell you I'm gay.'

Johnny puts a hand out towards me. I'm not sure what he's doing.

I think he wants a handshake.

'Congratulations, mate.'

'You're not surprised…?' I shift awkwardly, let Johnny keep pumping my hand up and down.

He's grinning from ear to ear. 'Not really. But I'm glad you've told me. Well done.'

I'm not sure you should congratulate someone on being gay, but it's gone better than it did with Mark. At least Johnny let *me* do it. We sit in silence for a bit, enjoy the sun on our skin.

I speak again, my voice feeling loosened by the sunshine. 'So… Saturday just gone…'

'When you and Mark disappeared together and you came back grinning like an idiot? Yeah, what about it?'

I sit bolt upright. 'Do you know? But you were out of it!'

'It was a bit obvious, mate, to be fair. Even for me! Anyway, here comes the man of the hour.'

My voice tightens again. It's like there's a stone in my throat as Mark pulls himself out of the water and joins us. As soon as he sits down, Johnny launches himself to his feet and throws himself off the riverbank, swimming towards Luc under the bridge.

Another long and awkward pause, in which it's Mark's turn to pick at the grass. Then, 'So…'

'Yeah. Totally. Right.'

He leans over, as if his shoulder might bump mine. But he pulls back. 'You alright? You seem a bit quiet.'

As if you'd notice, I think. But what I say is, 'Yeah, fine. Just enjoying the weather.'

Then we sit for a bit longer, 'enjoying the weather' together.

But I need to ask. 'That night … when I was … when we were … you know. Did you…?' But I tail off. I can't.

There's a picture in the David Hockney book that

Dad leant me called 'Pool with Two Figures'. In it, a man is standing on the edge of a swimming pool in the middle of a beautiful Italian valley or wherever, and he's looking down at another man, swimming towards him, underwater. I don't know if they're meant to be the same person – there's something similar about their old-fashioned haircuts – but right now I feel like I'm both of the people in that picture: one of them trapped in the cool of the swimming pool; the other one looking down, watching.

'Did I what?' Mark's trying to keep his voice quiet. I can tell. 'Yes, I enjoyed it if that's what you're asking. I think. I don't really remember that much.' He looks at me for a split second, then back out to Luc and Johnny in the water. He scratches the back of his neck. 'But I just … I don't know … maybe can we not make a thing of it, yeah?'

'Yeah, sure.' There's a swirling in my stomach.

Something in me starts to strain a little and it gets harder to breathe. It's not like I expected us to be a 'thing', like he was about to be my boyfriend or whatever, but still…

Mark lies flat on his back, shielding his eyes from the sun.

'So, that girl from the train, then…' I say, a warm trickle climbing my spine. What *is* that? Jealousy?

'Yeah, it's just chat, mate. Nothing's going on.'

'Fine. You do what you like.' I go back to levering

up stones, throw them into the river where they're swallowed with a series of tiny gulps.

'Look, if it means that much to you, I'll delete her number.'

And he does. He actually shows me his phone – his new one he can't stop showing off, which *is* kind of hot in a geeky way – and he hits 'delete' on their whole conversation. And then he blocks her, too. 'Like Luc said, it's not going anywhere.'

I'm too surprised to know what to do, so I look somewhere else.

Luc's doing the same thing again, swinging under the bridge, but this time he's got his back to us, the taught coils of his shoulders, his biceps like bulbed bombs. Then he launches into the river again.

I take a deep breath, plunge back into my own murky waters.

'Did you film it, Mark? I remember your phone coming out, and the camera…'

'No.' He swallows. 'I mean … I can't remember. Maybe?' His hand's still shading his eyes. I can't tell if they're open or not. 'I mean, there was a video, I think, but I deleted most of the stuff from that night. I'll check when I get home, though. OK?'

'Oh.' Another pause. Why can't he just check now? 'So you're not sure if…'

'I didn't watch it, like I said. I looked at the pictures, then deleted most of them, and a few videos maybe.

I've been a bit busy, you know?' He looks away, across the fields. 'But maybe there was a video, yeah.'

'Really?'

Mark shifts his gaze to somewhere above my head. 'Really. Anyway, even if there was a video, and even if I haven't deleted it already, what do you think I'd do with it?'

Once again, I don't have the words.

Mark leans in, jabs the top of my arm with a finger, a little bit harder than is comfortable. 'Hey, what do you think I'd do with it, eh? I'm your friend, right?' His shoulders seem to relax a little, then he looks right at me, for the first time all day. 'Right?'

I look him in the eye, force myself to hold his gaze even though the moment feels weird and sincere, like something out of a book. Then I smile. Then I laugh but it's a thin kind of laugh.

Mark laughs too, but like mine, it's not a real laugh. It's like his jaw is clamped too tight. He jogs my shoulder with his own, actually connecting this time.

'Don't worry, mate. You'll be alright. But, like I said, could we not … you know? Not when Luc's around, anyway.'

Guess I'm not going to get my romantic reconciliation after all. We look at Luc, treading water, the whole machine of him coiling under the surface. Definitely a torpedo.

'Yeah, sure. Good idea.' I can feel my own jaw stiffen.

Glad we've got that sorted then.

Johnny finally lands a forward flip that he's happy with. Luc even applauds it, and he and Johnny haul themselves out of the water and lie panting in the late afternoon light next to us. The sun's still strong, but it's dropped in the sky and the surface of the water is rippling with warm oranges, rather than the harsh white glare of earlier on.

Mark and I are pretty much dry by now, but I wonder what the others are going to do. No one's got a towel, and Johnny's t-shirt's still soaking. He took it off after his first few jumps, but it's still in the same puddle he threw it in a few hours ago, on top of his once-dry shorts and shoes. He's still wearing his socks. Luc's clothes are still dry, and, as always, neatly folded. It's just his boxers that are wet.

I don't have to wait long to find out their solution. 'Look away, boys!' Johnny calls, pulling his boxers down, exposing everything to the world. He leans over Mark, who recoils and scrambles to his feet. I can't help laughing. I turn away, equally reluctant to get a face-full, and spot two people in the distance: an old couple out for an evening walk. They're too far off to actually see anything, but it's clear what's going on and they stop. The man puts his hand on his wife's shoulder, protectively.

Luc hasn't seen them, and follows Johnny's lead, throwing the wet ball of his boxers into the long grass and stepping into his cut offs, buttoning the fly. 'Here, Johnny. Do you reckon some queer perverts'll come down here and steal those?' he says, loudly, nodding towards their discarded undies.

Johnny laughs, wringing out the worst from his t-shirt and placing it like a scarf around his neck. And, because Luc's looking right at me for some reason, I smile too, and laugh a little bit, despite myself. I'm back in that painting again, definitely watching myself underwater this time.

Johnny's socks have joined the growing pile of wasted fabric. They're black with dirt, so would probably just have ended up in the bin at home anyway. Regardless, I don't want to leave this spot worse than we found it. The old couple, who've now resumed their walk towards us, slowly, will find all this rubbish here and will think exactly what they already think of us. It would be nice, perhaps, not to justify their view completely.

While Mark's putting his clothes on, I step over to the boxers, the socks, and pick them up. There's some comment from Luc about me touching his pants, but I don't hear it properly. I pick up his empty can of Comeup, too, and jog over the bridge. There's a bin about twenty metres down the footpath, just through a hedge where the river meets a country road. I run in my bare feet, just my boxers on, lean through the gate, drop the wet things and the can in the bin, then run back.

From further downstream, I hear voices. It's the four kids from earlier, heading back from the other swimming spot, pushing their bikes, their hair wet and glistening.

I smile as I cross the bridge and say 'hello' to the walkers as we meet in the middle.

They glower back at me.

The others have thrown my shorts into a tree, which is undeniably hilarious, and there's no sign of my t-shirt. I jump up to get the shorts, pull them on, then jog slowly after the others. At least they left me my shoes. Luc's got my t-shirt round his neck, and the rules of boy-friendship dictate that I need to pay them back for the shorts, so I shout 'backpack' and throw myself at Luc from behind.

It was a game we used to play called – inventively – 'backpack'. The higher you can get when you jump, the better. If you're really confident you can turn sideways a bit, so your full weight hits the person you're 'backpacking' on the shoulders. The reason you shout is to let the person who's being 'backpacked' prepare a bit. Or, if they don't know the game, they'll turn around to see what's going on, which means you're more likely to knock them over. Which is kind of the point.

But Luc never misses a beat. Before I'm even airborne, I see him drop an inch or so and it's like trying to push over a wall. I go almost fully sideways too, and end up just rolling down him, ending up in a heap on the floor.

Luc looks a bit annoyed first, but Johnny and Mark are laughing so Luc joins in too.

'Loved that game,' says Johnny. 'What happened to the kid we used to play it with all the time?'

'Greg Hunter?' I offer.

'YES! *Greg* Hunter!'

I'd noticed it first, and mentioned to Mark, that if you called Greg Hunter by his full name it made him sound like his job was hunting Gregs, especially if you put the emphasis on the 'Greg'. '*Greg* Hunter, can I borrow a pen?' or '*Greg* Hunter, what are you having for lunch?' Luc backpacked him once and sent him sprawling along the science corridor at school. Luc said it was like a rodeo, that there was a raging bull under Greg Hunter's small appearance. Must have been all the *Greg* hunting. So he did it a few more times after that. And then a few more. We all did.

'What happened to Greg Hunter?' Luc asks.

Everyone knows that Greg went to another school halfway through year nine. It was about the time that Luc had a conversation with Mrs Clarke about backpacking. By that point, Luc was backpacking Greg at least twice a day. The rest of us a little less. The headteacher even mentioned backpacking in assembly as something that would be added to the zero-tolerance list. But not until after Greg had left.

Maybe those walkers judged us right.

12

Mid-August, and we're up on the school fields again.

Everyone's setting their socks on fire.

Everywhere I look there are little flowers of orange flame, and the squeals of people's laughter. There must be ten, maybe twenty little groups of people in their threes and fours, all setting their socks on fire.

Johnny started it. Of course. But he's gone left on whatever Mark sold him earlier and is now lying on the grass near the long-jump pit. Amy's rubbing his back.

It's not really the socks that are on fire, of course. Johnny turned up at Mark's with a slab of deodorant cans that he said were lying on the loading dock at the back of the Co-op, and said he had an idea. You spray a bunch on your socks, then spark them up.

Luc wanted to do a flame-thrower fight instead, but no one was really interested, thank God.

I did it a few times. Mark gave me half an orange one again – he charged me a tenner this time – and I liked the weird hot tickle of the burning aerosol up my legs, the sweet-sharp smell of singed hair mixing with the heavy muskiness that reminded me of primary-school discos. But I'm coming down now and just want to sit here on the grass with my eyes closed.

I'm waiting for Mark – seems like I've been waiting for Mark for weeks now – who's doing the rounds, making sure everyone's OK. He's got this whole new look that seems to have evolved overnight. There's the big headphones he wears around his neck, the clothes that he always dusts off when he stands up, and I've counted three new pairs of trainers. He keeps rubbing stains off them with a licked thumb. But he's got this confidence to go with it all now, this spiel he slips into. I can hear him, off to my right a little way, his voice like a purple ripple against the orange flames. It makes me smile.

Not that I'd show him that.

I don't know the people he's talking to. These nights up the Lanes or on the school field are busy now. Every week – or every other night, now it's summer – new people show up. People you know from school, but you've not really spoken to before, or people from somewhere else entirely. Which all means more people for Mark to talk to. Sell to.

Which means I have to wait for him some more. Farewell, summer romance.

I wonder if he knows I'm waiting.

The little orange flares register inside my eyelids like mushrooms, and the laughter peels away into the night. I follow it with my ears. Below my hands, the earth is warm. I trace a crack in the soil with my fingertip, pretend I'm a tiny ant. It's been scorching for weeks now and the grass has started to turn brown, shrivelling into itself for protection. Even at night, the heat doesn't really leave. It stays in the ground.

I tilt my head back, open my eyes. The moon is a thin gash in the sky.

'Matt?'

I turn. It's Amy. She's beckoning me over.

'John's not well.'

I walk over. Johnny's lying on his side in what looks like the recovery position that we all had to learn in the first aid unit in PSHRE last year. 'Did you put him like that?' I ask.

'Yeah, but he didn't put up much of a fight. Do you think we should call someone?'

I bend down, shake Johnny's shoulder.

He groans a bit.

'I dunno. Maybe. Has he had anything to drink?'

'He had some of my vodka.'

'I mean *to drink* drink, not *drink* drink.'

Amy starts giggling, 'Drinky, drinky, drink.'

I smile, almost giving in to laughter. But then I give my body a good shake to find some seriousness.

Johnny groans again. I pinch his ear lobe, which, they said in those PSHRE lessons, is a good way to test for consciousness if people have passed out.

Johnny swats at me with the arm he's not lying on.

'I think he'll be OK. Want me to take a shift with

him? I'm off on holiday tomorrow, so was going to ease off now, anyway.'

Amy shuffles onto unsteady legs. 'Thanks, Matt. You're the best. One day, you'll make a girl very…' She tails off. Everyone knows now, I think. Not that I've mentioned it.

Amy's hazy eyes flick past me. 'My QUEEEEENS!' And she's off, wobbling across the field towards Megan and Niamh, who are just arriving. She gets halfway towards their outstretched-for-a-hug arms before going over on her side and cry-laughing about pins and needles, moaning about how long she's been looking after Johnny. Then they're all passing a bottle of vodka between them and looking around for Mark.

'Good luck,' I mutter. More to myself than to them.

I sit down next to Johnny.

'You alright, mate?'

Another groan. This one sounds a bit more like a 'yeah'.

'Good call on the socks-on-fire-thing.'

He gives me a short laugh, tries to haul himself upright, but ends up rolling onto his back. I push him over into the recovery position again.

'You've got gentle hands,' he says.

'Thanks, mate.'

'And you're in love with Mark.'

I stutter a bit. 'Pardon?'

'Got anything to drink?'

There's a half-drunk can of Comeup by Johnny's feet. I give it a sniff to assess its alcohol content. It seems clean. I help Johnny sit up and he gulps at the can, greedily.

'Does he know? Mark? That you like him?' He slurs between mouthfuls.

'Er… I don't know. I think so. We've … er…'

'You snogged. Pashed. Played tonsil tennis.' Johnny makes loud sucking noises around his tongue. 'Yeah, I know.'

'It's not funny, man.'

'Sorry, mate. Dropped a whole orange and a half earlier and things have run away from me a bit, you know?'

One and a half? No wonder he's so spaced out.

'Affairs of the heart, as they say…' Johnny tries to carry on, but can't seem to remember what 'they say'. He switches metaphors. 'I can read you like a book, Matt.'

'But you don't read books, Johnny.'

He likes that one, and snorts into the Comeup. But the snort catches inside his stomach somewhere, and with a quick roll onto all fours, Johnny's emptying his insides onto the grass in spectacular waves.

I rub his back as he heaves again.

Johnny's chundering draws a few looks in our direction, including from Mark. He flashes me a quick thumbs up, with an 'is he OK?' face. I nod at him. Smile. Think about waving him over. But he's already turned back to the group he's talking to.

They all laugh.

Johnny retches one more time, but it doesn't seem that there's anything else to bring up. A thin trail of saliva dangles from his nose. His wipes it on his t-shirt.

'Come on, mate. Let's get you home.' I stand up. Amy wasn't wrong – I'm already getting the beginnings of pins and needles. 'There's nothing here for either of us tonight, I don't think.'

'Do you ever…' Johnny starts, rolling onto his back again. He's not done yet, it seems.

'Ever what, John?'

'I dunno.' He pauses, arms flapping about a bit like he's doing dry-grass angels. He does manage to avoid the sick, though. 'Ever just wonder at the sheer … *audacity* of it all?'

I sit down again. 'That's a long word, Johnny. Please elucidate.'

'You know, the *balls* of it? The sheer fucking *cheek* of all this?' He gestures at the clear, night sky. 'All of that, up there. All that … space!' He laughs at his own joke. 'And then us, scuttling about down here, feeling all trapped and pushed up together as if there's nowhere else to go.' He starts to laugh. 'It just seems like … I dunno. Like *bad manners*, sometimes. All that nowhere, and us, now, here.' Then he stops, takes another swig from his can, and gets unsteadily to his feet. 'Come on then.'

I can't say I follow Johnny's argument, but I manoeuvre him off the field easy enough, steer him home across the heath and plunge his head into a few dewy bushes on the way to try and sober him up. As whatever he's taken starts to ebb a bit lower, he starts to shrug me off. He walks with his head tipped back, eyes on the stars again. Then he spots something, points off to one side. 'Look.'

The copse where we used to build dens is silhouetted against the sky, like a cardboard cut-out in the windless air. 'Oh yeah.' We stand and look at it for a while.

I used to imagine all the trees up here bending over at night, flailing their branches like limbs. I even had a few nightmares about it. I still find trees a bit scary sometimes, especially in the dark. A small shiver runs up my spine. We get moving again and walk in silence for a while.

As the lights of the road grow steadily closer, I ask, 'When's your mum off on holiday?'

'In a few days. Three, maybe.'

Johnny's parents always take at least one trip over the summer holidays. Johnny's mum always says she needs a holiday from the kids' summer holidays. Then she and Giles go away again in early September, usually.

'Your nan coming this time?' I ask. We're off the heath now, onto the wide avenues of his estate.

'Nah, we're old enough to look after ourselves now, Anna and me.' Johnny's started picking at bushes now, clumsily shredding leaves as we walk.

'Oh, right.' I want to ask Johnny if he's OK with that. 'That's good, though. You can do what you like. And Anna's cool, isn't she?'

'Anna'll be working most days. Wants to get a head start on revising, she says. Reckons year thirteen'll be really hard work.'

'Has she done the forms for uni yet?'

'Almost, she says. The ones for doctor courses have to be in pretty early, I think.'

'Is it just medicine she's applying for?'

'A few biology courses, but mostly, yeah.'

'But you'll be OK? Keep yourself busy?' I don't know why, but I always feel a bit guilty for going away in the summer with my family, leaving Johnny on his own.

We're walking between the orange globes of light from the streetlamps when Johnny stops.

Outlined on the ground at our feet are two shadows – one cast by the streetlight in front, and one by the light from behind. Johnny takes a few steps forward and, as the shadow behind him grows shorter, the one in front gets longer. Johnny takes a few steps forward, then backward, then walks between the lights like a crab, watching both shadows at once.

'What are you doing, John?'

'I'm trying to work out if the shadows are always the same length – added together, I mean.'

'And…?'

'I'll need a few more tests before I can say for sure.'

I look up at the lights for a bit, wonder how you'd even start to work that out. I can do words, but numbers don't come quite so easily. When I look back at Johnny, he's found a long stick and a piece of white stone from somewhere and is using it on the pavement like chalk, marking the length of the stick's shadows at paced-out intervals between the lights. He's got that concentration look again, his tongue between his teeth.

'G'night, Johnny.'

I cross the road, head for home.

MARK

13

So, I told Matt I'd deleted that video. But I haven't.

I don't really know why. It's not like I want to show it to anyone, and it's not like I've watched it. Not that many times.

But for some reason, I like that it's there. Especially that bit where Matt's looking straight down the lens. Straight at me.

I try not to think about it too much, though. Mostly because I'm really busy, playing the game, getting paid.

It's like I've gone up a level. There are new routes, new tactics, but the rules are basically the same.

You wait for a message, then you do what the message says, then you collect rewards. Simple. It's like an old video game – one of those 'bring me the stone of Aramoth and I shall give you this key' adventure ones. Or maybe it's more like one of the really old ones, where you go across the screen, jumping from platform to platform and picking up coins or whatever. Like I said, easy stuff.

But it's mind-blowing how many rewards you can collect. I've not been playing very long, but the money's just the start of it.

The Guy's still keeping hold of the money for me. I looked into bank accounts, and he was right about me needing Mum's signature and stuff. She's been far too busy for that. Anyway, she'd probably have some questions that I'd rather not answer. And the card works fine on contactless. No one ever checks the name on cards, do they?

He says there'd be a problem with transferring my money, too. I'd be waiting for days – weeks, maybe – if I wanted him to transfer my money to my own account, in my own name. He knows how the online banking stuff works. And he said the only account I could get would be a cash account. I'd have to take cash out of the wall and wouldn't be able to use the card in shops – you have to be eighteen to get one of those accounts, he says. Johnny's got a card he can use in shops, but that's in his step-dad's name. So it's what everyone does, I guess.

So I could get the cash card account, but The Guy also says that no one professional uses cash anymore. He's right. The more I look, the less cash I see. I like the feel of those crisp twenties, but I'm the only one in shops that pays cash, and it's embarrassing having to pocket a handful of coins. So until I can get it properly sorted out, I told The Guy to just keep putting everything I earn into that account and send me the balance. I love seeing that balance every week. What a buzz! It keeps going up, up, up! It's well into four figures now. It'll be five before I know it! And I can just scan my card on the little machine – *boop* – and get what I need. Easy.

That's how I bought everyone burgers for lunch the other week.

Which absolutely blew their minds.

On my second city trip I picked up some new headphones to go with the new phone. Minds blown once again. Then, one day, The Guy's backpack comes out of the locker with some new trainers underneath it. Still in the box, too. I'd already got some new trainers, so these were bonus trainers, and worth triple-figures. And then I bought another pair a few days later because they were amazing. *Boop* – mine! That's the kind of rewards this game gets you.

My left pocket buzzes. Finally! I still love feeling the bevels of the handset in my grip, the cool metal of the case as I pull it out, like ice in my palm. It's almost addictive. The message is the same as usual, another collection at locker 22.

I'm kind of feeling that I've had enough of my own company though. Luc's been on holiday for a week, and he's got another week until he's home. His pictures look amazing – loads of sunshine, swimming pool that chemical blue colour. And there's a few selfies, because it's Luc and that's what he does. And Matt's off camping somewhere by the coast, I think, so I couldn't see him even if I wanted to. I've got the video, though.

That leaves Johnny, whose parents are away – again

– but they never take Johnny with them. Johnny's always around, which is cool.

I drop him a message, ask if he fancies an adventure – a mission – and head down the hill along the main road, into the new estate. When they started building it, just before I started at secondary school, Mum used to bring me here to watch the diggers. She'd let me stand here for ages, holding my hand. Back before she had to work all the time.

Johnny's house is at the bottom end. It's massive. There are two huge windows on the front of it that don't even have rooms behind them, just the big staircase that winds up from the hallway. And once you've climbed up that, you walk along a kind of balcony to get to the bedrooms. Our staircase is narrow and dark, as if it's been folded into the house as an afterthought when the builders remembered you needed to actually get to the tiny bedrooms upstairs.

There's five bedrooms in Johnny's house, all doubles. One of them is something called a 'guest suite' that's a bedroom and a bathroom and it's probably as big as our whole downstairs. There's even a sofa up there. That's why it's called a suite, Johnny said.

Johnny sends me a message saying he's up for it, and about five minutes later I knock on his front door.

His sister Anna answers it, invites me in.

'You look hot, Mark.'

I'm about to say something.

'Hot like warm, not hot like... Oh whatever. Do you ever take that hoody off? Or is it a wetsuit?' She grins. 'You could put it in your lovely backpack.'

'It was cold this morning.' I take off the top, giving myself a quick sniff under the armpit as I step through the door, pretend I'm wiping my nose on my sleeve. I am a bit tangy, to be honest.

'Erg, boys!' Anna goes off, leaves me in the hallway.

Johnny barrels downstairs a few seconds later in cut off denims and an old t-shirt, shouting to Anna that he's going out. As we're on the doorstep, Johnny has a sudden thought and shouts back into the house, 'What's for dinner later?'

Anna's voice echoes from somewhere deep inside the building. 'I'm not here for dinner. I told you, Mia's doing a barbeque. And it's not my job to feed you, either.' She comes back into the hallway, through a different door from the one she left through. 'There's money on the breakfast bar. Oh, Mark, while you're here, are you still ... y'know, *delivering*?'

I nod. You can even *boop* in taxis, I've learnt. Which is handy.

'Good. I'll be in touch later. Nice trainers, by the way.' Then she's gone again.

'Right then, money and supplies,' Johnny says, playfully. I follow him through the big hallway, into the even bigger kitchen. He grabs a few notes from a brightly coloured bowl on the counter. There are a couple of stools tucked underneath where you can sit and eat or have a cup of tea or whatever. That's where Johnny's mum sits most of the time, when she's here, flicking through magazines. We get the money and keep walking, through a set of double doors into the big lounge (it's not just called that because of its size; it's because there are two of them, and this one is bigger). Johnny grabs a zip-up hoody from the arm of the sofa. Then it's through into the little lounge, which they also call 'the snug', which is Johnny and Anna's own lounge where the Xbox and stuff is, and in one corner there's a fridge of Coke and a cupboard full of snacks and a kettle and a thing for making coffee, too. Anna's in there, reading a chemistry textbook. Johnny grabs a couple of bags of crisps from the cupboard, throwing one at me as we come back into the hall, the lap of the house complete.

Johnny kicks his feet into a pair of old flip flops and we're out of the door.

A little way down the road, crisps finished, we start talking.

'Which one's Mia's house?' I like to keep track of Anna's friends. They're customers, so it's good business.

'Big posh one in one of the villages. Can't remember which one. She's got a pool and a couple of donkeys.'

'You mean horses?'

'No, donkeys. Her mum adopts them or something. So Anna's spending the day by the pool.'

Even though Johnny's family have got loads of money, it's still nothing compared to some kids at school.

'Your parents away again?'

'Yeah. Hey, you want to get a takeaway later?'

'Yeah, maybe.' Takeaway means leftovers. Maybe I could bring a box or two home, put it in the fridge. I've eaten at Johnny's a few times. Anna and Johnny always over order.

It's much more comfortable at Johnny's without his parents being there. It's not like they mind anyone coming over, but they offer you snacks you've never heard of, or talk to Johnny about remembering to do something in the so-and-so room, or reminding him to keep his feet (and those of his friends) off the so-and-so piece of furniture and I don't really understand what's going on.

In my house, we've just got the normal furniture. But Johnny's house has got *chaise longues* and *ottomans* and *sideboards* and *dressers* and loads of other stuff. And, in our house, we've just got the living room, the kitchen, the bedrooms and the bathroom. That's it. Normal. But Johnny's got a *pantry* and a *boot room* and a *study* and a *snug* and even a room they call *the gym* which is just a room with a yoga mat and a big bouncy ball in. So when they're giving Johnny instructions or telling him off – and they're always doing one or the other – it's like they're talking another language, which is strange to be around.

And if it's the afternoon and Johnny's mum's at the breakfast bar with her magazine and a glass of wine, she asks you about the latest 'capers' her son has been getting into at school. The first time I was there, Anna had to explain to me what a 'caper' even was. According to his mum, Johnny's always in a 'caper' of some description, or another letter from Mrs Clarke has just arrived, and she asks you about it with this sideways smile on her face.

You have to be polite to friends' mums. That's part of the game. But it's also one of the rules that you don't snitch on your friends. So it's easier when Johnny's mum isn't around. Which is good, because she's not, most of the time. And Giles is there even less.

Giles is Johnny and Anna's stepdad.

I think Giles is OK. His house is tricked out, he drives this huge car with tinted windows, and he clearly makes loads of money. When he *is* around, he's normally on the phone, or in his office, which is a room I've never been into, off the kitchen, 'through the boot room and next to the pantry', or something. No one's allowed in there. And he's always well dressed – for an old guy, anyway. He always wears these light-coloured trousers like he's saying 'come on then, stain me. I can afford it.'

And he also lets Johnny and Anna do pretty much what they want.

I say 'pretty much'. There are definitely limits. People always ask why Johnny and Anna don't have more parties, especially when they see the size of their house and find out how often it's just them there. We used to nag him about it all the time. But then, after the four of us came back from the heath a few years ago, and Johnny was still a bit wired and forgot to take his shoes off before lying on the sofa in the kitchen (that's how big the house is – there's a sofa in the kitchen) we found out why they don't. That was the point when Giles walked in. He must have heard us. He started off being all 'lads' with us, like Luc's dad does, offered us a can of Comeup to share between us.

Then he saw Johnny lying there with his shoes up on the sofa, and he stopped dead. He did an 'oi' and clicked his fingers at Johnny – actually clicked his fingers, like Johnny was a dog or something – and Johnny did a face like I'd never seen before and unlaced his trainers straight away and took them out of the room. Giles watched him all the way, even held up a finger when Luc started talking, then he watched as Johnny walked back again.

But there must have been some dirt on his shoe or his knee or something, because there was a little smear on the edge of the sofa, and across one of the cushions.

When Giles saw the mess that Johnny had made, he went mental. Well, we didn't see him go mental because he told us all to leave, pretty much told us to fuck off. Luc almost said something, but the look on Giles' face was a bit scary, even for Luc, so we went quietly. Then we just heard the noise of Giles' shouting as the kitchen door closed behind us.

So maybe he is a bit of a prick.

We walk down to the station, and Johnny doesn't even blink when I buy the tickets at the machine. It's not like I'm trying to show off, or could even compete just with his stash of 'emergency money', but it grates a little bit that Johnny hasn't realised I'm paying for loads of stuff. It's like he doesn't even *see* money, sometimes.

We scan through the barriers and wait on the platform. Johnny gets his phone out. There's a new message from Matt, wondering what we're doing.

'You didn't invite Matt?' Johnny asks.

'Thought he was on holiday.'

Most of the train seats are empty so we spread out at a table. I put my backpack under the chair but keep a hold on the top handle. I put my feet up, show off my bright white kicks.

'Anna's right, man, they are nice trainers. Thanks for the ticket, by the way. I'll get the next one, yeah?'

'You can add it to what you owe me for those two oranges you had off me last week.'

Johnny grins, puts his phone away, pulls out his 'emergency money' and puts it on the table. 'Hey. You got any more?'

'Well, as it happens...' I dart a quick look around the carriage: empty except some old dear at the other end, facing the other way, her white hair like a little snowy hill above her seat. I swing the bag up onto the table, undo one of the inside pockets.

So that's the game for today, then.

14

And then the game changes.

The orange kicks in as we get off the train, the platform swimming beneath our feet as we make for the left-luggage lockers. Johnny can't stop giggling but I'm trying to keep a straight face. Because I've got a job to do.

But when we got to the lockers, my key won't fit. I don't know if someone else has already put something in there, or if the lock's been changed, or if I'm too early. I look at my phone to check, nearly dropping it. But no, I'm on time. I try again. The key just won't turn. I look at the number on the key, check it against the locker.

Like any good businessman, I use my initiative and decide I'll have to wait for whoever The Guy's friend is. So I lean against the wall, opposite locker number 55, and pretend to be on my phone. I don't know where Johnny is, but I can hear him occasionally, giggling to himself or shouting at me from what seems to be a long way away. People are walking past me, blurry legs and loud shoes.

About five minutes later, someone stops a few metres from me. He clocks me leaning on the wall, then turns, hunches into the jacket he's wearing, takes a key from his pocket and opens a locker with a slightly battered door. He peers inside, looking confused. I laugh a bit, like he was expecting to see a whole civilisation in there or something. Idiot. He even puts his hand in, has a good rummage. I laugh a bit more. I can't help it. Then he looks right at me and slams the door shut again, quickly walking off in the direction he came from.

The locker door hasn't been shut properly, and swings on its hinges. I call after the figure, 'Excuse me, mate. You've left that open?'

He doesn't turn around but quickens his pace.

I haul myself upright, take the few steps on stiff legs to the open locker, push it closed. Then I see the number on the front. 22.

Pulling my own key out of my pocket, I look at the label. 22.

Then it hits me.

I've been reading my key upside down. But how? I've done this plenty of times already. The orange has messed with my head, messed with the game.

I sprint after the figure as he starts up the footbridge that crosses over the tracks. 'Hey!' I call. 'Wait!' I wave the backpack over my head. 'You're looking for this!'

But he doesn't look back, and he's taking the steps two at a time.

By the time I get to the top, he's most of the way across. He glances back at me as he pushes through the door to the multistorey car park. I can feel a tingling in my arms, my heart pounding in my chest, but my head still feels like liquid. I bounce off one of the hand rails, almost fall into a woman walking the other way, the bridge pounding as I run, steel girders booming like a huge drum.

When I get through the doors, the figure is getting into the passenger side of a blue van. It starts to pull away. 'Wait!' I shout, waving the backpack again, my voice echoing around the concrete car park. 'Wait!'

The van slows as it nears the exit, then its engine revs loudly, tyres complaining as it swings a dangerously sharp turn and comes back my way.

I step forward as it comes to a sharp stop in front of me, glad I managed to avoid disaster. I even smile at the face of the figure in the passenger seat. Seeing him close up for the first time, I guess he must be about my age, maybe a year younger. But he won't catch my eye, his face frozen, eyes dead straight. If I was thinking clearly, I'd have said he looks terrified.

But I'm not.

I put on my charming grin, reach for the passenger door, ready to apologise and hand the bag over. Then the side of the van opens like a giant black throat and swallows me whole.

*

It's pitch black inside the van.

How could I have been so stupid? There's no way a 22 looks like a 55, even if you squint at it.

There's something digging into my back. It feels like a coil of rope or something. I try to pick myself up but the van swings around a corner and I'm thrown down again, crashing into the metal struts of the van's internal panels. The pitch of the engine rises sharply, then the throaty jolt of a gear change.

There's a smell of oil and petrol, like how Luc smells when he's been working on his dad's car. And it's hot. Really hot. My top lip is wet with sweat, and my forehead feels tight. I try to stagger upright.

'Stay down,' growls a low voice.

'I've got the –'

'Stay. Down.'

There's a small section cut out of the wooden partition between the back of the van and the cab. A small square of sunshine. Silhouetted against it I can just make out the outline of a large man. With one hand, he holds a strap attached to the van's roof and he sways easily with the van's movements that are tossing me around the floor.

The van lurches again and my head is thrown into the side panel with a thud. I groan, seeing stars for a second. The orange is still going strong, and the flash of light I see in front of me is intensified.

'Sit still,' the voice rumbles at me.

Wincing, I manage to pull myself to a slouch, holding onto the sharp edges of the van's metal ribs.

'Now, give me the bag.'

Shakily, I hold the bag up towards him and he snatches it from my grip. I can't see a single detail of his face.

The man knocks heavily on the partition, and a hand appears at the opening, holding a small parcel of something. The man crouches, and for second it's like he's disappeared into the darkness. I force my eyes to pick him out, and see the man squatting with his back against the partition wall, my backpack at his feet. He pulls my hoody out, tossing it towards me.

'This stinks, kid. Wash more,' he grunts.

'OK, yeah.' I manage to whimper. Where are they taking me? The van has reached a relatively steady pace now, swaying gently. I have an odd feeling of sea-sickness. I close my eyes tight, but the feeling gets stronger inside my head. Faces swim at me behind my eyelids: The Guy asking me what I've done, the silhouetted man and his grim voice, and Matt. Matt, looking straight at me, concerned, worried, tender.

When I open my eyes, the man is taking another package from the hand at the opening, putting it into my backpack. Then a third. Or is it a fourth? A fifth? Then the man stands, holding the roof strap again, my backpack swinging in his fist. He turns briefly, takes a look through the opening.

'Hold tight,' he mumbles.

But I don't move quickly enough. The van breaks sharply then swings hard to the left. I lose my grip and my face is driven into the floor before I can get my arms out for protection. As the van comes to a standstill, I pitch forwards again, my head knocking against what must be the man's boots.

He flicks me off like I'm a leaf.

'Now listen. You get one fuck-up, right? One fuck-up, and one fuck-up only.' His head is close to mine, his hand on the back of my neck, angling my face upwards.

'S-s-sorry.'

'Don't be sorry, Mark. Be better.' He pats me on the cheek a few times, hard, then pulls me up by my t-shirt so I'm sitting.

The van engine is idling, making the inside rattle in a way that juggles my stomach. I feel I might be sick.

'Any more fuck-ups and you're finished, right? You and that boyfriend of yours.'

'Boyfriend...? What?'

'We've seen that video. The two of you fumbling around on the grass or whatever. Do you think we're not watching you, Mark?'

Something drops like lead in my gut, the van not spinning anymore, but falling, plummeting, like a broken lift.

'I don't know what you're talking about,' I stutter.

The man gets his phone out of his pocket, the blue

light flashing across his square head, his small eyes, narrow and clean-shaven chin. He sees me looking at him. 'Don't try to remember this face, boy. This isn't a face you remember, right?'

I look away.

The man thrusts the screen at me, a video playing. My video. I see Matt's face, the top of his head. It's lit up like a halo.

'You get it?' The man growls in my ear. 'We're watching you. What you see, we see.'

I nod.

With a grating roar, the side door opens and daylight floods in. I put my arm up, covering my eyes. I'm hauled upright then flung from the van and it's so bright I can barely see. Managing, somehow, to land on my feet, I stumble into a chain link fence. I turn quickly, arms raised ready for the next assault.

There is a thud as something hits my chest. Then the sound of the van door slamming shut, an engine gunning, tyre squeal, then nothing except the roar of traffic passing fast and close and me gulping for air, filing my lungs until its painful.

I drop my arms, blink. I'm at a petrol station, a dual carriageway in front of me and another road behind the chain link fence at my back. The backpack is at my feet.

I pick it up, my shoulders aching as I put it on. I close my eyes against the pain and see the video playing again, that short bit of film, not even a minute. What will they do with it, or with me? What will they do with Matt?

My hoody is at my feet. It must have been thrown out with the backpack. I pick it up, see it's stained with oil or something equally dark and tar-like, sticky against the dirty material. I drop it to the floor again, where it can stay.

I reach for my phone. The one that they are using to watch me. When I pull it from my pocket, there's a crack down the middle of the screen. I think about launching it over the fence into the middle of the oncoming traffic. But something makes me stop, put it back in my pocket. Then I take it out again and check the time.

How long was I in the van?

Not long. Five minutes maybe.

I look around again, the floor starting to feel more solid under my feet. Opening my maps app, I wait for the blue circle to come to rest. From where I'm standing, I can just make out a big blue road sign that points to a motorway.

Was it only five minutes?

My phone tells me I'm five miles from the station, somewhere in the city's sprawling web of roads.

My stomach does a backflip, and suddenly there are waves of sick coming up my throat. I let it all out against the fence, fingers curled into the mesh, keeping me upright. Some of the sick is going on my new trainers which, like the hoody, have got some kind of black tar on them from the floor of the van.

I use the hoody to mop up some of the sick, then I kick the damp mess towards a bin a few metres away, wipe my mouth on my bare arm.

I'm staring at my phone screen, trying to make sense of all the lines when I hear another engine pull up close to me. I flinch, force my head to stay down, but it's not the van men come back for another round. It's just a taxi.

I keep staring at my phone as it works out the walking route back to the station. It says I have to go across the road behind me, so I look for a way over the fence.

On the forecourt, someone's getting out of the taxi's back seat, saying something to the driver about how they're meeting their dad here and not to worry, it's all fine. I hear the driver say that it's a strange place to meet, the passenger replying, but their voices aren't clear, then the door closes and the taxi accelerates away.

I pocket my phone, put a hand on the top of the fence, try to pull myself up, but the chain is sharp and it cuts into my palm. I think someone shouts my name, but I don't really register it and I drop down from the fence and look at my hand as a small pool of blood starts to form at the base of my thumb and I suck at it, the thick, metallic taste almost making me sick again.

Then I hear it again, clearly this time. I close my eyes and a familiar voice is saying my name.

Then there's a hand on my shoulder.

It's Johnny.

LUC

15

I met a girl at the airport.

She was in the duty-free shop while I was buying sunglasses. She had this pink bag that was too small to carry anything except a phone, and long wavy hair that she had brushed over one shoulder. Like everyone, she was wearing her comfies for the plane, but hers looked really nice and she wore a tight top that showed her belly button. I was glad I'd put on some new shorts and a decent t-shirt. When I saw her in the café later, I looked at her and she smiled back.

When we went to our departure gate, she was there again with her mum and dad. She saw me arrive and smiled right at me, pulling her hair across onto the other shoulder in the way girls do when they like you, then she went back to her phone. I sat quite near her and turned on my Bluetooth. There was a phone nearby called SaraGurl06, so I searched the name and found a few social media profiles. The pictures were definitely her, so I liked them and followed her, and she followed me back straight away.

On the flight she was sat way in front of us, but we

both had aisle seats, and I saw her looking at me a few times. I'd kept my new sunglasses on though, so she couldn't see me looking back. Once, I even saw her little brother's head peer around the side of the seat. He pointed at me and smiled, before SaraGurl06 pulled him back and I heard her shout-laugh at him. It must have been their mum in the aisle seat behind them because she turned around too and smiled in my direction, then SaraGurl06 sat with her hands over her face for a while. I waved at the mum. It's always good to wave at mums.

My mum sat next to me on the flight and held my hand when we took off. Dad sat in the window seat. I could hear his breathing get tight every time Mum winced at the tiny pockets of turbulence we passed through. When the pilot said we were starting our descent, she held my hand again and didn't let go until we'd landed.

SaraGurl06 was there at the baggage collection, and she was on the coach too, so she must be staying at the same hotel as us. I decided then that it was worth sending her a message. And she replied, of course. Her family were staying for a week. We were staying for two, but I guessed a week was OK and we arranged to meet at the pool the next day after breakfast.

But there were two pools at the resort, and we hadn't said which one to meet at. I was out of data, and I couldn't get the guest wi-fi to work until after ten am and three trips to reception to talk to the guy there who's English was really bad. But I got it sorted and was waiting at the bigger pool with my new swimming shorts on, a sleeveless t-shirt and my new sunglasses. The shorts were a bit tight maybe, but I looked good in them.

A minute later, the girl turned up in a baggy t-shirt but with this really hot bikini underneath.

'Hi.'

'Hi.'

'Sorry I'm a bit late,' I said. Girls like it when you say sorry.

'But you were here first,' she smiled, clearly checking me out. The tight shorts were a good idea. Then she put her arm on the shoulder of the kid standing next to her. 'This is my brother, George.'

'Oh, yeah. Cool. Hi George.' I hadn't even noticed him.

She said something about her parents wanting to get some time to themselves to work out how the resort worked. I said it was fine, and George was carrying a rugby ball so I thought he'd be OK.

The pool was packed, but we found a couple of old sun loungers on the patio of an unused, ground floor room, dusted them off and dragged them to the poolside. Me and George talked about rugby for a while and Sara – who's name actually was Sara, I asked – showed me some pictures on her phone of her and her friends from

147

school. She'd just finished her GCSEs and was on holiday to celebrate her results, so I told her the same. I'm only a year away, and it's not like she'll find out.

I asked her what she got and she gave me a list of 7s, 8s and 9s. I told her I got mostly 7s and a few 8s and said I was in top sets for most things, like she was, and I said a few things that I remembered Matt saying. Who knew listening to that guy might be useful one day? Sara looked actually impressed by my take on some of the poems from English lit, and I said I was looking forward to sports science for A level. She's starting sixth form in September – Maths, Physics and French.

We went for a swim: the edge of the big pool has a kind of river you can swim around, and at some points around the river there are these little benches built into the side. Me and Sara sat on one, underneath a potted palm tree, while George went on the waterslide.

She told me she had a friend called Luke, so I told her about how you spell my name different. 'So are your family French then?' she asked.

'Not really,' I answered, which was a shame, because I remembered she said she was doing French next year.

'Sounds good though, having a French-sounding name. *Luc.*' She said it again, her lips pouting as she put emphasis on the 'c'. 'Your girlfriend must like it.'

I guess she'd seen the pictures on my profile of me and Alice. It annoyed me that Alice tagged me in all the selfies she took of us together. There was one of me with my tongue in her ear that I'm surprised she posted in the first place.

'She's not really my girlfriend. More like ... more like a "girl mate", I guess.'

'Oh right. With benefits?'

'Something like that,' I smiled. 'So what about this other Luke, then? Is he your boyfriend?' I leant forward on the bench. A strand of Sara's hair had fallen out from behind her ear. I put it back, let my hand rest on her cheek.

'No. He's just a "boy mate", y'know?' Her eyes didn't leave mine.

I dropped my hand. She caught it in hers, gave it a little tug.

'Your hand's shaking.' Her voice was soft and low.

I leant in, catching the warmth of her breath, sun glowing on her lips.

'Are you coming to try this slide or what?' George was suddenly above us on the poolside, water from his wet shorts dripping in my ear.

I could have punched him.

'Yup, coming now.' Sara stood up. 'Coming, Luc?'

'Going to swim a bit first, I think.' I pushed off the bench, back into the water and started an easy breaststroke. I shouldn't have worn those tight shorts.

*

Sara's family are one of those families who like going out and doing things together – going into town, or down to the coast. Mine aren't like that, but I manage to see Sara every day, even if only for a little bit. The best days are when she comes back from the beach and she has this amazing salty, spicy smell on her skin, beneath the suntan lotion smell, and we spend the evening by the pool, before dinner.

She hasn't held my hand again. Yet. But actually, I'm weirdly OK with it.

We talk, agreeing to talk about anything but school, which suits me. I've done a good job of faking it so far, but I'm definitely no Matt. So we spend mornings sunbathing, sharing headphones before Sara's mum calls from reception that their taxi's arrived, and she has to go out to lunch. Or we sit on the same sun lounger really close to each other, letting George have the other one, if he's found us. Sara always leaves their room first, and tells George to meet us at one pool when we've actually arranged to meet at the other one, or in the games room, which buys us a bit of time to be on our own. But, like I said, we haven't done anything yet. I don't know why – it's obvious she wants to – and I don't know why it feels OK not to, either. It feels different to being at home, to the girls there. Like I've got less to live up to, maybe.

When we're sitting together, she puts her hand on my thigh sometimes, squeezes it when she laughs at something I say. And sometimes she'll swim right up close to me in the pool, bump against me in a way that feels deliberate, but she makes it look like an accident. Like, on the third day, I'd agreed to throw a ball in the pool with George. She joined us after a while, and we played a game where George threw the ball in the air, and Sara and I would see who'd get to it first. While we were waiting for the throw, Sara stood right in front of me and pushed backwards into me with her bum. Then, when she got the catch, I tackled her from behind, wrapping my arms around her and taking us both underwater like I'd seen a couple do in a film once. But Sara came up spluttering, saying she'd got water in her nose and called me a dumb jock. I helped her fish out her sunglasses, but she got out after that and went for a shower before dinner, leaving me and George to toss the ball between us again. I felt like I should have apologised, but we were only playing. I didn't mean it.

She got over it anyway, because the next day we played water volleyball against her dad and George. I'd set her up for a smash, but she mistimed her jump and pretty much landed on me on purpose, pushing me over into the water with her hands on my shoulders. When we both surfaced again, laughing, her arms were around my neck. She didn't let go, even when we'd stopped laughing. I wiped the hair out of her eyes. Her dad said there were rules against heavy petting in the

151

pool. George found it hilarious. I wasn't even that bothered if we won or not after that.

But Sara leaves tomorrow night, and her parents are insisting on going into town for a final dinner – they didn't get the all-inclusive deal that Dad got us.

It's the middle of the afternoon, and Sara and George and me are by the pool again – we've got a sun lounger each this time. I'm feeling tetchy – like I do before a game, almost – and Sara's put a song on the headphones that's crap: all whiny lyrics and guitars and stuff. I think I'm supposed to listen to the words, but I can't really concentrate. I go for a swim.

I do two lengths of the main pool, then see Sara's watching me, leaning on one arm. She's wearing the really hot bikini she wore on the first day, and even though there's a bit of burn on her shoulders and her thighs and she's not wearing any make up, she looks beautiful.

But she's leaving tomorrow, so what's the point in thinking like that?

George's head's buried in a book; he's going to turn out like Matt, probably.

I swim off towards the river bit.

When Sara's feet appear on the poolside next to me as I'm swimming along, I pretend I haven't seen her. But she's started wearing this thin little ankle bracelet she got in town which I can't stop looking at, and as soon as I turn my head I know I've lost.

I stand up in the water. 'What?'

'What do you mean, what? What's up with you today?' Her arms are crossed. She's looking down at me.

I don't like it. 'Nothing.' I bob down in the water, dunk my head, then float on my back, looking up at her, wait for her to speak.

Sara sits down on the edge of the pool. 'I've had a really nice week, Luc. With you, I mean. I don't want to spoil it.'

'Who's spoiling anything?'

'I know it's not easy. With George, I mean. But he's my brother, and he deserves a holiday too. I can't just leave him on his own.'

'What about your mum?'

'Mum and Dad? They're ... I don't know. Busy. They've both been busy at home a lot recently, too. They spoke to us in the car on the way to the airport. "Sara, George, we need some time this week to reconnect," they said.' Sara does a pretty good impression of her dad's voice. It sounds a bit like he's got a cold. '"So here's the deal – half of each day we'll be a family, then the other half, you guys are on your own." Then Dad put his hand on Mum's shoulder and twiddled her hair and I did a bit of sick in my mouth.'

I put my mouth underwater for a few seconds so she can't see me smile.

Sara slips into the pool, dipping her shoulders under like mine. Our chins are really close together. She had

153

a can of lemonade a minute ago and there's a tingle of it left on her breath. She takes hold of one of my hands underwater and interlinks our fingers. 'Let's not argue, OK?'

'Fine. I just ... you're leaving ... and—'

'Tonight. I'll come and see you after dinner, OK? Meet me at that door by reception at 9?'

'Yeah, what'll we do? You sure "Luke" won't mind?'

'Like I said, he's just a boy mate.'

We're closer than we were that first time. I feel her squeeze my hand. I reach for her other one, find her wrist and pull her towards me, pushing my mouth towards hers. She meets it and I feel her tongue against mine, the lemonade and the heat and the chlorine from the pool all mingling. Her arms are around my neck, mine are on her arse, one inside her waistband and I slide one round the front and I feel one of her hands on the bulge in my trunks but then she's pushing me away, moving backwards through the water.

'You're a naughty boy, Luc,' she says, pouting to emphasise the 'c' again. 'Tonight. Nine o'clock. We'll say goodbye properly.' Then she's out of the pool. 'No need to follow me,' she says over her shoulder. 'You might have someone's eye out with that.' And she's gone.

*

I know where we'll go. Always move forward, Dad says. Use what you know, turn things to your advantage, have a plan.

Matt's house has these sliding patio doors that are really old, and don't fit the frames properly. If you lift them in a certain way, you can get them open, even if they're locked. Anyway, there are some unused ground-floor rooms – where we took those sun loungers from on that first day – and they have pretty much the same doors. On the way back to my room, once I get out of the pool with decency, I push through the bushes onto the rooms' little balcony, try one of the doors and it works first time! I put my head around the thin curtain, have a look around. It's not much, but it'll do.

That night, I'm not really listening to Dad talk about how many lengths he's done in the pool or tell us about the call from one of his sites that he had to sort out (he's been on his laptop, working, for at least a few hours every day; his phone too). Mum's being quiet, as usual. I watch the clock and head back to my room just after half eight while Mum and Dad go to one of the hotel bars. I have a shower, put on the best clothes I've brought, rub some scuffs off my trainers and make sure I've got a condom or two in my wallet. It's going to be a good night, I can tell.

There's a door between my room and Mum and Dad's, so I have a look in their mini-fridge before I head out. There's a bottle of wine that's only got a bit out of the top. I don't want to look cheap, so I top it up with a few miniature vodkas. I take the plastic cups that the maid puts on my bedside table each morning, and make sure I'm at reception just a couple of minutes late.

Sara's already there, wearing this yellow dress that looks amazing. She's put her hair up and smells like perfume, and my stomach goes a bit funny, just looking at her. She's also holding a bottle – hers is smaller and whatever's inside is clear.

She nods at my wine. 'Oooh, very fancy!'

I blush a bit. What is *happening* to me? 'What's that?'

'Something from town. I was in a shop getting some other stuff – presents for people at home – and this was by the tills so I thought I'd chance it. The guy serving winked at me and put it in my bag like it was nothing.' She passes it over for me to look at, puts her hand on my arm, squeezes it.

'Wish it was that easy at home.' The liquid looks a bit oily. There's a picture on the front of a bull sailing a little boat with a red sail.

'I know, right! Anyway, it says forty per cent on the side so it should be OK.' She squeezes my arm again. 'So, Luc, where are we going to enjoy these delicacies?'

I give her both bottles to carry. 'Follow me.'

I left the door open a fraction of an inch earlier, and we step into the cool dark of the empty room. There's a bed with no sheets, and the same table with two chairs that must be in every room in every hotel. Apart from that, the room is bare.

Sara shuts the door behind us, pulls the heavy curtain closed then goes to try the light switch; it works, and a warm orange glow comes from the sidelights. 'Simply divine, darling,' she says in a weird voice, then leans against the wall like she's a character in an old-fashioned film. She dangles the wine bottle. 'Shall we?' She sits down, sweeps a loose strand of hair behind her ear, and pats the bed next to her. I sit down, open the wine and put my nose against her neck. She smells of suntan lotion and perfume. We kiss for a bit, then I put my hand on her leg and she pulls away, drops the bottle in my lap. 'You can pour.'

The wine tastes a bit weird with the vodka in it, but it's still quite cold and I've tasted worse from Johnny's concoctions up the Lanes. After two plastic cups each we start making out on the bed. Sara keeps guiding my hands back up when I try to get under her dress though.

'Slow down, Romeo. We've got all night,' she laughs. 'Hey, do you want to play a game?'

It seems a bit stupid, but I say OK. I hear my dad in my head: sometimes, he says, if you want to win with girls, you have to play by their rules for a bit.

'It's called 'firsts'. You ask each other when your first 'whatever' was, and if the other person hasn't done that yet, they have to drink. I'll go first.' She rearranges herself on the bed, leans to the table for the little sailing bull bottle that she brought, cracks the screw cap and pours both of us a generous glug. 'First time you broke a bone.'

'My own, or someone else's?'

'Alright, Iron Man! Your own, of course.'

'It's never happened. This is a perfect and unbroken specimen.'

'True, but you have to drink then.'

The alcohol is hot in my mouth, sharp and stinging. It feels like it's taking the breath out of me and burns a bit as it goes down, but I push back the whole cup-full, then shake my head in a grimace.

Sara giggles. I lean in to kiss her again but she dodges me. The room starts to lurch a little. 'No, not yet. Your turn to ask a question.'

'OK, fine.' I sit, cross-legged on the bed, facing her. 'First time you kissed someone.'

'Boy or girl?'

'Er, girl.'

Sara raises an eyebrow. 'Well...' then she knocks the cup back quickly, her whole body convulsing as the liquid makes its way down her throat. 'Blagh! That's *horrible*!' she says, pouring two more cups, bigger than the last ones. She spills some on her dress. 'Same question to you. First kiss.'

'My mate Johnny's sister, Anna. She's two years older than me.'

'Liar. Full story now or it's a lie!' Sara is swaying slowly. Or is that me?

'No, it's not. We were all round at Johnny's – me, Matt and Mark and him – and I went into the kitchen to get drinks. Anna had fancied me for ages, she still does, and she had some friends over, they were in the dining room, revising probably.' I told this story for weeks after it happened, impressing everyone. I'm still a bit proud of it now, even though it was years ago. 'I heard them all go quiet when I walked in, and then I'm at the fridge and one of girls said 'Luc', so I turned around, and Anna's standing there and sticks her tongue down my throat for, like, ten seconds or something. After, I just walked back into the other room with the drinks. I keep seeing her looking at me. She remembers too. Bet she loved it.'

Sara's eyes are wide. 'No. Way! My friends did exactly the same to George! We were at my house, and George had some friends over and Evie said she'd dare me to kiss whoever came into the room next, and I said no because if it was my brother that would be sick and Evie said she'd do it anyway and then George walked in and he must have only been eight or nine and he looked like he was going to explode afterwards and he just walked out afterwards, completely silent! It was so sweet and hilarious, him stood there not knowing what to do, all these teenagers giggling at him. Whenever Evie comes over now, she always blows him a kiss and he goes bright red! I can't believe the same happened to you!'

I flashback to the laughter I'd heard behind me as I'd carried the drinks back to the games room. I'd never told anyone about that bit. 'No, Anna definitely wanted it.'

'You tell yourself what you need to,' Sara patted my thigh. 'Your turn.'

I feel hot, itchy under the arms, as if I've just had something shown to me, then taken away. 'Alright then, who was your first fuck?' The word is out of my mouth before I really know about it. That blunt sound lands in the room, and part of me likes the effect it has.

Sara seems to have stopped wobbling. She looks me in the eye. 'You go first.'

The lights in the room seem to have gotten brighter as I tell Sara about the Lanes and about Alice and doing it against a tree while everyone else was about twenty metres away, smoking. But then the walls seem to get a bit closer, and I remember it wasn't that, and that it was actually Amy one night when we were both wasted and found ourselves up at the place we used to be build dens, and how we kind of did it awkwardly on the armchair we used to keep up there but that didn't really count.

'God, what a romantic life you've lived, Luc.' Sara tops up my cup, even though I've not drunk anything. 'Tell me it gets better.' She sounds a bit sarcastic, but we're both slurring a bit so it's hard to tell.

There's definitely a high-pitched hum coming from

the lightbulbs as I tell Sara about the house parties, and how there was the weekend when Alice's parents were away and she'd text me to come over in the afternoon and I was late because of a rugby match that ran to extra time so by the time I'd got there she'd already drunk the bottle of wine she'd got and was half asleep. And about the time we'd done it when we were swimming in the river and how Alice couldn't do it for a month after that because she'd gotten an infection or something, so I'd done it with Amy again, up the Lanes, even though Amy said she shouldn't because Alice was right over there. And I tell Sara about the others from school as well, at the Lanes, in their houses, in other people's houses. About how its boozy and warm and slick and then it's over and I don't know why I'm talking so much but it feels like there's something opened up in that room, between me and Sara, that I need to fill with my talking, but the more I talk the bigger the gap gets, and the further away Sara gets, and then I'm talking because I'm angry, and I'm using words I only use with the lads, and even then not all the time, and I start feeling really hot.

Then I say, 'OK, your turn,' and I stop talking.

Sara looks at me, a weird glaze over her eyes. She slowly and deliberately lifts the cup to her lips and downs the whole thing. I can see her trying not to flinch as it goes down her throat, and she keeps looking at me all the way through.

'But, I thought ... Luke? A boy mate with benefits, you said.'

'No. I didn't. That's what you said.'

So we sit quietly a bit more. Then I put my cup down on the bedside table and crawl over to her. She turns away, shuffles to the edge of the bed. She lets me kiss the back of her neck, but I don't think she's enjoying it.

'So you're not going to... I mean. Don't you want to...?'

'I did. I *really* did, Luc. I was thinking on the way to the airport that wouldn't it brilliant if I had a little holiday fling, get the whole virginity thing out of the way, and then I saw you at the airport and then when you sat at the departure lounge I thought "Yes, this is it!" and I even turned on my Bluetooth and changed the name to my Instagram account because I wanted you to find me, and you did, and then this week's been amazing and it was all going so well. Until about ten minutes ago. When you kind of killed the mood.'

'*I* killed the mood? It wasn't me that wanted to play that stupid kids' game. I've been trying all night but you've been knocking me back.'

'OK, fine. I'm just ... I'm a bit nervous, OK?'

Silence again. I kneel on the bed, looking at the back of her neck, the yellow dress and her bare shoulders. I feel completely stupid, and that feeling of losing comes back, white hot and quick, like Sara's tucked what I want under her arm again and won't let me have it. 'So you've been leading me on all night? All week?'

'No.' She turns, looks me straight in the eye. 'I did want to, but now I don't anymore. It's not a good idea. I think whatever was in that bottle wasn't a good idea, either.'

I look over at the bedside table. The bottle is three quarters empty. 'All right, fine. You can't leave me like this though.' I point to my crotch.

'What?' Her voice is quiet.

'You need to, you know, help me out. As payment, for being a tease. You owe me.'

'What am I doing here?' Sara stands, takes a few wobbly steps to the bathroom and leans against the doorframe. She flicks the light on. The glare of it makes my eyes hurt. She shuts the door.

It's Sara's fault because she showed it to me then she took it away and it's her fault that the anger is coursing through me now. It knows what it wants and it's going to take it. I knock on the door, then I pound on it.

Then I open the door with my foot.

16

The pool's getting pretty boring. The wi-fi keeps dropping out, too, and by the time most of the sunloungers fill up around mid-morning, it's so laggy that it's pointless. I tried downloading a bunch of stuff – boxsets and music – overnight, but there's a data limit and Dad's refusing to pay for the upgrade, so I re-watch old stuff and flick through my socials most days, post a few pics of the pool.

Sara's blocked me. I delete all the pictures of her from my phone. It's not worth posting them now, I guess.

Mum's suggested I read a book: there's a little library thing in reception. Sounds like something Matt would do. Completely pointless.

Apart from mealtimes, Mum doesn't really leave the hotel room, just props herself on the balcony and plugs into her Kindle every day. I can see her up there now. Dad got rooms with views over the pool, but they don't get any sun until the evening. Mum's fine with that. She doesn't really like the heat. She didn't mention the wine going missing.

Every now and again I see her looking down at me and she waves. That's when I get up and go for another swim.

Dad said he's sorted the stuff at work now, and can start to have a real holiday, so he's rented a bike for the last five days and has been out exploring. It's a full-carbon model with electronic shifters – says it's costing as much as my room is every day – and he says he's going to buy one when we get home. He's shown me his rides on his tracking app. The speed he's getting down the hills is amazing. He said I can go out with him this afternoon. He said it'll be good for my cardio and I've not really done anything but eat for days since Sara left and Dad said he's not paying for me to just get fat. He said all that last night, at dinner.

Mum said I was a growing boy and that Dad should leave me alone. Then she patted my arm.

Of the three restaurants on the resort, Dad likes the posher one, even though our all-inclusive package means we can only have the set menu. Sara said her mum thought it looked cheap and gaudy – but she was a snob, that's what Sara said. Dad always says that apples never fall far from the tree. Maybe he's right.

When we go to the posh restaurant, Dad makes sure Mum gets dressed up nicely and me and him both put shirts on and proper shoes, not just flipflops. That's where we ate last night. Dad picked a table in the middle of the restaurant – said he wanted to show us off, his family – and ordered a bottle of wine which he drank while telling me stories about how he and Mum first met, which made Mum blush and laugh quite loudly.

Dad said that the wine was getting to her. Dad's not mentioned the wine from the mini-fridge either. He probably thinks Mum drank it, so I think I've got away with that one.

The main course was a whole fish that you had to take the skin off yourself, and lift all the spine out with the head still attached. The waiters gave us these special knives to do it with. Dad said it was a bit different to fish and chips at home, and got pissed off with it after a while. Mum was doing OK, and asked Dad if she could help him, but he said don't worry about it. That's when Dad said the thing about me going for a ride with him and me getting fat and my room costing a fortune. He was pointing at me with his little fish knife. And then Mum stood up for me and he pointed it at her instead and said some other things.

Mum didn't really speak the rest of the evening. We ended up sending most of the fish back, uneaten. Me and Dad went to the other restaurant for a burger at the buffet.

Mum didn't; she went up to bed.

Before she went, she asked me if I want to go for a look around town the day after tomorrow, before we fly home. Maybe we could get lunch, she said. Dad said why would he want to do that? Dad's paid for all the meals already, why would be pay twice?

I haven't decided yet. About going into town.

I'm at reception, waiting for Dad so we can go for a

ride together. He comes in, the special clips on his cycling shoes tapping on the hard floor. He's carrying a pair of shoes for me, and a helmet. The shoes feel a bit small when Dad does the straps for me, but Dad says it's better that way. I walk across the reception, putting my weight on my heels and trying not to slip.

Outside, my bike is leaning next to Dad's. It's white all over, same as Dad's, and looks like it's been carved by an expert craftsman or something – all smooth lines, and you can barely see the joins. Dad says they cast them in one go, so there actually aren't any joins. He explains the process for a while. I zone out.

It takes me a while to work out how to get my feet in the pedals and, by the time I manage it, Dad's already halfway down the road. It feels strange, hunched over the handlebars like this, but I try to keep my back straight so I look OK if anyone's watching, and click through the gears that are built into the brake levers. I can feel the chain gliding across the different cogs. It's almost silent. When I finally get some speed up, it feels a bit like I'm flying. I smile. I could get into this.

I wobble up behind Dad at the traffic lights where he's waited for me, just managing to get my foot unclipped before I fall over.

'Get off the drops through town, son. You look like an amateur. They're only for when you're really putting the hammer down.'

'Yes, Dad.' I guess 'the drops' are the curved over bits of the handlebars.

We head out along a flat, straight road, following the bucket and spade signs for the coast. For a while we cycle side by side. We don't speak. Cars sweep around us in wide arcs, their tyres shushing on the tarmac, a slight thud as they drive over the white lines down the centre of the road. Then it's just the quiet hush of our own wheels on the road, the bikes' machinery turning all our power into pure speed. I look down at the little computer and see that we're already doing thirty kilometres per hour, and my legs aren't even aching at all.

The road is a dark line with sandy-coloured fields on each side. After a while, we make a right turn in front of a low hill, and there's the blue-green ocean glittering in the sun, close on our left. We're passing villas and little cottages on the right, all bright white and with the same red roofs. There's that salty, sweet taste on the breeze that Sara used to have when she came back from the beach.

We speed along the seafront for about ten minutes, then the road starts to rise, and we start gaining height, leave the beaches behind.

We stop on a wide, sweeping corner halfway up the first climb. We must have been going an hour at least. The air coming off the road is all wobbly with heat, like above the radiators at school in winter. Dad's chugging on one of his two water bottles, sweat running down the sides of his face. He grins, the white of his teeth glinting almost as bright as his mirrored sunglasses. He got himself a pair of proper cycling ones. I've just got my Ray Ban knock-offs from the airport duty-free, and I'm wearing an old vest top and a pair of rugby shorts that I brought in case I wanted to go for a run. But Sara got in the way of that.

Dad looks like a pro. He's got full lycras which he bought from the cycling shop on the morning he first hired the bike. He bought two tops, which he alternates, and he gets Mum to rinse them off in the evenings. Still, he's a bit stinky, and I don't look at his crotch because something weird happens to my stomach when I do, but he looks pretty cool.

I unclip, a bit more smoothly than last time, and reach down for my own water bottle. But it's not there.

'Didn't you bring water?'

'Yeah, one of those little ones from the buffet.'

Dad swigs hard again, then wipes his mouth with the back of his hand. 'Didn't fit the bottle cage properly. Probably fell out a way back.'

I look around, as far as I can into the wobbly-heat-wave distance.

'We'll stop in a bit. There's a place you can get another one. Will you make it to the top, do you think?' Dad gestures up the road with his bottle. The hill seems steeper here, where the tarmac rounds a corner and disappears. 'You can always turn back if you want.'

'No, I'll be fine.' Sweat is gathering on my upper lip. I lick it off.

'Good,' Dad clicks his bottle back into its cage. 'Race you to the top.' And he's off, gliding over the tarmac.

I try to keep up.

Forty minutes later, I finally limp to the top of the hill.

I'm glad Dad didn't see, but on a really steep bit I wobbled and fell over. I couldn't unclip my feet in time. Luckily, the graze on my leg didn't bleed much, and I didn't scratch the frame that visibly either, just a few black marks that I mostly rubbed off with what spit I could muster.

Eventually, the road levels out. I made it. Even if I didn't win.

Freewheeling along, I close my eyes for a bit, seeing white blobs and pulsing flashes behind my eyelids. I get those when I train hard after a heavy night down the Lanes sometimes, but today they feel more intense, each pulse going through my whole body like a wave.

I find Dad about a kilometre along the road, sitting in a white plastic chair outside a ropey-looking café. His bike is against the table in front of him. There are two pints of beer on the table, one half drunk. There are beads of water on the sides of the glasses – they're sweating as much as I am.

I almost fall again as I unclip my feet, and prop my

bike against another table, making sure that the side with the scratches on isn't facing Dad.

Dad takes his hand away from his forehead where he's been showing me the 'loser' sign ever since I rode into view. He pushes one of the beers towards me.

'Alright? What kept you?'

I smile weakly, sitting down in the chair opposite him. The table between us wobbles, and Dad puts a hand on his bike saddle, frowning at me. A little beer spills from the top of my full glass.

'Get that down you. I'd say you've earned it, but your mother would've been quicker up that than you were! Ha ha!'

I wonder how he'll react if I ask for some water.

'I've been here fifteen minutes. Did you stop for a piss or something? Some other tart catch your eye now that chick you were hanging out with had to leave?'

My head's swimming as I pick up the beer and take a few gulps. It's crisp and sweet, but my throat tries to close around the slightly bitter aftertaste and some of it goes up the back of my nose. I concentrate really hard on not letting it dribble out, squeezing my eyes tight shut.

'Jeez, Son. Can't take you anywhere!' Dad laughs. 'Thought you'd be able to handle a beer by now! Ha!'

I swallow down the mouthful, blink back the tears from my stinging, half-flooded nose, then try to laugh.

Luckily, someone from the bar comes out with a jug

171

of water. Slices of lemon bob on the top and I can hear ice clinking against the sides. She gestures to the closed parasol poking through the centre of the table. Dad shakes his head. The bar lady shrugs, mutters something under her breath, and leaves the jug and glasses. I eye them greedily, reach out to grab the jug, but Dad's there first. He lifts a bottle from its cage and starts to refill it. Then he does the other one.

When he's done, I pour what's left of the jug into a glass and down it in three seconds. The beer takes me a bit longer.

'What do you think then, eh? Not bad is it, this cycling lark. See a bit of countryside, work up a bit of a sweat.'

I nod, happy that I can't hear my heart thumping in my ears anymore. The sun is heavy on the back of my neck, and the skin on my arms feels tight. I topped up on sunscreen before I left, but I must have sweated that off miles back.

Dad gets up. 'Right, I'll have a slash, then we're off.'

He leaves about a quarter of his beer. I wait until he's gone inside the café-shack, then down it in one, panting like a dog.

It's easier going downhill, and I 'get on the drops', click into the lowest gear and 'put the hammer down', as Dad says. I manage to keep up with him, too. I could even overtake at some points, if I wanted to, but I can feel a headache creeping slowly up from the root of my spine. I try to focus on the white lines of the road flashing past me, and on the burn in my thighs.

After ten minutes of fast descending, we stop at a crossroads. I recognise the name of the town we're staying in. The sign says it's a right turn, and twenty kilometres away. 'Are we heading back?' I ask. The top of my head's starting to feel like a string's tied around it.

I must have sounded a bit too enthusiastic. Dad looks like I've spilled chips in his car.

'You can if you want.' Dad pushes off again, turning left. 'I'll be back by dinner. Tell your mother. And take your bike back before the shop closes, yeah? They charge extra for over-night rentals.' Dad shouts this last bit over his shoulder.

I watch until he's out of sight, then lie down on the roadside for a bit, holding my forehead.

My head is pounding by the time I get back to the town. The bike shop is a few roads across from the hotel and I stop a few doors down, use the bottom of my top to rub the last black tarmac-marks from the scratches on the frame. It looks OK. Still, I leave the bike leaning on the shop's front window, the shoes and helmet next to it, and say a quick 'Gracias' through the open door before hobbling off as quickly as I can in my bare feet. A few times, I have to put a hand on a wall to stop from falling over. I feel these waves of sickness pass up from my stomach, my vision is swimming, and the phantom string that's tied around my head is getting tighter and tighter.

When I get back to my room, I drink a whole two-litre bottle of water then pretty much bring the whole thing back up again into the toilet. I drink another pint, slowly, then collapse on the bed, the room spinning.

The next morning, I wake up to Mum sitting on the bed. I blink a few times, then the headache comes back, almost as bad as yesterday.

'How are you, love? Your father says you forgot a drink yesterday.' She puts her hand on my forehead. It feels cool. 'Bit of heat stroke, I think. You've burnt, too. Your neck and all up your arms.'

I groan, roll over, my tingling body suddenly too heavy on the scratchy, sticky fabric.

'I'll bring you some aloe vera for your sunburn. And there's a drink there with some special salts in it that your father got from the pharmacy last night. Drink that and I'm sure you'll start to feel better.'

I squint up at her, see Dad leaning in the doorway between my room and theirs. Mum touches my forehead again, places her other hand – air-conditioner cool – gently on my shoulder. It feels like needles. 'What a shame, the last day of the holiday and you in bed like this.'

She shuffles out, past Dad. 'Don't worry, love. Maybe you can have one last swim this afternoon before the flight tonight. Guess we won't have time to get into town after all...'

I try to nod, but my neck won't move properly.

174

Mum goes, and Dad closes the door behind them. I pull a cushion over my head to make the darkness darker.

Late afternoon, and after a cold shower, I feel well enough to leave the room before dinner. I walk around the big pool, past the bench where Sara and I sat that first day, then up to the smaller pool where George and I threw the ball around, back past all the places I walked with Sara, all the talking we did.

Last, I go back to the room where it happened. I pop the screen door off again, and everything's just as it was: the bathroom door still open, the light still on. The almost-empty wine bottle stands on the table; the other – Sara's bottle of local whatever-it-was – is lying on the floor by the bed.

Just where it fell after Sara hit me with it.

She'd caught me with the bottom of the bottle, where the glass is thickest, and it didn't smash. It was enough though, and I'd stopped. Stopped what I was doing. Stopped what I'd been trying to do.

And then I'd seen everything clearly.

Sara's eyes. The way she'd looked at me like something that was hunting her. Something she feared and hated. She took off through the door without looking back. I knelt on the floor, one hand on the place where she'd hit me, the sour, acrid smell of cheap alcohol glugging out onto tiles.

It's still thick in the room, covering up the suntan lotion, the salty-sweet smell of the beach, her perfume.

I blink hard against the tears that are forming in the corner of my eyes. What had I been capable of doing that night? What would I have done if she hadn't stopped me? And why couldn't I stop myself? It wasn't just the drink – I'd felt that, what it was doing to me. There had been something else behind it, too. Something worse.

I sit heavily on the bed, the hum of the bathroom light burrowing into my head. Closing my eyes, I see her again, the way she looked at me. The way I'd made her feel.

It didn't feel like winning, at all. More like I'd ruined something. Forever.

I push a finger against the spot behind my ear. For some reason, the bruise didn't come up – I've checked every morning in the mirror. Maybe it went inward. I push harder, the pain sharp and angry as a few tears splash onto my knees. I can still feel it – the thing that wasn't the drink – all coiled and lurking inside me somewhere. But I don't ever want to see it again.

As I turn to go, something on the floor catches my eye. It's Sara's ankle bracelet.

I put it in my pocket.

MATT

17

Mark won't talk to me.

I don't know what I've done or haven't done. For some reason, I'm always looking at it as something *I've* done. Why is that? It's *him*, after all, that's not answering *my* messages. Maybe I'm just annoying him?

Whatever it is, he's barely come near me since I got back from holiday: an uneventful two weeks camping in Devon, lots of galleries, lots of drawing. Drawings of Mark, mostly.

But he won't look at me when we're up on the heath or on the school field in the evenings. If he's even there, that is. He doesn't always turn up now. Johnny says he'd been hanging around with his sister and her friends or something, chilling out at pool parties or whatever it is they do at the big houses out in the villages, but he wasn't doing that anymore, either. Johnny says Mark's abandoned us for greener pastures, that he's moving up in the world. I think Johnny knows more than he's letting on.

Then suddenly it's the last week of the holidays, and there's Mark, just across the road from me, walking along with those huge headphones on – another one of his recent purchases – and the backpack he never takes off.

I'm out with Dad when I spot him. He persuaded me to join one of his 'plein air' expeditions this morning where he wanders around with his sketchbook until 'the muse descends' and he does a quick sketch of something that's 'inspired' him. It can't be any worse than pining at home, I think, and I take my sketchbook. Maybe it'll be good to get out of my own head for a bit, see what other muses there might be out there for me. A sketchbook filled with page after page of a boy who's ignoring you is pretty tragic, right? Best to break it up a bit, for appearances' sake.

When I'm not drawing Mark, I like drawing 'ephemera', which is a word I learnt last year for things that are 'transient and temporary'. In particular, I like drawing the stuff that winds up at the roadside, or under hedges. Plastic bottles, old tennis balls, anything thrown away, or broken. Or that's lost its purpose.

If something's lost its purpose, should it still have the same name as when it was useful? Is a broken umbrella still an umbrella? Or, if a crisp packet no longer holds crisps, is it still a crisp packet? No one in their right mind would try and use an old crisp packet to put crisps *back into*, right? So the fact that we still call it a crisp packet, makes you think it's useless and no longer has a function. So it becomes rubbish. Used up. Junk.

But I don't think that's true.

Johnny used to do this thing with old crisp packets, making shiny origami triangles out of them. We all started doing it, keeping them in the front pocket of our backpacks. Between us, we had hundreds of crisp packet triangles. Then Johnny asked if he could have them all and made this beautiful mosaic out of them on the last day of year eight. We'd been doing mandala patterns in RE, and Johnny said he was doing one of those, pretending to be a monk. He spent ages over it, and it covered the two picnic benches that he'd pulled together for the purpose. Then, at the end of lunchtime, he just swept the tables clean with his arm, pushed every last one of those shiny triangles into the bin. Which was the point all along, he said.

So a crisp packet *does* become something else when it's not a crisp packet anymore. And old cans – Johnny used to do a thing with them, too. So, what if we just gave old things new names? Would we look at them differently?

At one of the galleries we went to on holiday, there was an artist I really like called Filip Hodas. He does these pop-culture dystopias – a giant Spongebob or Mickey Mouse head in the middle of a jungle, like an ancient ruin. When I'm pretentiously drawing my 'epheme*rah*', I like imagining all this old stuff is recycled as the centre of some new civilisation. I've drawn little tribes of ants coming out to see this new cigarette-butt sculpture that's been placed in their town square, or a group of woodlice relaxing inside an old flip-flop against a stone wall.

So I'm out with Dad, turning a cracked old baby's toy into a shrine for praying beetles, when I see Mark, headphones and backpack on as usual. He doesn't see me. Or, if he does, he ignores me. I decide to follow him, so I tell Dad I'm done following the muse (!) and I'll see him at home. Then I set off after Mark, towards the heath.

He's walking quickly, slipping a bit along the sandy paths and heading – I'm pretty sure – for the bowl. I keep my distance, wait for Mark to disappear around a corner before jogging along after him. I kind of enjoy it. It feels like a game.

And just *watching* Mark, his head down, lost in his own world, it's like I'm seeing him completely off guard, in his natural habitat or something. Like I'm definitely the guy on the side of the swimming pool in that painting, looking down. I keep going back to it, 'Pool with Two Figures', and I don't think the swimmer knows he's being watched. He's completely in his own world. That's why the watcher is watching him, to see if he can understand what it feels like. Or what it used to feel like. And watching Mark is the same. He isn't being the Mark that I normally see. He's so vulnerable, like this. He's beautiful.

I decide to get ahead of him, try and bump into him coming the other way, make it look accidental. Fine, he doesn't want to make a thing of what happened, and I'm over the video that he said he's deleted now. But he's obviously avoiding me, and I want to know why. If he's heading for the bowl, then he'll probably walk out the other side, down towards Johnny's house and the new estate. I can take the next fork in the path, go around the bowl rather than straight towards it. So I take off at a run, my sketchbook a bit clunky under my arm.

I could even set myself up sketching next to the path, I think to myself. Mark will walk past me, and I'll look up, a perfect rendering of his face beneath my delicate pencil.

A bit creepy, maybe? Yup, bad idea.

So, which of my sketches might he like best? As I jog on, I narrow it down to the tennis ball wedged in a storm drain, or the beetle admiring himself in the mirrored insides of a split-open can of Comeup.

When I get around the bowl, I set myself up with my sketch book to wait: 'the dashing young artist in repose'. Irresistible. I practise my line, 'Oh, Mark! How are you?' Inventive, right?

But Mark never comes over the rim. I give it a few minutes, then pick a path up the side of the bowl, determined to investigate.

I hear voices from inside. They're not clear enough for me to pick up what they're saying, but I do hear Mark say 'sorry' a few times. The other voice sounds angry but trying not to show it too much. Or trying not to be too loud. It sounds how Dad sounds when he's frustrated over a painting that he can't get quite right.

Maybe it's his brother, Brendon, that he's talking to. Brendon's always scared me a bit. He's always angry or seems to be. Always scowling at people. I don't think I've ever seen him smile. He'd just left the school when we started in year seven, so it's not like I know him well. Even back then he was angry. So were his friends. Especially a kid called Vince. He was *really* scary, and never even got to the end of school – excluded for something, then moved somewhere far away, apparently.

I remember a few of the teachers clocking that Mark was Brendon's brother and making some kind of snarky comment. But Mark's never had that edge to him, that kind of toughness that you can't push against because it feels like it might shatter, and you know there'll be violence behind it.

Mark's not like that. He never has been. Mark can take a joke, and he's normally smiling, not scowling.

I slide back down to where I left my sketchbook and start on a half-hearted attempt at the leaves on the birch tree I'm sitting next to. I can get the shapes OK, but they keep coming out flat, dead and lifeless. I go back to one of my eyes instead. I like doing eyes.

Really close up. I've done this one really big, using a whole A3 page. Maybe I'll put something reflected in the iris while I'm waiting.

I'm working on the tear duct, how it reflects the light, when I hear someone coming down the slope behind me. It takes every bit of concentration not to turn around.

Just be cool, I think to myself.

'Nice eye.'

'Thanks.' I turn around, smiling, the 'M' of his name forming on my lips.

But it's not Mark. And it's not Brendon either. It's some other guy, smiling at me from behind sunglasses.

I flash a quick smile back at him, then turn to the picture again, suddenly hunching over it like a primary school kid who doesn't want anyone seeing his work.

The guy wanders off down the path, his feet rooting out a few pinecones and kicking them into the scrub as he goes. He pulls out an e-cigarette and a cloud of vapour follows him as he walks off.

I wait a minute, then sneak back to the top of the bowl. But it's empty. Mark must have gone back the other way.

There are two cigarette butts at my feet, and a scrag of sweet wrapper is caught on a bit of heather next to me. I flick at it and watch it wheel away in the wind, wondering what you'd call a person once they no longer have a function.

18

I resign myself to failure: clearly I'm crap at romance, or picking first boyfriends, and I'm glad when school starts again and I can get back to a game I'm actually good at.

Year eleven kicks off with little fanfare. But what was I expecting – trumpets?

Mark's not in on the first day, nor the second. Not that I care, I've decided, walking to school on Wednesday morning through the light drizzle that the start of term has brought with it. At least it's a break from the heat.

We're walking along like we always do, Luc and Johnny and me, heading towards Mark's house, closest to school. Luc's going on about the car, how it's almost ready to start showing, the topcoat done now, whatever that means. Him and his dad are going to do a few events in the autumn, maybe a race or two. I try to look impressed.

I'm the first to see Mark.

And Mark sees me. He shoots down an alley that leads up to the heath, taking the long way to school. I half expect Luc and Johnny to chase after him, leave me on my own. But instead they both just watch him go. That makes me feel a bit better.

'He's being a right prick at the moment,' Luc says, gesturing at Mark's retreating back with his chin.

'He's got issues, man,' Johnny answers. 'Demons to fight.' Johnny grips his usual breakfast can of Comeup like it's a sword and starts fighting demons with it. Drips go everywhere, including on Luc, who swings a fist at him half-heartedly.

Johnny doesn't notice, and downs what's left of the drink. 'Watch this,' he says, and puts the can on the floor, balancing on top of it with one foot. He taps the side of the can with the other foot and it collapses sideways. Johnny loses his balance, flailing wildly into a group of year sevens and dragging two of them into someone's garden hedge.

'Can't believe how shit you are at that.' Luc shakes his head.

John picks a few leaves out of his hair, checks the two kids he tackled are OK, then winks at me. I've seen him nail hundreds of those. He did that on purpose.

I can talk about Mark-stuff with Johnny, but Luc's a different species, almost. I've not told him specifically, but I'm pretty sure he knows. Like everyone knows, now. But it somehow feels … I don't know … better … or easier at least … not to talk about 'those things' when he's around, regardless of how many times he's regaled us with his own tales of conquest. He's being uncharacteristically quiet about his summer, though.

Johnny starts talking to Luc about whether an

185

RPG or mortar would be the best option when using infantry to attack a fixed machine-gun nest in level thirty-something of whatever Xbox game they're both obsessed with at the moment. I zone out. Think of Mark. I am trying not to, honest.

Whatever he's got — arrogance or confidence, depending on your perspective — he drips with it. He's just so sure of himself. It's magnetic. God, I'm being pathetic, aren't I? Such a bloody *cliché*! I imagine him now, probably bumping into some other group on the heath, falling into conversation with them about whatever, making them laugh, lighting up their mornings for a minute or so.

It's a gift he's got.

And one that I am completely lacking. Woe. Is. Me.

We get to school about ten minutes before the bell, so we wander down to PE and sit in the changing rooms before registration. It's PE first period. Not a GCSE lesson, the everyone's-got-to-do-it kind of mild and pointless exercise, and Luc's got to slum it with all us squares. Poor boy.

The changing rooms have their usual sour taste. It's too strong to be just a smell anymore, and you can actually feel it at the back of your throat — a mixture of sweat, deodorant and a sharp catch of something 'sporty', like Deep Heat. And there's that fungal, damp smell from the showers at the far end. Every now and then a kid gets pushed in there and forced to endure them close up. Hilarious, I'm sure.

It used to be worse when the showers still worked, and the ritual humiliation would involve turning them on. The victim could either stand at the far end, where they'd avoid the worst of the water whilst staring back at the wall of boys, all shouting whatever the insult *du jour* was. Or they could attempt to push and fight their way out, no doubt getting pushed back under the cold water and ending up even wetter, but maybe get some points for trying, or dragging someone else in with them. It happened most weeks in year nine, before they disconnected the pipes. And we all got a turn.

Johnny, when he was pushed in, had lain down on the floor, the water pooling around him, and pretended to go swimming. He was out within a minute accompanied by cheering and slaps on the back and cheers. Mark had gone for the 'fight' option and dragged Greg Hunter in with him. He was out in two.

So I'd planned mine, how I was going to 'perform'.

I was going to stand right in the middle of the showers and face my tormentors, smiling along with their taunts as if it was some initiation ritual that I was in on. Which, to some extent, it was. I wouldn't get any less wet, but there was a chance they'd let me out quicker and maybe accept me as 'one of the lads' from that point on because I was 'up for it' and 'took it so well'.

That was my plan, anyway.

It didn't work, and I was in there for about five minutes, hearing the slurs they used for everyone. 'Queer.' 'Faggot.' But, it sounded to me, with extra venom this week. The only thing going through my head was 'Do they know?', which turned into '*How* do they know?' and wondering if there was some smell or pheromone I was giving out, something that acted like a sign around my neck. I tried to smile through it all, despite the shivering. The water, of course, was cold.

As the bell went for the end of the lesson, the boys still blocked the exit, having got changed in shifts to ensure a continual guard and that the water stayed on. Eventually, they drifted off and left me. Must have lost interest. I had to dry off and get changed with the year elevens, whose lesson was after ours. They knew what had happened, and I was sure they could smell it on me too: what I was.

I wasn't on my own though. Johnny had waited for me, and helped pick up all my bits of uniform that had been thrown around and hidden: again, what *is* the whole thing with enforced nudity amongst groups of staunchly heterosexual men?

That weekend was when I'd told my parents. About how I might be gay. I didn't tell them about the shower incident, though. I left that out.

I didn't report it to anyone. There wasn't any

point. It would have just marked me as a target. Besides, it happened every week, so what made *me* any different? But I think Mr Hughes, who saw me leave the changing rooms late, hair still dripping, must have worked it out. But someone *always* left that changing room with wet hair, and sound *always* travels through walls, right? So why then?

Whatever, the next PE lesson we found out they'd disconnected the showers. And we had another assembly about bullying, this time with the glittering headline of 'Homophobia: Hate Crime'. Completely unrelated to my ordeal, of course. I almost died.

The only one who didn't get a turn under the showers was Luc.

Luc dumps his bag and slumps onto a bench. He looks completely at home in changing rooms. Like it's his natural environment.

'I really hope it's not cross-country today,' I sigh, sitting opposite him.

'Cross-country's not bad,' Johnny says, lying down on Luc's bench. Luc cuffs him around the ear when Johnny tries to put his head in his lap.

'It isn't if you hide in a bush until you see everyone coming back down the hill,' Luc scoffs.

'They should make it a circular course then; not out and back. It's their fault there's loopholes.'

'It is cross-country today. I saw the rota in the office last night. Had to pick some stuff up after school yesterday, advanced PE theory stuff, and I had a quick talk with Hughesie about the rugby this weekend.'

'Morning, lads.' A balding head emerges around the door. Mr Hughes, head of boys PE. 'You alright, Luc? Everything settling after that catch-up yesterday? Any questions? Can't have you tanking any more tests this year, can we?'

'No, sir. It's fine.' Luc flushes slightly. I don't know why he's hiding the extra work he's doing. I saw him talking to Ms Kelley the other day, too. It actually makes me think better of him.

'Bell's about to go, boys. Best get off to registration.'

'Can we leave our bags, sir? We're here first period?' Johnny asks.

'Not a problem with me.'

Luc goes one better. 'Do you mind if I just get changed, sir? I want to work on my warm-up routine for coursework. Thought I could use registration time if it's OK with you?'

'No worries. I'll mark you here.' It must be useful for Luc that the head of his favourite subject is also his tutor. 'The rest of you, hop it.'

I get a hundred metres or so across the playground when I remember I've left my History homework in my bag, and it needs to be in first thing. The fact that *my* tutor is also my strict History teacher clearly isn't as useful as Luc's arrangement. So I jog back towards the changing rooms as the first bell goes.

Again, the smell hits me when I open the door and walk in, but it's not that that stops me dead.

Luc is where we left him but undressed now. There's something in his hands: it looks like a thin bracelet; a black cord with a small charm on it. He's holding it to his lips, his eyes closed. And I think he's crying.

His eyes pop open, rimmed red. 'How long have you been there?' He's on his feet in seconds, crossing the room in three strides.

'What? I was—'

'You were what? Looking at what you can't get? You make me sick.'

'Luc, this isn't—'

'You think I haven't noticed you watching me? Trying to undress me in your head?' Luc pushes me back towards the door which comes up hard against my back.

'Luc, don't…' I put a hand to his chest, trying to stop him.

'What the fuck are you doing? Had enough of an eyeful, have you? Want a touch as well?' Luc knocks my hand away, grabs my arm, swings me around with it and pushes it behind my back, my face against the door. His breath is hot on my neck. 'Don't you dare tell anyone. Do you hear me?'

I nod.

'If you tell, I will end you. Do you understand me?'

He pushes my twisted arm an inch further for emphasis.

'Yes, Luc. Yes. I understand.' I want to howl out, get help, but it's like being underwater. If I screamed, I'd just drown. So I speak quietly. 'Luc that really hurts, please…'

His grip loosens, but his mouth is still right against my ear. 'I know what you are,' he snarls. 'Now get the fuck out.'

And I'm stumbling forwards into the empty playground, the changing-room door slamming shut behind me.

MARK

19

I missed the first few days of school. I didn't even realise, to be honest. Too busy. It wasn't until I got a message from Johnny that I realised. And if Johnny's the one telling you to get to school, maybe you should listen. No one does anything in those first few days though, so it's fine.

A few days after the actual start of term, I've spent the night at home, had a shower and put my uniform on. I still feel a bit grimy, despite the shower. And the uniform doesn't seem to hang right on me. I must have grown.

I take the long walk to school across the heath to avoid anyone else. I spot the other guys, but I don't think they see me. Can't be dealing with hassle this morning – all their questions. Definitely easier to avoid them. I time it perfectly, the bell for registration just fading away as I jump the fence onto the back of the field.

I make a plan. First, go see Miss Amber and get my new timetable, hoping Mrs Clarke's not in the office too, but she shouldn't be as she's normally telling someone off at registration, normally Johnny. Then I'll hang around in a bathroom or something until first period starts, hoping it's not a lesson with Matt in it. Or Luc. Thirdly, if it's a lesson where I can sit at the back, maybe I can even get some sleep.

As I get onto the playground, the door of the sports hall opens so quickly it bounces against the wall. The clang of it echoes across the empty concrete.

I see Matt running along the side of the building. It's not like him to be late. He looks a bit panicked.

Almost like he's been crying.

Something flips, then, in my stomach. I have to fight the urge to follow him.

Even though I haven't got time for the hassle, there are things I want to tell him.

I want to tell him about the crazy incident when Johnny had to pay for our cab home from some random petrol station on a dual carriageway. About how I'd got there. About how I'd seen his face – Matt's face – when I was rolling around the back of that van. His eyes, looking at me, worried.

I want to tell Matt how I watched that video a hundred times in the week after, pausing on that look he gave me. My phone had been like a silent weight in my pocket for seven days. I kept getting it out, checking for messages, missed calls. But there'd been nothing. So I'd watched the video. Which had helped a bit.

At first I thought I'd blown it, thought I'd fucked it all up and there'd be no more easy money. No more playing for prizes. No chance of getting out of this shithole house. And, worse, that I might lose that video. I had no doubt The Guy would want his phone back, now I'd been fired. Losing the phone didn't really bother me; you've got to be easy-come, easy-go in the world of business. But, for some reason, I didn't want to lose that video.

So I'd moved the video of me and Matt to a cloud account I set up and protected it with a password. Then I'd deleted the original. Finally.

Then, out of nowhere, while I was walking up on the heath late one evening, kicking around at the old spot where we used to make dens and feeling sorry for myself, the phone went off.

I want to tell Matt that I'd run all the way home after that call, and when I got there the blue van was parked outside my house as The Guy had said it would be, the engine idling. It wasn't properly dark yet, and behind the glare of the headlights, I could just about make out two outlines in the cab. I'd been a bit nervous, to be honest. Part of me wanted to run, then. But I didn't. I had to be brave, didn't I? Get back to work.

The passenger window rolled down as I approached.

'Job for you.' The Guy's voice was crisp, curt. 'You up for it? Or are you going to fuck it up again?'

I nodded, still out of breath.

He opened the door and stepped down. 'Give me your phone.'

I handed it over. I knew it.

'In.' He gestured with his head.

'You not coming?'

'What difference does it make to you? Get in.' He weighed the phone in his hand for a bit, then he gave it back to me. 'You'll still need this.'

I didn't say anything. I couldn't, could I? So I just climbed up into the cab which smelled of musty tracksuits and old farts. The Guy shut the door, jogged around the front of the van and disappeared into my house through the unlocked door. The Guy must need a quick piss, I thought, then he'd come back, and we'd go.

But then the engine gunned, and with a jerky start, we pulled away.

I looked to my right, at the driver. He had rings under his eyes and a black beany hat low on his head.

I tried to get comfy, put my feet up on the dashboard, put on a front. Tried to see myself the way Matt sees me in the video. 'Alright?' I said. 'I'm Mark, by the way.'

He didn't even acknowledge me. Just leant down and turned the radio to some crap station belching out pop music. 'You want to get a better van, man. Get some proper tunes in here.' Again, he ignored me, so I took my headphones out of my backpack and plugged in, turned the volume up and watched the streetlights flash past in time to the beats as we headed out of town. I have to admit, I was excited.

We'd been driving about ten minutes before we pulled into an industrial estate. There was a sign for a tyre shop and an aquarium supplies centre, but it was way past closing time, and the concrete car park was empty.

Except for one car.

A white Mercedes was parked under a tree on the far side. My driver (that's how I tried to think of him, ferrying me to my next meeting) pulled up alongside and gestured with his chin towards the white car. I climbed down from the cab, and I hadn't even closed the door properly before the driver put it in first, not even looking at me as he headed for the gates. He must have had some other job he needed to get to.

The passenger's window on the Merc slid down.

'What's your name, kid?' The man in the passenger seat was in his twenties, short hair, neat beard over a lean, almost pointed face.

'I'm Mark.'

'Adam, did you say? Look, Frank. It's Adam.'

Fine, I thought. I can be Adam. It's all part of the game.

'I'm Tom, by the way. And this is Frank.' Next to him, the guy in the driving seat laughed to himself.

'Where're we going?'

'Just get in the car, Adam. Got a job for you.'

Frank pressed a button and with the faintest electronic whirring noise the doorhandles of the Mercedes emerged from the body. It was beautiful. And the back door opened with a satisfying 'clunk'. I climbed in. The seats were black leather, and it was like they'd been sculpted to me exactly. The dashboard was lit up with red and blue lights making the whole car glow like the

197

cockpit of a jet, and there was a new-car smell, half carpet, half freshly cleaned glass. Frank pressed another button and the engine growled to life. Now *this* was the kind of car I should be travelling in, right?

'Buckle up, Adam. Safety first.' Frank and Tom laughed again.

Another solid click as the seatbelt went in, and the car glided out of the car park towards the main road. Tom put the sound system on. It was like the car was surfing on a wave of bass. I couldn't help thinking of how jealous Luc would have been. His dad's Subaru's pretty cool, but it's got nothing on that machine. Even Johnny's dad doesn't drive anything that tricked out.

This was going to be an easy job, I thought.

But that's when it started to go weird. I want to tell Matt about it, but he's almost running across the playground as the second bell goes for registration and something stops me from calling his name. Maybe it would be too weird, saying it out loud.

So I watch him go.

Just before we'd got to the motorway, the car had pulled into a petrol station. Tom opened the glove compartment and handed me a plastic bag.

'Now, Adam, have you ever put anything up your arse before?'

'What?' There was a sudden ringing in my ears. Frank turned the engine off and got out. I watched him through the tinted window as he picked up the pump nozzle and slotted it into the car, his fingers tapping on the roof.

'Adam, look at me, not him. I said have you ever put anything up your arse before?'

Do they know about me and Matt? Has everyone seen that video? It was just a kiss. Well, a bit more, maybe, but we didn't go that far.

'No,' I said. 'Never.'

'That's OK, Adam. It's really easy. Easiest thing you've ever done. Doesn't even hurt.'

My heart was beating in my throat. I wondered how far I'd get if I just ran, took off over the fields into the rapidly darkening night. I glanced down at my door handle, but a red light winked up at me. Locked.

'Here's the kit.' Tom's hand rustled around in the plastic bag. He pulled out a tube of something. It looked like cream. 'Just use a load of this. It's lubricant.'

'What the fuck?' I started to say. 'What are you...?'

Tom dropped the tube back in the bag. He was holding a condom, now. 'Make sure you put the package in here first, right? No one's buying if it stinks of shit.' He dropped the condom back in the bag and holds it out to me.'

Package? What package?

'The package is in the bag with the rest of it. There's a toilet in the garage you can use.'

I took the bag, silently. Apart from the tube of lubricant, it felt like there was nothing in it at all.

'Don't show that off.' Tom pointed at the bag, still in my outstretched hand. 'Keep the kit under your top when you walk in.' He passed me a ten-pound note. 'And get us some coffees on your way out, will you? Frank'll have a latte. I'll have an Americano, no milk. Get yourself one too, if you want.' He smiled, almost friendly.

Tom pressed a button on the dash and the red light on my door turned off. I could have run, then. Just got out and legged it. Couldn't I?

My left foot was out of the car when Tom spoke again. 'Oh, and Adam? Please don't make me have to come and help you.'

I stuffed the bag under my t-shirt, tucking it into the waistband of my trackies as I crossed the forecourt. The double doors slid open, and the bleachy smell of the garage made me shake my head a bit. I clocked the 'customer toilet' sign next to the coffee machine.

*

'I hope you washed your hands,' Frank said as I handed him his latte.

'Yeah, course.' I forced a smile.

It took a while to get comfy on the back seat again. I think I used too much of the cream and I could feel a wet patch growing in my boxers. In the front seat, Tom and Frank talked in low tones as the car accelerated into the motorway traffic.

Tom leant around the seat. 'How are you with police, Adam?'

'What do you mean?'

'I mean can you handle yourself, or do you get all twitchy?'

I thought back to the police officers at the train station, the sweat under my arms as they came closer and closer, the relief when they passed me by. But I shrugged. 'Fine, I guess.'

'I used to hate them. Always felt like I was under suspicion or something whenever I'd see one. Even if they were parked at the other end of the street, I'd make a mental checklist of what I had on me, in my bag, even if I knew I had nothing.'

'Same,' grunted Frank. 'It's normal to get a bit nervous.'

'Yeah, I guess.' I was getting a strange, heavy feeling in the bottom of my stomach.

'Fact is, Adam, they can't touch you if you know your rights. Once you realise that, you'll never be nervous again. I'm not saying we'll see any tonight, but just follow our lead, right? You're with us. Untouchable.'

The car was speeding along – and I mean *really* speeding. I could see the dashboard over Frank's shoulder, the needle hovering above ninety. I watched the faces of the drivers we passed, their mixture of anger and envy. I tried to focus on the envy. Me, speeding along in that car. I was living the dream, right?

'So what's school like, Adam?' Tom asked.

'Fine, I guess. I'm doing business studies, so this is all...'

'Ah, a supply and demand man!' Tom laughed. 'An entrepreneur! You don't need school for all that. Look at us. We barely went to school and look where we are.' Tom used the cuff of his top to rub a smudge from the touchscreen console in the centre of the dashboard. 'Fuck's sake, Frank. Didn't you use the gloves when you filled up? Tsh. Messing up our nice new car.'

Frank weaved back across the lanes and turned off the motorway. We were driving through built-up streets, houses at first, then flats and office blocks, then those were replaced by the glowing signs of bars and clubs, and pavements full of people and the noise of shouting and laughter all around us. People bent down and squinted through the tinted windows. There were a few shouts of 'Nice car, mate.' Frank nodded to them in acknowledgment. So did I.

Frank swung into the kerb outside a glass-fronted bar, its interior glowing a soft orange colour. Tom jumped out and walked straight up to the bouncer on the door. They shook hands, bumped shoulders. Tom said a few words, gesturing towards the car, and the bouncer said something into the radio on his shoulder. Tom came back to the door, opened it and leant in, talking to Frank.

'Round the back. Same as usual.' He turned to me. 'You alright, Adam?'

'Yeah, fine.' My boxers were starting to get pretty

sticky now. I hoped I wasn't leaving any marks on the seat.

'See you in there.' Tom shut the car door. The bouncer opened the rope and let Tom in. A few angry gestures from people in the queue, a big group of lads trying not to shiver in t-shirts. I smiled at that – actually smiled. Even though we weren't in the line, we were still at the front of it. And those lads couldn't do a thing about it. We were untouchable.

Frank turned the car into a narrow alleyway. A tight corner, down a ramp, then he parked between a couple of dumpsters, turning off the engine. 'In there,' he said, pointing to a closed, steel door. He pulled a packet of cigarettes from his shirt pocket and lit one. 'And don't tell Tom I'm smoking in the car, or I'll shove something much more painful up there, alright?' From the slight smile on Frank's face, I'd say he was joking. But I shuffled out of the car silently, and I rubbed my cuff across the seat just in case I did leave anything behind.

The back door of the club opened with a groan. Tom was standing there, and instantly pointed at Frank, the orange glow of his cigarette visible through the front window. 'Put that out!' he said, calm and firm.

The orange tip sailed through the window, landing almost at Tom's feet. 'You put it out. Don't be long this time, OK? I want to get home.'

Tom ushered me inside the back of the club, into the darkness and the smell of vape smoke and something

203

sweet-sour that I didn't recognise. Then he shut the door behind us.

20

It was OK, though, Matt. I passed the test! You're probably in tutor time now, but I'm going to sit out here for a few more minutes. I don't feel like being seen by anybody right now. They wouldn't understand.

You might, though. If I actually talked to you.

Anyway, the drive home was even quicker than the way up, Frank pushing the car over 100 miles per hour, weaving back and forth across the lanes.

'You did alright, Adam. Not bad at all,' Tom said from the front seat. 'Especially for your first time.'

The sound system was up loud again, and I was glowing a little bit, trying to keep the smile from my face. Maybe it was the adrenaline or something, do you think? It had been OK in the end. They'd sent me to a toilet – not the real club ones, but a much nicer, backstage one – and I'd got the stuff out, binned the condom, rinsed off the little cylinders and given them to Tom. He'd gone to see the club owner and come back a few minutes later with an envelope. Then we'd gone back to the car and headed home. The whole thing probably took twenty minutes.

'Think you could find your way there again, next week? On your own this time?' Tom asked, turning in the front seat to look at me properly.

'Yeah, sure,' I shouted over the thrum of the bassline. 'No problem. So what was in the envelope?' I knew the answer already, but I wanted my share. The businessman in me was coming back.

'Do you think we should show him, Frank?' There was a cheeky smile on his face as he spoke.

Frank nodded, smiling as well.

'Pull on that strap next to you.' Tom pointed to a wide strip of leather next to my seat.

I pulled it and the middle of the back seats folded down into a wide armrest with cupholders and a dial to control the temperature in the back. Honestly, Matt, this car was a spaceship!

But that wasn't all.

'See that back panel?' Tom pointed to the space between the seats where the armrest had been. 'Push on it, then let go.'

The back panel seemed to slip a little bit under my fingers, then sprang forwards and clattered onto the cupholders. I heard Tom 'tsh' in the front seat.

Behind the panel was another wall made of a strange grey-white material with orange stripes. Or that's what I thought it was. Tom told me to take one.

'Take one what?' I said.

'Just reach in and pull on one of the orange bands.'

So I did. And, like a wooden block from a game of jenga, a thick brick of cash slid out from the rest of them. It was money, Matt. You've never seen so much of it. Must have been tens of thousands of pounds in there. Hundreds, probably. It was amazing.

I ran a finger over the edge of the brick, rifling the crisp edges. I couldn't keep the smile from my face. My mind was blowing all over the place.

'You can unwrap it if you want,' Tom said. 'Run it through your fingers, see what it feels like.'

So I did, and do you know what, Matt? A weird electricity ran through me, starting at my fingers and going right up through the back of my neck.

Tom had his phone out and took a few pictures of me holding the wedge, half in each hand and all fanned out like a real boss. 'You're a natural, Adam,' he said.

I couldn't stop grinning. It was like I'd been plugged in to something, like that time on the heath when we…

'Ah, shit. Cops,' exclaimed Frank, peering into his rear-view mirror. I looked over my shoulder at the red and blue flashes of a police car, creeping closer. Frank pulled into the slow lane and wound the car right down to the speed limit. 'Maybe they'll go on past,' he said.

I was fumbling the orange band back onto the stack of notes, scrambling to get the panel back in the compartment. I could feel my heart beating against the seatbelt.

'Hey, Adam. Chill, OK?' Tom fixed me with his eyes, the cheeky smile still on his face. 'It's going to be OK. We're invincible, right? They can't touch us.'

I nodded at Tom, wanting to be convinced.

'Do you trust me?' Tom asked.

I was still nodding as the police car swung in behind us.

Tom picked up the envelope from the club, still on the dashboard in front of him. It was full of money – fifty-pound notes – and he slipped two out. He put the envelope back on the dashboard, then handed the two folded notes to me.

'Put this in your mouth,' he smiled. 'If you can keep your mouth shut for the next few minutes, you can keep it.'

'But what if—'

'I trust you, Adam. It's just a game, right? Do you trust me?'

I nodded again. The electricity was back. Of course it was a game, and I was going to show them how well I could play it. I put the notes in my mouth, their dry edges catching a bit on the inside of my cheeks. Fifties are quite big, you know. I wanted to cough but held it down.

'Follow our lead, Adam,' said Tom. 'Untouchable, remember.'

Frank pulled over to the hard shoulder, bringing the car to a smooth stop, then turned off the engine. The inside of the car was filled with the stuttering lights of the squad car. Frank pulled his wallet from his pocket, put it in his lap and rolled his window down. 'Don't want that getting smashed in,' he smiled.

Tom smiled back. 'Let's try avoiding that, this time.'

Between the occasional whoosh from the opposite carriageway, I could hear the police officer's feet approaching. The money was hard and pushing down on my tongue. I had to breathe through my nose, blinking back tears against wanting to choke. And then a face was at the window, the yellow of the police officer's jacket flaring in the light of a car passing close.

'Do you know why I've pulled you over?'

'Yes, I was going a little fast, Officer. I'm sorry.' Frank's voice had changed, gone up a bit, sounded softer at the edges.

Tom leant across. 'Sorry, we were taking our nephew out for a quick spin. Just picked up our new car yesterday and he was desperate to see what it could do.' Frank's hand was on the gearstick, and Tom placed his on top of it.

The officer flashed his torch across Tom, and then to me in the back, before turning back to Frank. 'At this time of night?' There was a pause. Tom and Frank smiled up at the officer. 'Licence and registration, please, sir.'

Frank opened his wallet and took out his licence while Tom passed across a bundle of papers from the glove compartment. 'Here you are, Honey.' Frank passed them on to the officer.

'Is this your car, sir?'

'It's ours, yes. Just picked it up yesterday.'

'Wait here, please.' The officer went to the front of the car, checked the registration number, then took the paperwork and Frank's licence back to his car.

Tom turned to me. 'Frank gets a bit nervy at this bit.' He gave Frank's hand a little squeeze. 'But it only seems to happen when he's driving. I wonder why that is, Frank.'

I smiled. One of the notes almost slipped between my lips.

'Take a breath, Adam. He's on his way back. You're doing brilliantly by the way. Here, see if you can get a few more in.' Tom picked another two notes from the envelope, still on the dashboard, and pushed it into my palm.

Frank moved uncomfortably in his seat, and I just about got the cash wedged into my other cheek before the officer was back at the window.

'Can you tell me how fast you were going, sir?'

'About eighty, I think.'

'My colleague on a bridge about ten miles back clocked you at ninety-two miles per hour, sir. I'm going to issue you a fixed penalty speeding fine.' The officer turned to me in the back seat. 'And this is *your* nephew, sir?' he said to Tom.

'*Our* nephew. He's my husband's sister's son,' said Tom.

'Right.' The officer waited a beat. 'And how old are you, son?'

'He's fourteen,' jumped in Frank.

'And does your Mum know where you are?' asked the officer.

My mouth was getting a bit painful, like the notes

had dried all my spit up and left me with a mouth full of sand. Tom jumped in. 'Yes, she does, doesn't she, Adam.'

I nodded, keeping it cool, even with the torch light in my face and my throat on fire. But I managed a little smile.

'And your name is?'

'Adam Groves,' Frank stated, clearly and without flinching.

Another beat. 'OK then. Wait here, please.'

Tom waited for the officer to be out of earshot. 'What a happy family we are this evening.'

He wasn't away long this time,and handed a piece of yellow paper to Frank along with his other documents. 'You have twenty-eight days to pay, sir. I'd advise you to take a minute before continuing on your way this evening. And please drive carefully, gentlemen.' He tapped the doorframe twice with his palm before walking back to his car.

'Thanks, Officer.' Frank grumbled out of the window.

Tom added, 'And sorry again. You have a nice evening.'

The patrol car pulled out onto the motorway, the blue lights switching off as it moved away. As soon as it passed, I pulled the money from what seemed like the back of my throat to the laughter of Tom and Frank. The notes lay glistening in my lap. Four of them. Two hundred quid.

Tom and Frank watched the taillights dwindle into the distance, then disappear over a hill. I couldn't stop staring at the money.

'Good job, kid,' said Tom, his hand still on top of Frank's. 'You OK?'

I nodded. So did Frank.

And that's it, Matt. I did it. We got away with it. And I got two hundred quid just for keeping my mouth shut. Un. Touchable.

We did a few more pics on the way home. I told Tom where I lived, and they dropped me back outside my house. Frank even let me take a selfie in front of the car.

'Sorry about the speeding ticket, Frank.' I said, putting my phone away.

'No worries. I'm sure Frank will be delighted to pay up.' Frank laughed, dryly. He pulled something out of his pocket. 'Here. Souvenir for you. Something to remember us by.' He passed me his driving licence and the speeding fine letter. 'Do us a favour and put them in the bin for us. Cut the licence up first, yeah? We don't want some crook getting hold of it, do we?' He laughed, again.

It took me a few seconds to get it. The picture on the licence didn't even look like Frank. Not if you actually looked. It did say 'Frank' on it, though.

'See you next time, then?' I asked.

'Afraid not. G'night, Adam. And good luck,' Tom said as the Mercedes pulled away, leaving me on the kerb. The engine roared at the end of the road, tyres squealing off into the night.

It was past midnight. Mum still wasn't home; working a double shift again, probably. Nor was my brother.

I went upstairs. On my bed was another phone. Not like the last one The Guy gave me. Not new and in the box. This one was old, really old. But still, I've got three phones now. Who's a proper businessman, eh?

Under the phone was an envelope with three hundred pounds in it. I put it in my wardrobe, where I've been keeping the rest of the cash so Brendon can't find it, and put the still-wet notes from the game we'd played in my wallet.

The new phone lit up almost immediately. A text message. Just an address. This phone didn't even have maps on it, so I opened my old one.

Also on my bed was a plastic bag. I didn't have to open it to know what was inside. A tube of lubricant, a condom, and the same black cylinders as earlier.

I headed for the bathroom.

So this is the new game, Matt. It's a bit more effort, but the prizes are bigger.

And if it keeps them away from you, then it's fine.

LUC

21

Matt's a prick.

How dare he barge in on me like that, trying to see me naked.

But it's not just that, is it?

I punch the wall a few times. It helps.

Once I've calmed down, I get my kit on and focus on my breathing, wait for everyone else to arrive.

There's a little white-hot stone in the bottom of my stomach the whole morning. It helps me destroy everyone else on the cross-country, which feels good.

But not as good as it used to.

Dad's fitness training is definitely paying off, and I don't even feel sick very much after the run. A few glugs of water from the water fountain and I'm fine. The spout smells and tastes of metal. Like blood.

Blood's the best taste to have in your mouth if you want to win something. It gets your own blood pumping faster because your body thinks it's under threat and has to fight to survive. That's what Dad says.

When Dad's standing on the scrum machine and he's getting me to push him along all on my own, he says it's good to have a bit of blood in your mouth. It makes you want to fight. To win.

So sometimes I bite my lip, or the inside of my cheek. And it helps a bit. Or, maybe, the taste of the blood makes his voice seem a little quieter. If only for a few seconds. Either way, it's better.

I don't have lessons with Matt for the rest of the morning, and at lunchtime I go to see my science teacher, Ms Kelley. She's doing a pile of marking, all spread out across the second row of benches. I have to do this twice a week, she says, use the time to catch up, and not just in science. It's not a detention though, it's an opportunity. And Dad would probably agree, but it's best he doesn't know yet, Ms Kelley says. At least not until I'm 'on top' of all my work.

Last year I was probably a bit too interested in sport to concentrate much on my schoolwork. Hughsie – my tutor – didn't mind. Said I was invaluable. And he looked out for me. But my other teachers started getting a bit worried. That's the word Ms Kelley used – *worried*. She said she didn't want to involve home yet, but that she was going to offer me her time each day so I could 'catch up' and 'keep on top of things'. I don't know why she didn't want to call home about it. Mum wouldn't have minded much, and school always calls Mum, not Dad. And she almost never tells Dad about this kind of thing. So it would have been fine.

I'm staring at a Chemistry textbook, no idea what

I'm looking at. Every now and again I write a few things down to make it look like I'm busy. I've been doing this for just over half an hour.

'Everything OK, Luc?' Ms Kelley looks up.

'Fine, miss. Yeah. I've done the Chemistry stuff now.'

'Good. You're working quickly. It's good to see you so focussed,' she smiles.

I smile back.

'Maybe you'd like to give me a hand with these year seven books?'

I smile again. I think she's joking, but I also think she might want to keep me here longer because she fancies me.

And she's not *not* fit, Ms Kelley, in a fit mum kind of way. Like Johnny's mum. I've got the strongest dad, and we all agree that John's got the fittest mum.

'What's next after Chemistry?'

'English. *Macbeth*.'

'You're supposed to say the Scottish Play, aren't you?' She smiles at me. 'Bad luck to say 'Macbeth' out loud. What do you think of it?' She's asking me questions. She doesn't want me here to work, she wants the company. My company.

I pack my Chemistry away, take out the battered copy of *Macbeth* with some old guy on the front staring into space like a moron – it's the same picture on the front of all Shakespeare books, Matt says. 'It's alright, I guess. I like the ending, just before everyone dies, where he – Macbeth, I mean – just keeps going even though he knows it's pointless.'

'Ah yes. "Blow wind, come wrack, at least we'll die with harness on our back,"' she says in a weird voice. 'That was supposed to be a Scottish accent, Luc.'

We both laugh. She definitely fancies me.

'How's the rugby, Luc? Season started again yet?'

That's the other thing about Ms Kelley – she likes rugby. She even goes to watch Premier League some weekends and always tells me about it when she sees me. She knows all the players' names, and actually gets what she's talking about. Not like Matt, who just pretends so he can talk to me. Or Mum, who's just embarrassing when she mixes up rucks and mauls and should just stay quiet.

I tell Ms Kelley about how Dad's letting me train with the men's team this Sunday.

'Really?' she sounds surprised.

'Yeah. Dad says I'm ready.'

She frowns. 'Are you sure that's a good idea?'

'Miss, I'll be fine. Don't worry about it.' I drop my head back to my work again. What does she know about rugby, anyway?

I open the play to some random place and start copying a few bits out. I don't know what any of it means. Matt would know. But he's a prick.

I put my hand in my pocket, touch Sara's bracelet

with my fingertips and this strange jolt goes through me. Maybe not a jolt. More like a wave. It starts in my stomach, rises up my throat. I can feel it pushing at the back of my eyes, like it did when Matt barged in on me this morning. When he saw me crying.

I remember Matt, standing against the door, the stupid look on his face as I stared him down, wouldn't let him go.

If he'd wanted to fight back, he could have. But he didn't. Just looked at me like something else I was hunting.

So I won again.

Not that it feels like it.

22

Sunday morning, and I feel fresh. I stayed in last night instead of going down the Lanes. I wanted to give myself the best chance of making a good impression with the men's team. And with Dad.

Dad likes to get to training early, and I practise my kicking like always while Dad sets up the cones for the first drills. I'm on good form, nailing drop-goals from the edge of the twenty-two yard line. Dad notices. 'Impressive stuff, son. That's 9 from 12, isn't it?'

I got 10 from 12, but I don't correct him.

There's a new guy coming this week – his first session, just like me. Dad says the new guy was on the brink of going pro, then picked up a dodgy knee and had to stop. He's just moved to the area, round the corner from us, and looking for a regular game. I know most of the lads from going to watch them for the last few years – I normally practise passes with the subs, or run the line if Dad lets me, so they all know me pretty well already. As they start arriving, they all say hello. No one's shocked to see me in my kit.

Rumours about the new guy have circulated, and we all joke about how we'll have to go easy on him for his first week, or how he'll need a proper induction at the pub later on. I laugh along, until we all see him arrive.

We all go a bit quiet as he steps out of his car.

I'm shocked he managed to get in it in the first place. He's huge. Everyone's impressed, shaking hands, making jokes about being glad he's on our side. When he shakes my hand, he holds it a second longer than the others, looks at me a bit off-hand. I try to drop my voice a bit when I say 'alright'.

'How old are you, mate?'

'Eighteen.'

Dad steps in, put a hand tight on my shoulder. 'This is my boy, Luc. He's going to start training with us today as well.'

The new guy nods, looks convinced. Kind of.

Dad puts his hand on the back of my neck. 'Don't go easy on him, though,' he says to the new guy before raising his voice so everyone can hear. 'That goes for all of you. Luc's joining us for training today. He's harder than he looks, and can probably run rings around most of you, so don't give him an easy ride.' He gives my neck a little shake.

I try not to blush too much with the pride.

Dad sets us off. 'Three laps then, boys. Go get warm.'

As we head off, I find myself next to the new guy. 'So the coach is your dad then?'

'Yeah, it's alright though. He used to coach our under 14s team then starting doing the men's instead.'

'Tough breaks. My dad coached my team for a while, when I was a kid though, not adult league. He'd always be on my back. Pissed me off sometimes.'

'Nah, he's alright, my dad. Pretty strict on the fitness, but it's all good.'

'So what do you do, still at school? College?'

'Yeah, sixth form – it's my last year.'

'I'm Dell, by the way.'

'Cheers, Dell. Good to meet you.' We do an awkward handshake on the move.

I've been practising the lies about being in sixth form, about being eighteen. Dad says if a ref ever asks me about it, I'll need to be convincing. It helps that Dad's the coach, obviously, but I'll still need to be pretty confident and have a back story. This is a good test. Dell's completely taken in.

Dell picks up his pace and trots alongside someone else for a bit, getting round everyone by the time we've done our three laps. He seems nice.

After some shuttle runs and a couple of sprints, Dad gets on the scrum machine again and makes us form up. Dad tells me to stand in at second row because Nick's kid's birthday is this afternoon and he can't make it. 'Probably has to get his clown makeup on early', Dad says, and everyone laughs.

I line up next to a guy called Brian, we crouch behind the front row and he wraps his arm tight over my shoulder. I feel myself wince a bit as he grips under my arm, suddenly realising the size of him crouched next to me, the closeness of the other bodies around me all much bigger than what I'm used to.

'Alright, kid?' Brian must have felt me pull away.

'Yeah, no worries. Just a bit tight that's all.'

Brian goes again and I manage to bite my lip. I'm winning.

When we make contact with the scrum machine, the padded bags give a sigh of air. Dad's giving the count from the platform on the back. *Push, two, three, push, two, three* and there are grunts from the pack. The rest of the team, all the back row who don't scrum, are standing with Dad and Dad's yelling for more. But I start getting a bit light-headed, a bit dizzy, and I have to close my eyes for a bit. But the legs, the sweating torsos, the grunting doesn't go away.

'Keep it level! Luc, go harder!'

I dig my studs in and push forward, my eyes still locked shut. A wave of darkness washes over the darkness that's already behind my eyes. But I can beat it. I force myself on.

It's OK, I tell myself. This is normal. And then it's over. Next drill.

Dad gets the tacklebags out, and we all pair up.

In my team – my age group, I mean – no one wants to face me when we do these contact drills. They're all avoiding me here, too. And they're all avoiding Dell as well, probably for the same reason. So we pair up.

'Go easy on me, Luc, alright?' Dell laughs as he takes up the stance, the tackle bag in front of him like a shield, digging his studs in.

We're supposed to be practising how to roll with the contact, take a change of direction, but I line up to run a bit closer to Dell's body than most others. He looks like he can take it. I go in pretty strong.

When I hit him, dropping my right shoulder, it's like running into a wall. I roll away, eyes glued shut and biting my tongue, a lance of white pain through one side of my body. I make it to the line of cones, feeling like my whole right side has fallen off.

But I can't show Dad.

I line up again, spit out a big gob of phlegm. My throat's feeling dry and my spit's got a metallic taste.

'You alright, Luc?' Dell stands up behind the tackle bag.

'Yeah, fine. Ready?' I try to get the blood in my mouth to spark up the old fire, but something's different this time and my head feels light.

Dell drops back down. This time we're taking the hit on the other side. I half cradle my arm as I run, pretend like I'm carrying the ball. I push through the tackle bag and roll out the other side.

Then we swap over. Dell gives me another concerned look as I ease my right hand through the straps. Needles of pain shoot through my shoulder and down my back, but I get the bag on.

'Lance? Luc's not looking great. He's gone a bit pale.'

'Luc, you OK, son?' Dad shouts across.

I nod.

'He's fine, Dell. That's a tough kid there. Don't go easy on him.'

Dell settles on the start line. I flex my knees, lean forward to take the contact, my left shoulder behind the bag as Dell starts running towards me, but just before Dell strikes the bag, the world swims up and to the left. When it settles down, Dell's face is above me. He's kneeling on the ground, asking if I'm OK.

*

Later, in A&E, Dad makes me phone Dell and apologise. Not straight away, obviously. That would be cruel. He waits until the doctors have popped my dislocated shoulder back into its joint, and until my arm's been X-rayed and until a nurse has put it in a tight sling that I have to keep on for four weeks so my broken collar bone can heal straight.

He waits for all that to happen, then passes me the phone. 'I thought you were ready for the big boys' game, son.'

'Sorry, Dad.'

'It's not me you should be apologising to. Poor Dell was about to run straight through you. You just crumbled. How many times have I got to tell you, if you don't do this properly, you don't do it at all.'

I mumble another apology.

Dell's really kind on the phone. I can hear a couple of kids shouting 'Dad!' in the background so he can't talk for long. But I tell him it wasn't his fault. When he asks me whether I felt it on the first contact, I don't reply. Dad's coming back from the drinks machine with a couple of coffees. He asks if I'll be OK doing my schoolwork with a sling on.

I say 'yes' without thinking about it. Now I've given my age away. Dad'll be furious.

'Thought so,' he says. Then, after a pause, 'You take care of yourself, Luc. I'll come and see you soon if that's alright, check how you're doing?'

I say he really doesn't need to do that. No need to put himself out. I find it hard to control the pitch of my voice.

'It's no bother. You're only round the corner, mate.' Then his voice shifts, drops a bit, like he's tensing his jaw. 'And I'd like to catch up with your dad too, at some point.'

I don't say anything. Dad's right next to me. I get that light-headed feeling again as he looks down at me with a thin smile.

Dell's voice gets even quieter. 'Sorry. He's there with you, isn't he?'

I manage a soft 'uh-huh.'

Dell's voice bounces right back to cheerful again, and loud. 'I'll see you soon, kid. Get well.'

I give the phone back to Dad, who hands me my hot coffee, then claps a firm hand on my good shoulder. 'Well, son. Home then. Let's go and show your mother.'

Dad's friendly shake spills some of my drink. I grimace, try to win against the pain as the boiling liquid trickles down my hand. With Dad's hand on my shoulder, I can't lean over to put the cup down. Dad watches, holds me upright. 'Fish and chips on the way home? Or Chinese?' He lets my shoulder go and turns for the sliding doors.

I pick up my kit bag. The paramedics had to cut me out of the two tops I was wearing so as not to move my shoulder again, and Dad's insisting I show my ruined clothes to Mum so she can tell me off for wasting her money. My boots are in there too. When I lean down, I spill some more scalding coffee on my hand. There are a few pink lines across my knuckles where it runs off. I drink a few quick sips, almost burning my mouth, then put the flimsy cup down under the chair, lick the drops off my skin. It's not even worth asking if Dad will let me drink it in the car.

'Hurry up, son. Do you need a hand or something?'

'No, Dad. I'm alright.'

My kit bag knocks against my knees as I hobble across the car park in my socks, and the evening air is cold across my bare chest. I've got Dad's fleece over my shoulders, but I can't zip it up. Dad drains his drink and slings his cup into a bush before getting in the driver's side. I keep knocking my bag against the door, trying to open it with one hand, and the gap between the Subaru and the next car isn't very wide.

'Don't chip my paintwork, you pillock.'

MATT

23

I send Mark messages, but I'm pretty sure they just fall into the bottomless pit that seems to have replaced Mark lately. He never replies to anything, and his 'last seen' on the messaging apps is always some obscure time, either very late, or very early. And Luc's not coming out tonight, so this Saturday is just me and Johnny.

I don't really fancy sitting on the school field rubbing Johnny's back and looking after him again. We wander the Lanes for a bit, see if anyone else is about. But they're not. They're up on the school field, of course.

So, faced with no alternative, we jump the fence just as the sun's dropping below the horizon.

Everyone's there, as usual. They're gathered around the long-jump pit. I wonder if they're sparking up their socks again, or if they're trying to get a proper fire going like last week. But there's no tell-tale orange glow, and there's a strange feeling in the air. A kind of tension.

People are having conversations in low voices,

their heads dipping towards each other but their eyes always forward, on whatever's happening in the middle of the circle.

'Who's *that* kid?' Johnny exclaims. He's pushed himself up on James King's shoulders, but James shrugs him off.

I spot Alice and Amy. 'What's going on?'

'Have you seen Mark? Is he with you lot?' Amy looks twitchily over my shoulder, into the darkening evening.

'No. Why?'

Alice is slightly calmer. She explains, 'This new kid's turned up with loads of green and other stuff. Says Mark's busy and we need to buy from him.'

'That's a bit weird. And you've not heard from Mark?'

'No, idiot,' Amy snaps. 'That's why we're asking you.'

'Ignore her,' says Alice. 'She's not eaten. She's hangry.'

'If I give you a tenner, Matt, will you go get me some chips or something?'

I wonder how I got this role: chip-fetcher, back-rubber, person-who-knows-where-Mark-is-so-people-can-score-drugs-from-him-er.

'Amy, stop being rude. We need that tenner anyway. He says they're not doing pre-rolled anymore, like Mark did, and his smallest bag's twenty quid.' Alice steps forward towards the new kid. People are drifting away to small huddles across the field. Barely anyone is laughing, which is weird. 'You want to join us, Matt?'

I shake my head and Amy barges me out of the way. 'Fine.' She pulls a ten-pound note from the back of her phone case.

Alice has to tug it out of her grip.

Amy moans again. 'Fuck, I really want some chips or something. I'd kill for a burger. Has he got any 'baccy? And skins?'

Alice takes a tin from her coat pocket and tosses it to Amy. 'Check in there.'

Amy struggles with the lid while I take a proper look at the new kid.

He's probably not much older than us. A few splodgy patches of hair are showing down the side of his face. In places, they get lost in fields of pretty bad acne. Some of the spots looks really painful. His dark hair is mostly kept under a black cap, a few oily strands peeking out under his peak, and he's got his hood up, too. It's hard to tell if his jeans are supposed to be as ripped as they are. They, too, are black. And he's wearing trackies underneath – black as well. His trainers aren't though. Nike Airs from the looks of it – powder blue with a white swoosh. They look almost new. I think he spots me looking at them, uses his cuff to brush a bit of sand off.

'You want anything, mate?' His voice is hard but quivers a bit. He sounds cold. Maybe that's why he's wearing two pairs of trousers.

'No, thanks. Do you know where Mark is?'

'Who's Mark?' He takes Alice's money, passes her a small plastic bag from his backpack.

She rises quickly, turns back to Amy and mouths 'He stinks' at her. Amy's got the lid off the tin and the pair of them sit down cross-legged to start rolling a joint. 'Sure we can't tempt you, Matt?' Alice asks. Amy has popped open the top of the bag and gives it a deep sniff. Her eyes widen and she starts giggling.

'No,' I reply, still looking at the new kid.

His eyes hover on me for a while, as if he wants to look at me but can't quite focus. Then someone else is leaning over him, a twenty-pound note in their outstretched hand. I watch him reach into the backpack and come back up with a smaller bag, two orange pills inside it.

'What's your name?' I ask. The kid looks confused, so I add, 'So I know you next time.'

He seems to find this funny, 'Yeah, sure. I'm Adam.'

I smile. 'I'm Matt. Are you sure you don't know Mark?' But he's gone, his hand diving once again into his backpack, Johnny standing over him with a twenty in his hand.

I manage to talk Johnny out of the orange pills, but I can't stop him buying a bag of green.

After everyone had bought what they wanted, the kid – Adam – takes a call on his phone and disappears. A few minutes later, the noise of a powerful car comes from the direction of the school car park, echoing through the school buildings before drifting across the field to us. I say 'us', but it's really more like 'me sitting on my own' and 'some other groups of people in various states of quiet inebriation'. No one else looks up from the studied task of getting high, not noticing the engine and tyre squeal.

The noise unsettles me a bit. Johnny says I'm getting paranoid, that it must be a new batch of weed and I should just smoke a bit more and get through it. But I haven't had any.

'That must be the problem then,' he laughs, offering me the last few draws on his rapidly dwindling joint.

I shake my head. 'Not tonight.'

Johnny tilts his head, narrows his eyes at me. 'You OK?'

I shiver against some imaginary wind. 'Not really. You fancy a walk?'

Johnny drops the end of his smoke and grinds it into the ground with his heel. In the grass next to it, the sharp edge of a twisted can catches in the glow from the school lights. 'Let's go,' he says. 'Where to?'

24

We hop back over the fence onto familiar paths and are soon deep into the dark heathland.

'Bramble,' I say, holding a dangling strand up while Johnny passes beneath it, into the lead.

It was another game we used to play. The four of us would walk in a line, the followers having to go wherever the leader chose. For hours, the occasional 'branch here' or 'roots there' were the only words we'd say. Only there's no Luc or Mark tonight, just the two of us. Johnny slips through the tight weave of a silver birch stand and I follow, the papery bark warm against my palms. Then we switch again, wordlessly.

I duck under some pine trees and into almost total darkness. When I feel the ground start to rise, I steer us into it. The slope gets steep quickly. I stay low, use my hands, grip the roots of the trees that cling to the bank.

'Pinecones,' I say, as a couple roll down behind me.

Johnny is silent. I imagine his tongue wedged between his teeth.

The hill steepens further, the sand starting to slide under my trainers. After not very far, we're through the trees and back out on the scrub, the ground still rising, the moon risen, and a silvery glow shows the creeping black roots of younger heather bushes fanning out across the sandy soil. I push my fingertips in between them, and Johnny and I climb, our breaths sharpened by the night air.

Soon after the ground levels out, a fence rises up in front of us. We turn around, backs to the chain-link. The black-purple heath yawns in front of us, the orange lights of the school maybe half a mile away, then the dull glow of the town beyond that. We can see the bypass from here, the wink of headlights and the soft woosh of far-off cars drifting on the still air.

I shiver.

'Don't remember this fence being here,' Johnny says.

'No. Me neither.' My breath billows out in front of me. I watch it fade.

'Wonder what's behind it.' Johnny tries to pull himself up and over it. But it's a half-hearted attempt and he soon sits down next to me. 'Nice view.'

'Do you think it'll always be here?'

'What, the heath? Yeah, it's protected, isn't it? Remember those Geography lessons in year nine. Something about the butterflies and lizards.'

Above us, a bat twitches erratically against the sky. A few stars show through gaps in the clouds. The sweat of the climb starts to cool under my arms, and I shiver again.

'Come on. We're close.' Johnny stands up, starts following the fence line away to his right.

'Close to what?' I call after him, my voice too loud in the darkness. 'I thought I was leader.'

No reply.

'Close to what, Johnny?' I call again, suddenly not wanting to be so far from him, the wind-bent trees bent over in the darkness around me, like they're worshipping something.

Johnny's voice drifts back. 'You'll see.'

It takes another ten minutes until we're there, the copse rising up ahead of us, looking weirdly familiar but with the details not quite right, like something drawn from memory. It's smaller than I remember.

I lose sight of Johnny as he ducks under the outer branches. My heart beating a little harder than I'd like, I follow him in.

When my eyes have adjusted to the darker darkness, I see Johnny kicking around at the base of a tree, pulling a half-rotten plank from one of them. 'Look,' he says. 'The ladder from the high den. Remember when we collapsed that one?'

I do. It was terrifying.

Against another tree lean the remains of the armchair. It's lying on its side, the seat cushion long since fallen out and lost. The ends of a few springs have pushed through the fabric, and it looks like something has chewed at the headrest – there's a spill of stuffing running out of it, all speckled brown and grey from age and leaf litter. I give it a kick. The loose springs quiver softly.

Something falls out from the back of the chair. It bounces and rolls to a stop at my feet. I bend down and pick it up. It's weighty and solid in my hand.

Mark's old penknife.

It's pretty stiff, but the blade has survived relatively well. There's a bit of rust along the top side but the sharp edge winks in the dimness when I open it. I push its point into the nearest tree trunk.

The first centimetre slips in easily and the sweet smell of sap fills my nose. There's a sugary glisten on the end of the knife when I pull it out.

Behind me, Johnny's kicking at an old pallet that's tied to a tree with dusty, green rope.

'Here.' I tug the knife through the fibres and the rope gives out with a cough. The bark of the tree it's tied to has grown around it, and holds onto the frayed remains like an old Christmas decoration. 'I didn't do the high den, remember? I sat that one out.'

Johnny pulls the pallet towards the edge of the copse and sits down, patting the wooden board next to him. 'Probably best you did. Mark was limping for a week, remember?'

We sit, looking out across the heath, the fence we followed to get here slicing through the mounds of gorse and heather. On the other side of the chain-link barrier, where the land used to drop away, there are new and strange mounds looming out of the darkness. On the soft breeze, an acidic smell – half rotten, half plastic.

'What's that?' I point.

'Landfill,' says Johnny. 'They sold it off a few years ago. Giles says they're going to fill in the whole lot, flatten it then probably build houses on it. Probably call the estate 'Heather Fields' or 'Gorse View' or something. Maybe we can buy one each. Be neighbours. We could all rig our houses to collapse, just like old times.'

We sit in silence again. I check my phone. Still no reply from Mark.

'You miss him.' Johnny's words have the quality of a brick – heavy and physical.

I get a sudden image in my head of Mark, hunched over his own backpack on some other school field, or at someone else's Lanes, surrounded by strangers waving money at him. No doubt he's loving it.

'Want to talk about it?'

'Not really.'

More silence.

'Why are you avoiding Luc? Did he say something to you?'

A beat. I say nothing.

Johnny tenses beside me. 'You know what Luc's like. He's all bark, right?'

'Yeah, maybe.'

It's Johnny's turn to shiver now. He pushes his hands deeper into the pockets of his hoody, pulls out a crumpled joint, puts it between his lips. His face glows for a second in the flame from the lighter. 'Shall we kill his dad? You know, destroy his god or something?'

The moon flickers behind a cloud as Johnny passes me the joint.

The tree sap on my finger sticks to the paper. 'How shall we do it?' I inhale deeply, warmth running down through my stomach.

'Cut the brake cables on his car? Push him off his scaffold?' Johnny pauses. 'Hit him over the head then bury him in his own garden?'

I exhale, the harsh smoke catching in my lungs. I cough until my eyes water.

Johnny pats me on the back, then leaves his hand there.

We stay like that for a bit, staring off into the night.

I fiddle with a loose nail, can't shake the feeling that the pallet we're sitting on might disappear from under us at any moment.

MARK

25

It's Sunday, I think. The Guy's keeping me busy, so I sort of lose track of which day it actually is. But who needs days when you're untouchable, right?

A taxi drops me at home as the sun's just coming up. I don't know where I've been. I have a shower, then fall onto my bed. My dreams are a bit weird: full of winding passageways and running after things, and faces floating up at me from dark rooms. They've been like that for a while now.

If I wanted to, I could probably take a day off, get some proper sleep. But the messages come so close together sometimes, and most of the time I'm not sure where I even am, so getting home normally means a lift with someone else. And they don't take me home – not straight away. There's another job to do, first, they say. Besides, it's all money, so it's all good, you know?

And the travelling's fine. I've never really been far from my home, and we've lived in the same house since I can remember. I like watching the dark go by on the motorways, or the backs of houses slip past train windows, or the telegraph lines dipping and rising between the poles, following a kind of rhythm.

Sometimes, though, to work out where I am, I find a quiet place and open my maps app, slowly zooming out from the little blue dot until I see a place name I recognise.

But it's no big deal. And when I get where I'm going, there's always someone who's got some green. Or something else. I was at this huge house, waiting in this really plush lounge once – glass tables, leather settee, the owner even had a bar set up in there, in his lounge! Anyway, someone there took a hit from a pipe and slid right off his chair onto the floor. I didn't think you could fall over if you were already sitting down. Haha! The smoke made me gag a bit, and I felt a bit lightheaded, even from the other side of the room. He was still lying there, not really moving much, when the owner came in with my envelope.

I just walked out, then took the cash to where I was told to go. I didn't even look back.

I was cool as anything.

Untouchable, like I said.

But I'm pretty sure it's his face I dream about and keep dreaming about. His, and a few others.

Mum's there when I wake up. It must be late, getting on for evening. I can hear her downstairs, ready to head out on a shift. I wait for her to leave, put some clean clothes on and go for a walk. It's nice to be in the fresh air, and somewhere familiar.

The Guy says I'm valuable in this new role, and I'm making better money. I don't see so much cash, but The Guy's still running the bank account for me. He sends me screen grabs as usual and he's getting me to take selfies in all these places I go to – especially the real high-end ones, like that bloke's lounge. He says I'll need a strong online presence when I step up to the next level and need to project an image of success if I want to attract more business. That selfie in front of Frank's Merc was a good start, he said. Honestly, being taught this stuff in the real world is so much better than school. That's why I've stopped going. But I guess I miss seeing people I know. And I suppose it was more fun when I was up at the Lanes. I wonder if anyone's up there now?

I'm walking past Luc's house when I see his dad's car pull into the drive.

The car door opens, and the house door does too. Luc's mum stands in the front porch with her arms across her chest. I can't tell from this far off if she's angry or upset. Luc's dad barges past into the house before Luc's even out of the passenger side, the passenger door closing on him a few times. Why can't he just push it open?

Then he gets out. I don't see the bandages at first – Luc's got his back to me – but when he turns to shut the door, I see the sling and another bandage holding his arm close to his chest. Must be a broken collarbone. Brendon broke his once on one of those death slides at an adventure park. He was about twelve, and the noises he made in the ambulance were so awful I was really scared he might die. I was five, I think; maybe younger. But I remember wondering what would happen if he died, and that I really wanted him to be OK. He was fine in the end, obviously, but he had to spend four weeks sleeping on the sofa in the front room, and he had a sling just like Luc's.

Luc's mum is on him almost as soon as he's out of the car. He shakes off her hug, wincing a bit, and I hear her apologise, putting her hands on his cheeks, delicately, like she's afraid she might break him.

I take a few steps closer, and Luc's mum spots me as I cross the road, smiling at me. We don't see much of Luc's mum. She always disappears into the house when any of us arrive – says she has to do some ironing, or laundry, or whatever – but she's always really nice. She seems kind. Which is lucky for Luc because I'm not sure his dad is.

'Hi, Mark,' she says.

'Hi, Mrs Durel,' I reply.

Luc turns around. His eyes are red, like he's been crying or is about to, but I look away pretty quickly, so he doesn't have to pretend that I haven't noticed. He passes his kit bag to his mum and rubs the heel of his hand into one eye socket. 'Alright, Mark?'

'Yeah,' I reply. 'What happened to you?'

'Oh, it's nothing. Just a collarbone. Went in too hard. Knocked the other guy flying, though.' He tries a laugh.

'I'll get your kit washed, son. And don't worry about the shirts. Are you staying for tea, Mark?'

The mention of food makes my empty stomach rumble. 'Is that alright?'

'Of course. The boys brought fish and chips home, but there's always far too much for me. I'm sure Lance won't mind.'

I can't tell from Luc's face whether he's happy to see me or not. Mostly he's looking at the ground, or rubbing his eyes, one then the other, pushing hard with the back of his hand.

'Sounds brilliant,' I smile. I really am hungry. Food on the road doesn't come too easy. It's normally a case of grabbing a sandwich and a chocolate bar from a train station kiosk or a corner shop. If I haven't got someone waiting for me or taking me somewhere.

In the kitchen, Luc's dad is plating up the takeaway, and it takes him a beat to register me in the doorway, and for his face to go from thunderous to sunny.

'Mark. Good to see you, lad. You staying for dinner?' He's already bending down for another plate, pouring on chips from the huge bag, shiny with grease. 'Helen normally leaves most of hers anyway. Be good not to waste it for a change.' He picks up what is a truly enormous battered fish fillet and plonks it on top of the new plate's mountain of chips. 'I went for large this evening. Luc needs his protein, for the healing. Right, son?

Luc gives a weak nod.

'It'll be ready in two minutes. Go and help the invalid into something warm, would you, Mark? He can't manage himself. Wonder if he'll need his arse wiped for him for the next four weeks too. Think you can manage your own arse, Luc?' Luc's dad's jokes are always harsh, but you have to laugh when you're a guest in another man's house.

'Yes, Dad.' Luc's already on the stairs, taking them two at a time.

I catch up at his bedroom door. 'So what happened? Get a tackle wrong or something?'

'Yeah, something like that. Was the other guy's fault, really.' Luc's rifling through his wardrobe for a jumper, pulling three off their hangers by mistake. He bends down to pick them up, then shoots straight back upright, drawing in a sharp breath.

'Careful, mate. Just go slow. Was that the bones scraping each other?'

'I think so, yeah. I'm fine.'

'Of course, mate, but just go easy, yeah?' Something in my own stomach turns a little bit, too.

Luc bends again, slower this time, and picks up the jumpers. But he can't get them back on their hangers with only one hand. If I step in and help, there's a good chance he'll hit me, so I sit on the edge of his bed while he fumbles for half a minute before tossing the jumpers in the corner. He picks up the third jumper, a hoody with a zip all the way up the front, and gingerly puts his good arm through it, then tries to swing the dangling end around his back and catch it, shrugging it onto his shoulder.

'Do you want me to...' I ask.

There's a beat. Then, 'Please.'

I don't mention the yellowy-blue bruising that's already coming up on his shoulder like an ink stain, and it's fiddly doing up zips from the outside, or undoing them – everything's back to front. I'm about to comment on it, but I don't. I know that just because I'm doing Luc's zip it doesn't mean anything. But still, it's best not to mention it.

Instead, I say, 'Remember when we were in cubs, that old guy who turned up every now and again to do the boring badges with us?'

'What, One-Arm?'

'Yeah. He always had the sleeve of his shirt – the one he wasn't, y'know, *using* – pinned in this weird fold thing.'

'Yeah, he pinned it with a couple of paperclips, didn't he?' Luc's smiling a bit.

'Want me to do you like that?'

'No, I've got a better idea.' Luc grabs the flopping sleeve, tucks it into the front of the hoody. 'Ta-dah!'

'You look like you're touching yourself up, mate. Squeezing your own tit or something.'

'Fuck you,' Luc gives me a shove. Even with his left he pushes me onto the bed pretty easily.

I bounce back up, but Luc pushes me down again, smiling.

I roll off the bed backward and come at him. We're both grinning, so I know that Luc's actually fine. I move in, my guard up. Luc's left arm, the one not in the sling, is tracking my bobs and weaves, his hand wide open to grab mine. But I stay clear, fake a right then stick a light left jab to Luc's kidney. Luc laughs out loud, rolls away from the punch. But then he pulls up suddenly, that same sharp intake of breath. Even I heard the bones scraping against each other that time.

'Sorry sorry sorry. I forgot.' I put my hands out, palms up, backing away – the universal sign for *please don't hurt me*.

'Ah, shit,' Luc grimaces. His right hand balls into a fist again and again, quickly. Then his whole body tightens, and a shudder runs through him, top to bottom.

'You OK?'

'Yeah, fine. I think my shoulder just popped out and in again. Again.' He presses his fingers gingerly around the joint.

'Shit, that must have been some tackle.'

Luc's dad calls up. 'When you girls have stopped making out, would you mind coming down for dinner? Come on, it's getting cold.'

When we get downstairs, there's a can of Comeup next to our plates. I pop the ring pull on mine and swallow a few mouthfuls. 'Cheers, Mr Durel, Mrs Durel. Thanks for having me.'

'It's no problem, Mark. It's nice to see you.' Luc's mum sits behind a plate of food half the size of any of ours. She picks at it as we three men shovel food into our mouths.

Then Luc's dad stops, mid chew. 'Luc, what is going on with that hoody? You look like you're squeezing your own tit. Can't I even trust you to do that properly?'

Trust. The word sounds weird all of a sudden. But I laugh, and Luc laughs, and even Luc's mum smiles a bit. But it feels like my laughing doesn't go any deeper than my skin, if you know what I mean. I can feel that my eyes aren't laughing. It's like they're blank, like the eyes of that kid I watched slide off his chair in a dark room with a mattress in the corner. When was it? Who knows.

But I'm seeing it over again, the way his eyes rolled back in his head, and the noise he was making when he was lying on the floor. And then, rather than happening in a dream, it's like it's happening right there in front of me at Luc's dining-room table. And there're other things too, other faces and voices in my head all seem to be spilling out around the table. People giving me things, asking me to do things for them.

And they always say the same thing. 'You trust me,' they say. 'Don't you?'

I push my chair back. 'Sorry, I've got to go.' And then I'm through Luc's front door and out into the early evening, the streetlights glowing and the air slightly damp. I get a few hundred metres down the road and lean against someone's front wall, pulling in lungful after lungful.

I pull my phone out of my pocket. I'll be fine in a minute. My head feels like it's full of scrunched-up plastic bags, but this isn't the first time it's happened to me.

The last time, I'd been in the back of a cab and some guy was driving me to a party. He kept looking back over his shoulder at me.

'Are you OK, man?'

'Yeah, fine.'

'You look tired, man. You can sleep if you like. It's quite a trip. I'll wake you when we get there.' His eyes flicked between the rear-view mirror and the road as he negotiated a roundabout.

I tightened my grip on the backpack in the footwell. The Guy has been pretty clear about being careful, especially around people who seem 'nice'. He'd said something else about trust.

'No, it's fine,' I said to the driver. 'I'll be OK in a minute.'

I did then what I'd done the previous time, and the time before that. And I do it again now. I log in to the cloud and open that video of Matt, pause it on the shot of him looking straight into the camera, the phone light reflecting in his eyes. I stare at that image for as long as it takes me to calm down.

And, in a few minutes, I feel OK again.

Untouchable, see?

26

Mum's kept her coat on, even though it's pretty warm in Mrs Clarke's office, and she's hunched into it like it's a kind of armour. It's an old coat, the same one she's had for years. Every autumn she says she's going to replace it but never does.

You wouldn't catch me wearing the same coat for so long.

It's hard to work out where Mum's looking. Her hands are held in her lap, and she keeps playing with one of the rings on her fingers, her nails tapping against it. She's looking at that, or her knees, or maybe at the carpet just in front of her, or the edge of Mrs Clarke's desk.

She's definitely not looking at Mrs Clarke, or at the police officers who are sitting next to her, filling up the room with all the stuff attached to the stab vests they're wearing.

And she's certainly not looking at me, even though Mrs Clarke and the police officers are looking at me, hard and extra-serious, like the more they look at me the more likely I am to answer any of their questions.

But that's not going to happen.

I don't have to answer any of them.

They want to know names of the people I've been going to see. Details of the places I've been going to. They want to know where I've been when I've not been at school.

But I'm not going to tell them.

They pulled me out of registration first thing this morning. It's Monday. I fell asleep pretty soon after getting back from Luc's last night; something about having some hot food in my belly, maybe. Mum woke me up with a cup of tea, which was strange. I should have worked it out then, I suppose. I didn't even ask why she wasn't at work.

I walked to school on my own, got here well in time for registration. Matt looked away when he saw me in our tutor room.

When Johnny came in, I asked him what the time was, and he just looked at the clock and told me. Then he went and sat next to Matt. Maybe they're not playing that game anymore. Whatever. Fuck 'em both.

Then, pretty much as soon as the register was done, Miss Amber came to the door and asked to see me. She said I should bring my bag.

Mum was already in the office when I arrived.

They say my attendance is low. That I've only been in school on a handful of days since the start of this year, which was weeks ago, apparently. I shrug. They ask, again, where I've been.

Again, I shrug.

They clearly don't actually know anything, or they wouldn't be asking. It's just like The Guy said, and other people I've met. They don't *know* anything, so if you don't *say* anything, they can't *do* anything. I'm untouchable.

Mum says nothing, just keeps looking anywhere but at me.

The male police officer asks Mum if she consents to him searching me.

Mum asks what for.

For drugs or other controlled substances, the police officer says.

I think maybe Mum looks at me then, just for a second. I don't see, because I'm looking at the ceiling, wondering how long this is going to last.

Mrs Clarke says that the police officer can use Miss Amber's room, next door. Miss Amber's here too, leaning against the wall on the other side of Mum, looking concerned. I'm not sure if that's for me, or for Mum.

The police officer gets up. Miss Amber says there's a blind on the window in her door. For privacy, she says. I follow him into the office.

He won't find anything, no matter where he looks.

I'm untouchable.

*

When he's finished, and I've put my uniform back on again, I stand in the corridor outside Mrs Clarke's office while he goes back in to talk to them, peeling off his latex gloves as he steps through the door. My backpack, which he also checked, is dangling from my hand. He didn't find anything, of course. I idly kick the backpack.

In primary school, I used to take a football in every day of summer term, for the field. My football was the best one: it was a Mitre, a size 4.

I remember opening it on my birthday morning. It came in a cardboard box, like an Easter egg, the words 'official' on the side of it. And it had its own pump and special adaptor for pumping it up. My brother helped me, put the special adapter in some soapy water first, just like I asked him to because that's what the PE teacher at primary school always did.

I'd carry the ball in my PE bag, and practise kicking it all the way to school, the PE bag's drawstring held in my fist. Sometimes, I'd do the commentators' voices as I practised volleys, or swung the ball up and headed it, imagining the ball sailing into the top corner, scoring the winning goal under floodlights a long way from here.

I kick my backpack again. There's a dull thunk from my lunchbox.

Because I had the best ball, I was in charge of the game. I'd be first onto the field at lunch, everyone behind me arguing about whose team they were going to be on, everyone really wanting to be on my team because it was my ball. Every evening I'd get home and make sure it was properly pumped up before I went to bed. I'd try to get the worst grass stains off at the kitchen sink with paper towel, then I'd dry the ball off and put it back in my PE bag, ready for the next day.

I kick my backpack again, twice: thunk, thunk.

Then, one day, it had been too wet to go on the field, and we'd had to play on the playground. Mum says she warned me, but I don't remember that, only the hollow, sick feeling as I ran my fingers over the deep gashes in the ball's leather that evening. Some of the stitching was really frayed, too, with holes between the little panels. And when I tried to blow it up, a pink bubble came through one of the holes like a bit of the ball's guts had popped out. I tried to push it back down but it was too hard. The next day, the ball wouldn't bounce right. It had gone oval, Luc said, and we should play rugby with it instead.

I didn't want to do that. But Luc took the ball and threw it to someone else, and they threw it to someone else, and soon everyone was playing – a whole, school-wide game of rugby. Even the girls joined in, running away when the ball came near them. I remember watching from the edge of the playground as the ball skidded and twisted over the snakes and ladders and number grids that were painted across the tarmac. I think Matt was with me, just watching it all happen. He said it would probably be alright and we'd play football again tomorrow.

Then Luc got his Maths compass out of his bag.

253

When the game was over, the ball was an airless, off-white sack that felt like an old slice of bread. Matt had gone off as soon as the bell went. He said he didn't want to get into trouble.

I put the ball in the bin and one of the dinner ladies took me back to our classroom. I got told off for being late.

That evening, Mum said she wouldn't buy me a new one and I should have been more careful. Then she went to work.

Through the window in the door of Mrs Clarke's office, I see Mum's head drop. Her shoulders hunch even further and they start going up and down, up and down, like she's doing a funny dance. It looks pathetic. Miss Amber has her hand on Mum's now, on the arm of the chair, and she's crouched down next to her. She's offering her a tissue. Mum can barely get one out of the box and has to be helped. She can't do anything for herself, and my brother completely ignores her, so how could she *ever* do anything for me?

I kick the bag again. It bounces against the door. I kick it harder, and the books jump around. Harder, and the lunchbox crunches. Harder, and then I'm kicking through the bag and just kicking the door, again and again and again.

The police officer has to make me stop.

LUC

27

Mark comes into the science lab looking like shit. He's got these big bags under his eyes and he's dragging his backpack after him like it's some kind of dead dog on a lead, knocking against his legs. Miss Amber's escorting him, so it must be pretty bad. She says something to Dr Coles, who's halfway through explaining something about electrolysis that's going way over my head, even though I've caught up in the textbook now, thanks to the lunchtime sessions. I didn't think it would make a difference, but it feels strange actually understanding what Dr Coles is going on about. And the other teachers. Must be the kind of feeling that Matt gets all the time. It's kind of nice, I guess.

But when Mark comes in with Miss Amber, Dr Coles stops, and they talk in hushed whispers in the doorway.

Everyone's watching Mark as he lumbers up to my bench, swings his bag under his stool and sits down. He crosses his arms on the bench top, then lets his head fall on top of those.

It's a bit pathetic, to be honest. He smells less of green than he did yesterday, when he came over for dinner, but there's still definitely a bit of a stink rising off him. The BO isn't so bad though. He must have had a shower when he went home.

'Thanks for dinner last night, mate,' he mutters from the bench top.

'No worries. You alright?' I watch as Miss Amber and Dr Coles look our way.

'Everything OK, Mark?' Miss Amber is doing her chirpy 'it better be Ok or we can discuss it in my office' voice.

Mark raises his arm in a thumbs up. The rest of him doesn't move.

'Will you keep an eye on him, Luc?'

There's nothing I hate more than teachers trying to turn you against your friends, but I force out a, 'Yes, Miss.'

Dr Coles goes back to electrolysis. Mark asks if he can go to the toilet. Dr Coles says no.

Five minutes later, I'm pretty sure Mark starts to snore.

On the way to our next lesson, I ask if Mark's heard about Johnny.

'Another holiday? Again? His mum is literally never here.'

'I know, right?' Johnny had told us this morning on the way to school. He said Giles had found this last-minute deal, which is why it's such late notice. I'd spotted Anna, then, on the other side of the road, with her friends. I'm sure I saw her looking at me. Ever since telling that story to Sara I can't help thinking back to it. There's no way Anna would've kissed me like that if she didn't want to.

'What does that guy actually do that means he can take so many holidays?' I say, trying to keep Mark's spirits up. He's walking a bit slowly and hasn't totally lost his sad-puppy look. 'My dad says he must be a front for a cartel or a drug trafficker or something. He says there's no way anyone who runs a real business can take so much time off.'

'I don't know, but it sounds like a job I'd want to do.' Mark has brightened a bit. I don't think he'll tell me what happened, though. I wonder if the police car parked out the front of the school this morning is anything to do with it. Maybe that's why everyone keeps looking at him – to see if he's snitched on any of his customers.

We push through a bunch of other students on the way to Maths, and I wince when one of the little ones bounces off my arm. It's strapped under my school jumper, so I guess no one can see it, but I still aim a cuff at the side of his head as he disappears into the crowd behind me.

'Yeah,' I continue. 'So they're off for two weeks to Gran Canaria or somewhere like that. They leave tomorrow.'

'How did Johnny seem?'

'Yeah, fine. But listen, what do you say to a party at Johnny's place, next Friday?'

'Really? At Johnny's?'

'I know. I think the kid's finally flipped. Got a death wish or something. Remember that time with the shoes?'

Mark laughs. 'Yeah. Not sure I'll be able to make it, though. I'll try.'

'Ah, c'mon, Mark. It's been ages since any of us have seen you. Properly, I mean. It'll be good, promise. You bring the green, like old times. Yeah? Johnny's on board, and I reckon I can get Anna to agree to it.'

'You still think she's hot for you, man. It's tragic.'

'Hey, how could she say no to this?' I grin.

'You're damaged goods, mate. Anyway, thought you'd fallen in love or something over the summer. That girl you met? Sara, was it? You not trying the "long-distance" thing?'

'Nah, she was a bitch in the end. A right stuck-up little bitch.' My whole body tightens up, saying it. I turn a bit sideways so I'm leading with my good shoulder and drive through the slow-moving crowd.

Mark trots along in my wake. 'Hey, slow down!'

Never, I think. Not for anybody.

28

Mark agrees in the end. 'Subject to availability,' he says. Whatever that means.

On the way home that night, we all walk together, just like old times. Well, year nine, at least.

We stop at the garage on the way back, Mark dropping in to get snacks. He comes out with a six pack of Cokes, sharing them round. It reminds me of when he insisted on buying us all burgers over the summer. He seems happy though, so I go with it.

Johnny downs his and then balances on the empty can, taps the side of it with his other foot, and crushes it flat underneath him. He picks up the slim, metal disc. There aren't even any scraggy bits around the edges – it's perfect. I've not seen him nail one like that for ages. He seems as shocked as anyone else.

'Can I have another one?' He bounds up to Mark.

This time, Johnny opens the ring pull, takes the smallest of sips, then puts the full can on the floor. He steps on top of it slowly, then taps the side with his other foot. When the can collapses under him, a fountain of Coke erupts in all directions, a frothy, creamy puddle spreading out round him in an almost perfect circle.

We actually cheer. So do a few other kids who were watching from the other side of the forecourt.

There's a shout from a woman coming out of the shop. She's wearing a hi-vis vest with the garage logo on it.

'Leg it!' shouts Johnny. He circles us, arms waving, then takes off down the pavement with a high-pitched scream.

We follow him down the main road, a loping, backpack-on-your-back jog up towards the estates, laughing all the way, the four of us. My shoulder hurts a bit though, and everyone slows down.

Then Matt tries to backpack Mark. He's as useless as he always was, doesn't jump high enough and pretty much bounces straight off. Mark barely flinches. I watch to see what happens, but Mark just laughs it off.

Then he takes an alleyway between some houses, and he's leading us up towards the heath.

*

We're sat at the bottom of the bowl, the autumn afternoon warm enough to be in shirtsleeves, our jumpers screwed up in bags. Johnny's sitting on his, cross-legged, like it's a picnic. There's a funny smell in the air, but we ignore it.

'So, party at yours next week, John?' I say.

'Yeah, definitely. It'll be awesome.'

'Do you reckon your sister will be OK with it?' Matt asks. 'And what about Giles?'

'Fuck Giles.' Johnny throws a stick into the ground like a knife. 'It won't be a big one, anyway. Just a few people.'

'What, like Harry's, last year?' says Mark.

Harry's parents had told him he could have a Halloween party last year because the pipes in his bathroom had burst and the whole downstairs of their house had been flooded. The insurance was going to cover it all, so once the water had all been pumped out, Harry's parents said that he could have some friends over as it would be the only time they'd not have to worry about the mess.

That's what Alice had told me, anyway. She'd been invited, but we hadn't. She'd come up the Lanes to see me before her and Amy and a few others were going to go over there. Only she didn't want to say goodbye to me.

So we all went.

And we found some other people on the way, looking for something better to do. So they came as well.

The way I see it, we'd actually been quite helpful. The sofas were going to get chucked anyway, so by putting them outside we were actually doing them a favour. And all the wallpaper needed stripping because of the water damage, and they were probably going to re-plaster, so the holes we made weren't really a problem.

'Johnny, did you really surf that cupboard door down the stairs?' Matt asks.

'Yeah, the look on Harry's face when you got to the bottom!' Mark joins in.

'You didn't have to be actually wearing his mum's clothes when you did it,' I add.

'I thought they suited me,' Johnny laughs. 'Thought it was the best way to make an entrance.'

'Then Amy did your make-up and everything. It was brilliant.' Matt laughs.

'Did we all go home with eye shadow on that night?' asks Mark.

'I didn't,' I say.

'Well, no. Not you, obviously. You might have caught something, Luc. Like a virus,' jokes Johnny. 'And I'm not sure your dad would have seen the funny side.'

We sit there for about another hour, talking and laughing, trying to ignore the strange smell that seems to be getting stronger...

Then Mark's phone goes off and he has to leave. Must be his mum.

And we all go our separate ways home.

MATT

29

It was great, walking home this evening. Like old times. And the party at Johnny's is going to be amazing, if we can persuade Anna. But sitting up on the heath, that acrid, yellowy smell from all the rubbish was making me sick.

It doesn't take me long to find an online group who are opposed to the landfill. They've got their own website and everything, not just a Facebook 'like' page, so they must be pretty serious, I think. Most of the homepage is photographs of the heath: arty shots of gorse flowers or heather in the foreground with a blurred digger blundering over a mound of stinking plastic behind it. There's an aerial one too, where the landfill site looks like a dirty scar against the greens and purples and yellows. But, in all the pictures, the landfill site looks much smaller than it does now.

There's a message board, but the newest thread was about three months ago. Its title is 'Mission Failed' and it's a rambling apology from the guy who must have been in charge of the group – a guy called Peter. I skim read it. It seems full of self-pity. Underneath there are a handful of comments, all starting 'Dear Pete' or 'Dearest Peter' and encouraging him to keep going, that everyone's behind him and they can't take the pressure off now as the heath has no other allies. That kind of thing.

But he did stop, clearly.

In school, we do studies on great world leaders – people like Nelson Mandela and Barak Obama – and everyone in that classroom would feel confident that the future was going to be OK. Yes, there were bad companies that were doing bad things – burning what they shouldn't be burning, or digging where they shouldn't be digging – but Nelson and Barak and the others were going to sort it all out and we didn't have anything to worry about. That seemed to be the message.

But Nelson Mandela had died, and Barak Obama hasn't been president for years, and the world wasn't really getting any better, was it?

And then we all got excited about Greta Thunberg, and we were told she was going to change things and talk to the world leaders about how we all felt. Which she does. And it's great – I'm very happy for her.

But still, not a lot's happening.

It's like all the adults do is find someone who's willing to put on the badge that says 'I've got this', then that person becomes a poster boy or poster girl for a better world and reassures us how we won't all die horribly in climate collapse or nuclear war. But what that actually means is that everyone else can stop caring or stop worrying because someone else is now in charge of that particular problem and we can all go on with our lives exactly as they were before. And nothing really changes.

I'm sure the people who were all 'right behind' poor old Peter are the same, just getting on with their lives, now they've failed. Peter probably is, too. Just getting on with his life, trying to ignore that smell drifting over his house. The smell that's only going to get worse.

Before I know what I'm doing, I'm writing all this in a comment on the website and clicking send. I slam the top of my laptop then go downstairs for a drink.

Dad's in the twilit garden, harvesting beans again. He keeps popping the shells open to look at what's inside, emptying a few into his palm for a closer look, then going to put the best ones on a dish he keeps in his studio. His bean paintings are actually pretty good. He's doing this series of really small pictures, about five beans in each and only just bigger than they'd be in real life, and they're almost 3D – the paint rising up in little ridges and blobs. He's done about fifty so far. And they're selling well, he says.

Mum comes in to the kitchen. 'Is that orange squash? Make me one, would you, love?' She looks frazzled. 'Honestly, if I see another spreadsheet today, that computer's going out the window.'

'I thought you were streamlining it all, getting that new system in place? It'll be better once that's done, won't it?'

Mum looks at me, smiling. 'How do you manage to be so bloody wise about these things? It's not my influence, I know that.'

'Well, just remember all this when I'm freaking out about exams next summer.' I hand her the glass of squash. She downs it in one.

'Deal. Where's your father?'

'Bean duty.'

Mum pulls her phone out, checks her messages, puts it away again. 'Can I tell you something? Just between the two of us.' Mum leans in, a conspiratorial smile on her face. 'I am *completely* sick of beans.' She rinses her glass, re-fills it with water. 'What you up to, kiddo? Homework?'

'No, done it.'

'Really? I honestly don't know where we found you. Maybe your dad cross-pollinated some child beans to make us the perfect baby.'

'Not a baby, Mum.'

'"Young Man" then. You look grumpy. What's up?'

'Not much. It's just…' I'm not sure Mum will be that bothered but I carry on anyway. 'Remember that place on the heath we used to make dens – Johnny and Mark and me?'

'Vaguely remember you mentioning it, yes. That's

going back years though, isn't it? I thought you all spent your time on the school fields now, drinking your parents' booze cabinets and making out with each other.'

'Mum, that's disgusting.'

'I know. Makes me sick. Anyway, what about the heath?'

'There's a landfill site there now. I went up with Johnny the other day and it stinks.'

'Yes, they just got permission to expand it, too. It was on the local news.' Mum's finished her water, is tapping the base of the glass on the countertop, keen to get back to work.

'I was looking online and found a group who tried to stop it.'

'That'll be Pete Thwaite. He's at the council. Different department from me, though. Nice man. Why are you interested? Is it those pictures you've been doing of all the giant bits of rubbish? They're very good, by the way.'

'Mum! They're not finished. You shouldn't have looked at them.'

'Wonderful though you may be, you still leave piles of old socks in your room that need washing. If your sketchbook's open on your desk, that's not my fault.' Mum puts her glass in the dishwasher, reties her hair on the top of her head. 'Please don't go traipsing across the landfill site for the sake of your art, Matthew.

That's a part of your father's "flâneur" tendencies you don't need. How's Mark, by the way? Is he speaking to you yet?'

'No.' I sigh, starting to think I shouldn't have told Mum about our kiss in the first place. But I guess I was mopey all summer, including during our holiday, and she'd wheedled it out of me on the beach one day.

Mum puts her glass down and looks at me carefully, puts her hands on my shoulders and moves me left and right, making a show of examining my temples or something, probing for outward signs of lovesick tristesse.

'Oh, teenagers!' she says eventually. 'Why don't you try giving him that sloe gin left over from Christmas? Maybe he'll let you make out with him again.'

I push her away, trying not to laugh. 'Mum! You can't use words like that. It makes me feel sick in my mouth.'

'Fine. Linking, then. Isn't that what you're calling it now? You can *link*.'

'Actually, that's worse.'

'Right, I'm back to work for an hour or so. See you later on. For the beans.' She makes a little vomiting noise when she says 'beans' and disappears back towards her study.

Dad's coming in through the garden door, carrying a colander filled with his little rainbow-coloured nuggets. 'What did you say about beans?'

I get an alert on my phone saying there's been a response to my post on the anti-landfill site, and would I like to read it, so I abandon Dad to his legumes and head back to my room, open my laptop and check the email that's just come through.

It's from Peter Thwaite, the big man himself.

It's basically another long apology, personalised for me this time, explaining how he feels he's let my generation down. There's a sarcastic line about how maybe we'll all appreciate the affordable housing the landfill company will no doubt build atop the rubbish dump and how we'll probably get discounted water rates as the ground water will be undrinkable for years, and that maybe they'll all have miniature methane burners to turn the noxious gases from the slowly melting nappies and food wrappers into cheap power. Pete finishes by copying some links to other charities that 'an engaged and motivated young man like me' might be interested in, then apologises one last time for being an old codger who's lost all his fight.

By the time I get to the end, I'm not even reading his words anymore, just scanning my eyes across the screen. But I've got an idea – nothing solid yet, but something is beginning to crystalise. Something that might make people take notice.

I delete the email and pick up my sketchbook.

30

It's pretty simple, really. A bit 'derivative', no doubt, but I think it could work. And all the best artists steal, don't they? I spend the whole evening sketching, going back to it straight after a dinner that I bolt down, hardly noticing the beany array of colours on the plate.

I'm not sure where I'll get all the materials for the models at this point, but I'm sure I can solve that. The models – sculptures, I should call them – need to be huge. Maybe I could get them made as inflatables? No, that would mean more plastic, ironically. Papier-mâché would be good – pretty biodegradable. Maybe those plaster-of-Paris bandages we used to use in primary school. I'd need loads though. Too expensive. The key thing is going to be size. They need to be so big that no one could possibly ignore them.

Then I'll have to put them in the right places. That'll be hard, but achievable. I'm sure Mum won't mind, really. It's hardly 'flâneuring on the rubbish dump' if I've got a purpose, right?

I don't have to think long about *where* I can make them, though, and that weekend I'm back at the copse as soon as it gets light.

Early morning sun slants across the heath, giving

everything a pinky, silvery glow. I start pulling the old pallets out from under years of pine needles and fallen branches. There's an earthy, peaty smell in the air as I work, and pretty soon I'm sweating, my jumper peeled off and hung in a tree. It would be useful if someone else could help. But no, it's probably best I'm here alone. It needs to be secret. Until it's ready. Until it's done.

By the time I've discarded the ones that are unsalvageable, I've got fifteen pallets in all, one half pallet, and a couple of old car tyres we used to use as seats, once upon a time. They'll be useful too. There's actually more here than I remembered. Where did we get it all from? It must have taken us hours bringing it all together.

Or years, I guess.

The sun doesn't last long, and it's threatening rain just before lunchtime. The tarpaulin's still here, bunched up under one of the trees with god only knows what growing all over it. It'll be full of holes anyway, pretty useless as a shelter. I'll have to get another one. If the models get wet, they'll be ruined. Maybe I could still use the tarp, though. For something else.

I spend a few minutes looking down across the heather to the landfill site, thinking.

After a quick walk to buy a sandwich at lunch, I'm back under the trees. I found another old tyre under a scrubby bush on the way back and rolled it here.

Then I get started properly, arrange some of the

pallets into a rough house shape, managing to put a 'proper' roof on the top by leaning two pallets against each other with a big stick holding them up. Getting them up there was pretty hard work, and I'm covered in sweat and dark green mould from the wood. I do the same thing with the other pallets. The roof on this one is harder to prop up, and one of the pallets slips, the corner catching my knuckles as it falls. I swear, loudly, and a squirrel stops her passage through the branches to look down at me.

She seems sceptical. Can't say I blame her, my knuckles speckled with blood and torn skin.

I breathe deep, calm myself down and find some barely recognisable bits of rope at the base of one of the trees to tie the pallets together before manhandling them skywards again. This time, they stay up. That's two houses done.

I've been putting it off, but I go over and give the old tarpaulin a kick. I swear something slithers out of it, but I take a pinch of the greasy, blue sheet between my fingers and ease it upwards.

The smell is awful.

Spread out, the tarpaulin's not in as bad condition as I'd feared. There's a big gash down one side of it, but it's mostly OK. I leave it to dry off a bit while I stack up the last three and a half pallets in a rough pyramid, then push the longest sticks I can find into the gaps, so it looks like some kind of massive hedgehog.

It's taller than I'd expected and loads of the sticks fall out or snap when I try pulling the tarpaulin over the top of them. I should have spread the tarp over first, then pushed the sticks up from underneath. Idiot. So I start again, standing under the tarp and pushing it up with one end of a stick, then wedging the other end of the stick into a gap in one of the pallets. A few times, the end of the stick goes through the tarpaulin, so I work out a technique of wedging a hunk of moss on the end of the stick so it's not so sharp. It's pretty grim, working under the old, damp plastic, drops of God-knows-how-old water dripping down on me. Once, a glob of old earth falls from the tarpaulin and I just manage to close my eyes before it slops onto my cheek. I can feel the bile rising in my throat, and come out from under the tarp for a few minutes of fresh air before ducking back under. But I get it done. Then I stand back for a look.

The dome I've made looks a bit crumpled in places, like it's deflating. It's perfect.

It's getting dark by the time I leave, and I feel mildly criminal as I open the big recycling bin at the back of the library on the way home. As I'd hoped, there are stacks and stacks of the week's newspapers in there. I pull out as many as I can, then decide it's best to take them up to the copse now. Tomorrow, I'll have the new tarp and a couple of buckets and tubs of PVA glue to deal with – I decided on doing papier-mâché in the end – as well as all the paint. So I lug the huge stack of papers back up to the heath. It takes twenty minutes each trip, and my arms feel like dead weights by the time I tuck the last of the papers under the least holey part of the old tarp dome and head for home again. I hope there'll be enough.

Mum complains about the smell when I get in. The shower runs brown for a full five minutes, and I'm sure I see something with legs circling the plughole.

But it'll be worth it.

MARK

31

Business was difficult last week.

School have been keeping an eye on me, and Mum's threatened to drop me off every morning to make sure I go. I've definitely been there this week, but I'm not sure when it was. Definitely Monday. And some of Tuesday too, I think. The police even came over one evening to check I was home. Luckily I was, that night.

But my phone keeps going off, and I don't know what will happen if I don't answer it. If I don't go where I'm asked to. I keep getting this tight feeling in my chest whenever I feel it vibrate. But that's probably normal, like adrenaline or something.

And it's better than school, in a way. Wherever I go, wherever they send me, they give me something to make me feel good – a bit of green or an orange one or some other stuff that I don't know. And the tightness goes away. The rest of the job or whatever they want me to do feels like it's happening to someone else.

But I wake up some mornings in my own bed, not entirely sure how I got there.

And the weekend doesn't start any better.

I wake up on Saturday to my brother and Mum going at each other. Brendon must have got in late – maybe he's only just arrived – and Mum's on the early shift again. Brendon says something about there not being anything to eat, and then Mum's screaming at him, and then the door slams.

I get downstairs and Brendon's picking up a bunch of coins from the floor that he says Mum threw at him before she stormed out. He puts the coins in his pocket, tells me I've got to go to the shops today, then he goes up to his room.

Brendon's right, there really isn't anything in the house. Some instant coffee and a couple of jars of pasta sauce in the cupboard, and half a packet of rice.

I make a coffee – two teaspoons and just an inch of water, like an espresso – and take it upstairs. The cash in the wardrobe is dwindling. I'm down to the last couple of notes. I'm sure there was more here than that. No worries, though; there's plenty in my account.

I peel a tenner off the thin roll and pull on some old trousers and a stained top. Maybe I could go shopping today, get some new gear. Or maybe do some laundry, save Mum the hassle.

At the shop I get bread, butter and milk, some tea bags, and a bag of apples because I feel like something fresh might make me feel a bit better. I also get a big bottle of orange squash and some washing powder. At the till I pick up a chocolate bar for the walk home.

The card beeps when I put it on the little machine, but then the light turns red. The cashier mutters something about how I need to put the PIN in. But I don't know it. I try the contactless again, but the same thing happens so I get the tenner out of my wallet. Good job I had a plan B, right? I have to choose between the apples and the orange squash, though, because I can't afford both. I go for the apples.

Back home, I make a note to ask The Guy what's up with the account, and if he can tell me the PIN again. It's probably been long enough that he's forgotten he never told me. He must have told me, at some point, I guess. Then I chuck four slices of bread under the grill, put the kettle on and start munching on an apple in front of the TV. It's not great, the flesh is a bit floury and crumbly. It's really sour, too. I should have got the squash.

I eat half, then go and turn the toast over. When I come back, the apple's gone brown. I put it in the bin.

I feel a bit more human as I crunch through the toast, the ticking under my skin calming down a bit – that might have been the coffee though. I make a cup of tea to take the edge off, putting in loads of milk and some sugar I find at the back of the cupboard. It's got black bits in but it tastes fine.

Then my phone goes off.

I ignore it at first – or try to – just let it vibrate on the kitchen table, its shrill little buzz filling the room. I'm finishing my toast, trying to focus on the crunch as my teeth go through the outer layer then sink into the squidgy bit in the middle. I'm really good at making toast, and always get it just right. With my eyes closed, I listen to the thick, crunching sounds in my own head, counting down the buzzes until I know it will stop.

Which it does.

But not for long.

The next time it goes off, I feel it in my veins. Like a little pulsing creature running through me, everywhere at once. My chest tightens and I get a weird feeling at the bottom of my gut, like a slow washing machine going round and round, sloshing and tumbling. For a second or two I'm outside of myself, noticing all these sensations, like you get when they give you something to make you calm down. Or like that moment when they leave you in a room on your own with the kit, so you can hide it, and when they walk out it feels like you watch a bit of yourself leave too. You know, that feeling like you're watching yourself on the CCTV as you do what you need to do. That's what hearing the phone go off feels like.

I'm on a weird kind of autopilot as I leave the room, like I'm watching myself get up and walk out. My brother's coming down the stairs and I partly register his puzzled look as I pass him. There's that welcome feeling of fresh air on my face as I step through the front door, kicking into my trainers, shrugging a jacket onto my shoulders.

'Are you not going to answer that?' he shouts as I

turn up the road, towards the heath, not really sure where I'm heading. 'Don't you think you should?'

I end up at Johnny's house. There's no answer when I knock on the front door, but I can hear something in the garden so I let myself round the side, reaching over the top of the gate to slide the bolt back.

Johnny's bouncing up and down on his old trampoline. It's been there years, since everyone had one, and – what with it being Johnny – it's one of the huge, almost-professional ones. We used to come back here after school to play on it, all of us doing front flips together and watching Luc do backflips and twists and everything. But it's been years since then. The springs are complaining as Johnny bounces up and down.

'You should have seen it when I started,' Johnny calls out as I round the side of the house. 'Little puffs of red were coming off the springs. Little rust clouds. I caught some. Look!' He shows me his palms, which look dusty and a browny-orange colour.

'How long you been on there?'

'Dunno. What time is it now?'

I go to check my phone, remember I left it at home. I shrug instead.

Johnny unzips the netting around the trampoline, hops down to the ground. 'I got really high a minute ago – just before you came – could see over all the gardens. There's a cat sunbathing three houses down, and the lady on the end's got her laundry out.'

'Great story,' I drawl, sarcastically. 'Tell me more.'

'Want a drink?' Johnny disappears through the open patio doors into his vast kitchen.

'Please.' I watch him go, leaning on the old-fashioned streetlight in the middle of the garden. I've never understood why his mum wanted it – the streetlight. It sprouts right up through the patio like a giant metal weed, and in all the years it's been there I think I've seen it turned on twice. At the bottom, there's a couple of pots of flowers. I stare at them for a while. The flowers are starting to turn brown. A little beetle crawls out of one of the flowers and my stomach does its slow whirring thing again.

Johnny comes back out with a can of Comeup, throws it to me before collapsing onto the garden sofa.

'How're things? How long's your mum been gone now?' I crack open the can and sit next to him.

'Five days. They left Monday.'

'Anna around?'

'No. She spent the night at a friend's. I played Xbox all night. Went for a walk up the Lanes to see if anyone was around but it was dead. Couple of people on the school field but they were year nines so I came home.'

'Doesn't sound like you, mate.' I smile.

'Yeah, must be getting old.' Johnny smiles back.

We sit for a while, nursing our drinks, the familiar tingling starting to come through as the sugars get into the blood. I see Johnny's foot start tapping, his leg bouncing up and down.

'So where were you last night?'

I shrug. 'Here and there.'

'Oh yeah?'

More silence.

'Ever see that blue van anymore?'

Straight away it's like I'm there again, body tense and buzzing in the train station car park, the ride to the petrol station, Johnny getting out of the cab, the silhouette of the man's face hovering in front of my eyes, indistinct and hazy. 'This is not a face you remember, boy.'

I shrug, maybe say 'no' to Johnny. I'm not sure.

These episodes and flashbacks are coming more and more frequently now, and even watching the video doesn't stop them every time. Waiting for a train last week, I felt this huge urge just to tell someone on the platform what was happening. I don't know why. There was a woman, about Mum's age, and she kept looking at me over the top of her phone. Maybe I could tell her, I'd thought.

Then she'd got up and moved down the platform, away from me.

And I'd realised I was still untouchable. But maybe not in a good way anymore.

'Are you alright, Mark?' Johnny's looking at me, looking at my hand in my lap.

'Yeah, fine. Why?' I realise my hand is shaking a little

bit, like something's tugging at it that I can't see. I've spilled some drink on my trousers which I try to mop with my sleeve. 'Yeah, fine.' I manage to hold my voice together.

Johnny looks at me, long and hard. I don't watch him watching me, but I can feel it. The back of my neck gets hot.

This lasts a long time.

Then Johnny speaks. 'I want to show you something.'

32

'What do you think they are?'

Johnny's standing next to one of the round ones, a thick circle of mushy newspaper that smells chalky, like a primary-school classroom. There are two house-shaped ones too, about head height, like children's playhouses dressed up as Egyptian mummies. Or ghosts.

'I found them yesterday. Look at this one! It's massive!' The biggest one is taller than me in the middle and looks like a crumpled dome that's slowly deflating. The newspaper on that one is drier, and when you flick it there's a hollow sound. 'What do you think?' Johnny says. 'Smash them up?'

I think for a moment, run a hand over the hardened newspaper surface. There are small ridges and dimples running through it, and it's warm. It's like skin, in a way. They're alive, these things. Like the whole of the copse is full of these little alien bodies that have beamed in overnight.

I wonder how to explain this to Johnny, though if anyone was going to understand, it'd be him. And Matt, maybe.

'No. Let's leave them.'

I give the big one a final pat. It sounds like a damp

drum. For a second, I want to crawl underneath it and live inside its echoey cave.

'Remember building dens up here, years ago?' I ask.

'Course.' Johnny's throwing pinecones at the large tarpaulin that's strung above the blobs. It's a pretty good job, the middle held on a high branch like a big-top at a circus, and the corners all tied off to tree trunks. It makes the copse feel like an event, as if a performance is about to start. 'This is where we first met, right?'

How could I forget. Johnny with his armchair, standing about where I am now. And me hiding in the best den ever, against that tree, there. I can't remember whose idea it was to start collapsing them, but I still feel the rush of bringing it all down on top of us, the ringing in the ears and the dull thud of a pallet to the head, the mad tumble and world-spinning weirdness of tipping backwards from a high place, not knowing where you're going to land.

I've been feeling like that a lot recently.

'John?'

'Yeah?' He's halfway up one of the trees, dangling from one arm as he looks down at me. He seems impossibly far away.

'Thank you. For that day. With the van and all that.'

Something moves across Johnny's face then. A shadow of something. I think he's about to speak, but he doesn't. Just smiles. 'No problem, mate. That's what friends do, isn't it?'

'I don't want to do this anymore.' I say this mostly to myself, facing the floor, kicking away at the leaf litter with the toe of my shoe.

'So don't,' Johnny says. He doesn't even ask what 'this' is. 'Stop doing it.'

Maybe it is that simple.

Johnny turns, carries on up the tree and sits there for a while. When he speaks, his voice seems to come all the way down from the sky. 'You should come see this, Mark.'

I swallow the lump in my throat, pull myself into the tree next to Johnny's and start climbing. The smell of sap feels real, solid almost. Pretty soon I'm level with my friend, and we look out from our tower across the heath and heather in the afternoon light.

'Where did that fence come from?' I ask, sun glinting on the wire. 'That's new, isn't it?' And beyond the fence, the ground has changed, too. It seems bigger than it was, and there are strange colours seeping through the sandy earth.

There's a dull rumbling sound from somewhere far off, and a yellow JCB slouches into view on the other side of the fence. It's pushing a heap of rubbish in front of it: piles and piles of bin bags, all rolling and spilling over each other as the digger shoves them along. Some rip slowly open and spill their contents, trailing entrails of trash.

As we watch, another machine arrives behind the first. It empties its load of dirt all over the rubbish that the first digger is spreading across the hillside. I look across at Johnny. He's studying the scene intently, his body perfectly still.

Both machines are driving forwards and backwards, forwards and backwards across what they've made, their engines thrumming and yawing, pressing the dirt and rubbish together until, from this far off, I can't even tell the difference.

*

When I get home, I let myself in through the back door. The Guy's at the kitchen table, spinning my phone in front of him.

'Got worried about you, kid.'

I freeze into the doorway, blood booming in my ears, my throat tightening. I think about turning on my heels and legging it. But a look over my shoulder shows me another guy standing in the garden. So I step into the room, try to sound as relaxed as I can. 'Yeah, sorry. Must have forgotten that when I went out. Is my brother in?'

The Guy fixes me with a stare. 'Nope. He popped out when I got here. It's just you and me.'

I fill the kettle, trying to calm myself down by doing normal things. 'Tea?' I look down the hall, towards the front door. Through the frosted glass I see a blue shape. The van on the road. No way out that way, either.

'No.'

I click the kettle on, then make a show of opening and closing cupboards, writing things down on a list on the back of an envelope. I see my brother's got through half the loaf of bread before he left.

Behind me, I feel The Guy move.

I'm leaning over the envelope, adding more fake food to my fake shopping list when my phone smashes against the cupboard six inches to the right of my head. The screen shatters on impact, showering tiny shards all over the worktop.

I turn, slowly, find myself caught inside the cage of The Guy's arms, one either side of me, biceps tight against the sleeves of his t-shirt and his thick neck pulsing.

'What...?'

My heart's churning in my ears, a sound like wind filling my head.

The Guy lifts the battered phone again, holds it right in front of my face, inches from my nose. He snaps the case in half like a twig.

'That's another two hundred you owe me.' He seems to speak through his nose, the voice cold, detached.

'What...? What do you mean?' I do a quick mental scan of all the places in my room I've stashed cash over the past few months.

'You owe me, Mark. Money. Lots of it. Best part of a grand by my reckoning.'

'What do you mean?'

'Think you can ignore my calls like that? You're costing me money right now, Mark. Do you think I'm going to put up with that?'

'But... What about the account? My account?'

'*Your* account...?' The Guy gives a dry laugh. Low and throaty, like the sound of a JCB engine. 'And I thought you were smart, kid.'

And then it hits me. He was never going to give me the PIN. There never was any money. Just pictures.

'I don't want to do this anymore,' I say, as clearly as I can. But it comes out as a tiny squeak, the opposite of brave.

The Guy laughs again. 'You'll be lucky to do *anything* anymore if you don't get me my money.'

I swallow, trying to think quickly. Then it hits me.

Johnny's party is this Friday.

'I'll get your money. Just don't show that video to anyone, OK?'

The Guy laughs. 'Think we're still interested in that? We've got more than enough to not worry about that anymore.' He reaches for his own phone, pushes the screen to my face and scrolls through picture after picture. And they're all of me – me in rooms at clubs, posing with stacks of cash and bags of green next to me, or me in rooms God only knows where. In some, it looks like I'm sleeping. In others, there are people with me while I'm asleep. I can't remember taking half of them.

'We've got more than enough here, Mark. No need to

worry about a skin flick of you and your boyfriend, mate.' He scrolls through more pictures, each image blurring into the next. 'More than enough here to make sure you can't get away from us. We're holding these on trust, you see? Now, about this money you owe me.'

'Just give me something to sell.' I blurt it out before I can think of anything else to say.

'I'm glad you said that.' The Guy smiles. He turns, leans down towards a small black bag at the foot of the table where he was sitting. Then he stops.

'You.' The voice comes from the doorway to the hall. 'Wasn't one of my sons enough for you?'

Mum is standing there, her eyes narrowed, her lips drawn back over her teeth in a scowl.

'Get out. Now.'

The Guy stands slowly, leaves the bag at the table. He grins at me once more. 'I was just leaving. Wasn't I, Mark?' He grabs my wrist, opens my palm and pushes the twisted remains of my phone into it. 'Until next time then. I'm trusting you, Mark. Remember that.'

He slides past Mum, putting his sunglasses on on his way through the front door. I hear the van pull away.

Mum steps into the room, walking straight past me and pulling out a chair at the table. The scrape of the chair legs on the floor makes me wince. But she doesn't sit down, just leans on the back of the chair, her shoulders hunched. I can't see her face, but I know her eyes are closed, tightly closed, her features pinched as if in pain.

I want to put my hand out to her, touch her shoulder, the crumpled uniform that always smells of whichever ward she's been cleaning on. But I don't. And then she moves and the moment's gone.

Mum throws her hospital ID badge on the table and moves through the kitchen. She's not seen the black bag yet, and I nudge it further under the table with my foot. She spots the half loaf of bread on the sideboard, looks back at me with a quizzical expression as she puts two slices in the toaster. Then she opens the fridge, pauses for a second before she pulls out the milk and butter. She opens the tea caddy, raises an eyebrow as she pulls out a bag.

'Kettle's just boiled,' I say.

Mum humphs.

As she walks back past me, she puts out a hand towards my chest. It stops just before touching me, then makes the last few centimetres of its journey very slowly, coming to rest just over my heart. Mum leaves it there for a second. 'Thanks,' she whispers. 'For doing the shopping.'

When the toaster pops and Mum goes to get a plate, I grab the black bag and slip out through the back door.

LUC

33

Johnny's outside, hiding behind the front bushes.

He's done this for years, waiting on the drive until he knows he's been seen, then hiding in the bush. My mum thinks it's charming. It drives Dad insane.

Maybe that's why he does it.

Dad's not home this afternoon. He's taken the Subaru out to a car-meet somewhere. He never tells me where they are or lets me come along anymore. He says not at the moment, with my collarbone like it is.

I can hear Mum downstairs, squealing with laughter. Johnny's found a tiny gap under the front bush and is trying to squeeze himself through it. From my bedroom window upstairs, I can just see his arms poking out. Mum laughs again. She must be standing in the front room window, watching him.

'Johnny's outside, love,' she says as I come downstairs. She's walking into the kitchen, wiping tears from her eyes with the heel of her hand.

At that moment, Johnny comes through the front door. He never knocks, which annoys Dad even more. His school shirt is all streaked in dust and dirt and old leaves from under the hedge. There's even a smudge on his cheek.

'Hi, Mrs Durel. I couldn't get through the hedge.'

Mum calls from the kitchen. 'Just be glad Lance isn't home. He'd have your guts for garters if he caught you.' She comes back through with a damp tea towel and starts mopping the mud smear from Johnny's face.

'Wasn't me. Must have been a badger.'

Mum flicks him with the tea towel. 'Why don't you two go out on the back deck? I'll bring you some drinks.'

Once Mum's stopped fussing and left us with a pitcher of lemonade and a plate of biscuits, I ask Johnny why he's here.

'Just checking in. Seeing how you are.'

'Whatever,' I laugh.

'No, honestly. I don't see much of you at school. Even lunchtimes. You still doing those extra sessions with Ms Kelley? Are they working?'

Actually, they are. In the few weeks since I did my collarbone, I've been going to see her most days, not just in our planned sessions. The first time she walked into her room to find me working away at my Maths homework at lunchtime, she almost spilled her tea.

'Luc?' She sounded surprised. 'What are you doing here?'

'Didn't fancy being outside, Miss. You mind if I work in here?'

She shrugged. I got a sense that she was trying not to look too pleased. 'Be my guest.'

I did twenty minutes straight and had almost got the hang of shape transformations by the time I was done.

Johnny's still looking at me, waiting for an answer.

'Yeah, they're fine,' I say. 'She's kind of making me do them until I catch up, but it's fine.'

'Good stuff.' Johnny takes a biscuit. 'It helps that she's fit, I guess.' Johnny says it like it's a question.

I laugh. Not long ago, I'd have felt the need to pick up on that, take it further. But I don't. Which is weird. I know the kind of thing I should be saying, form the words in my head, but I don't feel like saying it. Almost like I don't see Ms Kelley like that anymore. I don't know how to put it – it's not like I'm Matt and can do all that words stuff – but it's like she's actually a person.

This week, she kept checking her phone while I was getting on with some History. When I asked her if it was her boyfriend messaging her, she smiled and said it was her dad, actually. Turns out he's on a motorcycling holiday up in Scotland and she's making him check in twice a day because she's scared he'll get in an accident. He only started riding a motorbike when his wife – her mum – died a few years ago, and he's bought this huge, red bike that she said is terrifying. And he's up in Scotland on his own, going between bed and breakfasts on this big tour around the islands and stuff. And she's

293

worried about him. She just said all this stuff, and I listened and I wanted to make her feel less scared so we talked about engine sizes on motorbikes for a bit and I told her about Dad's car and how he lets me help with it and how I feel a bit worried sometimes when he drives really fast with me in it, and then I told her that I get a bit worried when he goes out for a drive on his own, especially late at night which he does sometimes, especially after he's had a shout at my mum, and I said I worried about him because I know he's driving really fast round the ring road, taking the roundabouts too quickly. And it was a really easy conversation. Then I went back to work, getting key dates on flashcards for Queen Elizabth the First's relationship with Spain. And now, for some reason, I'm telling all this to Johnny and getting this weird feeling in my stomach like a kind of excitement, but not really.

Johnny doesn't interrupt, just lets me say it all. 'How's the shoulder?' he asks when I'm done.

I roll it a bit. I can't feel the ends of the bones grinding together anymore, and I'm managing to sleep better at night even though I still have to sleep sitting up. 'Yeah, not bad,' I say. 'Hey, do you want to see something?'

'Always,' says Johnny, leaning in.

I unbutton my shirt and pull the skin tight over the place where my collarbone is healing. 'Feel there,' I say, and Johnny runs his fingers across the weird lump

294

that's forming. The doctor said it would do this, that the bone would have to form extra tissue to link it back to itself. 'It's called a fracture callous,' I tell Johnny.

'That's gross, mate.' Johnny does a pretend gag, but he doesn't stop touching it. 'So you made a gap in your bone and it filled up with more stuff?'

'I guess so.'

'Will you always have it?'

'Yeah. The doctor says it might go down after a while, once the bone underneath has sorted itself out, but there'll always be a lump there. Ow! Don't push too hard, mate.'

'It's like magic.' Johnny rubs his fingers together, like they're remembering the feel of my fusing bones.

I put my shirt back on. 'Some people have huge ones where the two ends of their bone don't go back together properly and end up overlapping a bit.'

'What, like this?' Johnny takes his left wrist in his right hand, and his right wrist in his left.

'Yeah, I guess.'

'That's amazing.'

We sit in silence for a bit, enjoying Mum's lemonade. It's even got real bits of lemon floating in it, not just out of a bottle.

'Is Anna still OK with Friday?' I ask.

'Yeah, she's fine. Invited a little group of her study friends over, says she's going to keep an eye on things, but she's already put an order in with Mark so....'

We let the name hang there for a bit.

Johnny breaks the silence. 'Does he seem alright to you? Mark, I mean?'

'What do you mean by "alright"?'

'He's been at school all week, which for him is unusual, and he's been talking to everyone about Friday, as if he's actually going to be there. So I guess he's fine?'

What I want to say back is 'He's better than he's been in ages', but that would mean talking about a whole bunch of other stuff, and I don't really know how that would feel. Instead, I say, 'Yeah, absolutely fine.'

Johnny's leg has started to twitch, and his eyes are darting around the garden, looking for something to do. I wonder how long it'll be until dinner, and if Johnny'll stay.

'He seems to be back in business, though. Lots of orders for Friday. It's gonna be a good night.'

'Yeah, definitely,' says Johnny, though I get the feeling he didn't hear what I said.

34

The next day, I get a text from Sara. I made new accounts on all the apps she uses but somehow she knew it was me and never accepted my requests. Her text doesn't say much; just *how's your head?*

My heart's in my mouth when I read it. It's the end of first period, and I'm standing in a full corridor, year eights pushing their way around me.

'Luc Durel, that's not a mobile phone I see in your hand, is it?' Mrs Clarke's wading through the crowd towards me, folder under one arm and a coffee cup held high over everyone's heads like she's the Statue of Liberty, which was a gift from France to the USA, dedicated in 1886, my History revision cards say. God, this stuff is actually going in.

I pocket the phone quickly. 'No, Miss.'

'Good. A word with you, if I may. Can you walk and talk?'

Mrs Clarke barks at a few boys for pushing and leans her head through one of the classroom doors to tell a teacher I don't know that she's got one of his tutees for a lunchtime detention today. He nods, looking as scared of Mrs Clarke as we kids are. I walk along in her wake, trying not to look like I've done something wrong.

We get outside the languages block and she starts talking. 'Ms Kelley tells me you've been working with her at lunchtimes and after school. Is this right?'

'Am I in trouble, Miss?' I don't want it to sound as rude as it does, but I'm strangely angry at her for getting in my face about my work again.

She turns, raises an eyebrow at me.

I look at the floor. 'Sorry, Miss.'

'Indeed. Sit.' She gestures to a cluster of picnic benches we're passing.

I do as I'm told, swinging my bag onto one of the tables and climbing up next to it.

Mrs Clarke perches on the edge of another table, facing me. 'What I *wanted* to say, Luc, is that I'm very impressed.' She takes a sip of her coffee, then puts the mug down carefully next to her. 'I know you didn't find last year easy, and I'm very sorry that you can't play any sports at the moment. I know how much that means to you.'

I look away. My body's definitely missing the activity. I swear my stomach's getting bigger, even though I'm doing sit ups most days. But there's a strange quiet in my head these last few weeks, knowing that I've not got a game or a match coming up. 'Yeah,' is all I manage to say.

'But I did want to say how pleased I am that you're showing this level of maturity. That you're *doing something about it,*' she taps her folder with each of these last words. There's a pause where she looks at me, then she carries on. 'And Ms Kelley says you're getting results already? Something about an English practice paper?'

I'd got a grade 5. My first ever. The paper is still in my bag, scrunched up at the bottom. 'Yeah,' I say again. I was going to show Dad, but now he'll be angry that I've not taken pride in keeping my work neat and won't even look at the grade. I showed Mum, though.

'Well, that's good.' There's a pause. 'Isn't it?'

'Yes, Miss.'

Another sigh. 'Well, there we go then. I've said it. Well done.'

'Can I go now, Miss?'

'Yes, you can go.'

I'm swinging my bag back onto my good shoulder as Mrs Clarke stops me again.

'Just ... keep going, Luc. Keep doing what you're doing. Can you do that?'

'Yes, Miss.'

I'm already walking away.

I find an empty toilet and lock myself in a cubicle. I have to use a girls' toilet, firstly because none of the boys' have doors on the cubicles anymore, and secondly because if I got found in a cubicle everyone would think I was about to have a poo and I'd never live it down. Another of the rules of the school game, I suppose. Sometimes they get tiring.

I send Sara a message back. *Head's fine. How are you?*

Then I wait.

Her message comes back a few seconds later. She must have copied and pasted it in.

You really hurt me, Luc. I don't just mean physically. You were the first boy I'd really wanted to be with. There was something in you that I really liked and what I thought would just be a holiday romance could easily have been much more, until that last night. It wasn't even the fact we'd both been drinking, was it? When you started talking about all the girls you'd been with, and what you'd done with them, something changed in you. Did you feel it? Something came into your eyes, like you were a different person. I couldn't believe it, how you treated Amy – was that her name? Alice, maybe? – as if she was nothing. I started thinking that that was how you saw me; just another conquest, another girl to tell your friends at home about. I just wanted to get out of there, and you were really scaring me. In a way I hope I did hurt you. I hope I left you with a scar. You've certainly left me with one. I haven't told anyone about what happened, and I don't even know why I'm sending you this. I'm going to block your number again after it's done, and please don't try and contact me anymore. It's taken me a long time to write this, but for some reason I wanted to tell you that I really, really liked you this summer. That's what hurts

300

so much. I don't want to think forever that I could have been that wrong. I'll never trust myself again if that's the case, and I can't live like that. So I need to tell you that there's something in you that's much better than the person you showed yourself to be on that last night. I never want to see you again, ever. But I hope you'll find a way to make yourself into that better person you can be. A part of me hates myself for writing this, but I know if I don't send it then I'll keep thinking about that night, and I don't want to. If what happened between us means anything, you need to do something about it, Luc. You need to make yourself a better person than you were to me. It's time to do something about it. Have a good life, Luc. S.

I read the message again and again. The bell rings for the end of break, making me jump, but I don't move for another ten minutes, my eyes roving again and again across Sara's words.

I try to reply, just one word. 'Sorry'. But the message gets rejected.

Then I type 'I love you' into the box, just to see how it feels.

Then I delete it.

I stare at the screen until it loses focus, feeling my pulse through my fingers where they hold the phone.

On the way out of the bathroom, I see myself in the mirror. It catches me by surprise – none of the boys' toilets have mirrors – and I wheel around to look behind me. For that split second, I genuinely think he's in here with me. For a split second, I think my reflection is my dad.

I go back to the mirror and stare at it. I pull my fist back, ready to put it through the glass and bring the whole image showering down.

But something clicks in my collarbone, like the bone scar has stretched and weakened a bit.

I lower my arm, breathe deeply, stare into those eyes. My eyes.

Time to do something about it.

MATT

35

I want to work on the sculptures for a bit before the party. The weather's been uncharacteristically dry this last week and the papier-mâché has pretty much all set. I got a coat of yellow on the houses and the big dome last night and used a whole tin of silver spray paint on the ones I've formed around the old car tyres. I should be able to add all the details this evening before I head to Johnny's.

I spot the yellow from way off. I should probably find something to hide them with. As I get closer, wading through the damp heather, the big one looms up massively. Goodness knows how I'll get it over the fence and onto the landfill site, but it's come out better than I'd hoped. All the crinkles and imperfections are perfect, like it's being slowly deflated. It's going to look great when I get the face on it. I brought black, blue and white paint, but I haven't quite decided what emoji it's going to be yet: a crying-with-laughter emoji or just a straight-up, smiling emoji? What emotion would you be if you were lying there deflating, half your face buried in landfill?

I run a hand over it, checking around for any more signs that someone's been here. When I came a few days ago, there were scuffs in the leaves that seemed fresh, and a dent in the side of one of the tyre sculptures. But maybe I'd made that. Or a badger, perhaps? I considered smoothing the dent out, but I left it in the end; they're supposed to look crushed anyway, like used cans. I get the paints out and start with those.

They look brilliant in silver, and ready for the ring pulls and graphics to go on. I've decided to do different brands on them, each one a slightly different, crushed can of Comeup. It's easy to make the logos look recognisable, even when they're crushed up. Anyone would know them in an instant.

Once they're done, I move on. I want the houses to look like toys, so I do red roofs and bright blue doors, and really simple windows on them with blue curtains. They look like something out of a Mister Men book, which is perfect.

It's getting almost too dark when I start on the emoji. I go for a big, grinning mouth in the end, with gleaming white teeth, like he's happy to be half buried. I mix a bit of the blue and black with what's left of the yellow to get a brownish colour for the mouth and eye.

As I'm finishing off the eye, maybe I get a bit carried away and, with a soggy, tearing sound, my brush goes through the thin layer of newspaper. It's

304

not a big hole, but I'm so angry that I almost put my foot through the whole thing. I catch myself, breathe deep.

The eye looks wonky now, the bottom of it curved up the wrong way like an upside-down eyelid or something.

Then I have a thought. I get the white and blue and put a dash of each in the bottom of the eye.

I step back. It's really dark now, so I can't see it too well, but it's worked. Despite the massive, goofy grin on its face, it looks like it's about to cry.

Before I go, I check the overhead tarpaulin one more time. We used to be up here in rain all the time, and always stayed dry under the trees, even when it was chucking it down. But I check the tarp anyway, just to be absolutely certain that everything will be OK.

Then I turn to leave.

That's when I see it, glinting in the dark. The light of the low moon creeping under the branches is reflecting off its surface.

It's buried in the leaf litter, just where I thought someone had been scuffing around the other day. I put the toe of one trainer underneath it and lever it up. Whatever it is comes out of the ground with a small pop. I put my phone light on to see it better.

It's Mark's old biscuit tin. All the paint's gone from the top, but there's still a bit of the familiar pattern around the side.

I pick it up, give it a shake. It's definitely not empty. Whatever's inside makes a series of light thuds.

I wonder what it could be. A pack of cards? Some old ropes, perhaps? No, they were never valuable enough to keep in the best tin. Books, then? It sounds like paper inside, a muffled *dumpf* against the side of the tin as I shake it. But when did we ever bring books up here?

Then it hits me: it's Luc's stuff. One week, it must have been before year nine started, he brought sheets and sheets of pictures he'd printed off the internet. He'd found his dad's laptop still logged into a porn site and he'd printed off reams of images, must have been fifty pages, thousands of thumbnails of girls doing stuff with other girls, or with men or groups of men. He'd poured over them for hours, asking us what we thought. We all went through this awkward show of laughing at them, making fun of the expressions, Johnny re-enacting the poses with himself. Then we'd all stopped – Johnny, Mark, me – grown tired of it. But Luc didn't. He sat there, in the armchair, the day growing darker and darker, cross-referencing the pictures, ranking them.

I don't want to look at that stuff, but it'd be funny to show a few of them to the boys tonight. I smile in anticipation, imagine the look on Luc's face when he recognises them. It might even bring him down a few pegs. Maybe I'll take the whole lot with me, present him with them as publicly as I can.

I'm still smiling when I pop off the lid.

Then I drop the tin. And scream.

An actual scream. Not a high-pitched, horror movie scream, but a from-the-gut, deep-shock scream that brings the sweat out cold under my arms and across my forehead.

It isn't Luc's pictures at all.

It's Mark's seagull's wing.

There are still a few recognisable feathers, their tips sticking out like pins. I think I can make out the end of a bone, round and smooth in the middle of the mess of old skin and tendon that's petrified to a treacly liquid. The whole thing looks like it's been dipped in tar. And there are speckles of what looks like red powder all over it; I don't know what part of the bird that used to be.

I swallow the nausea creeping up my throat, strangely drawn back again, closer.

Then I hear the buzzing.

From somewhere inside the sticky, half congealed mess, a fly emerges. Then another. A third follows. This one's got something stuck to its leg. Something that's moving. Writhing.

A maggot.

And then I see another, crawling around at the base of the bone. And three more, half covered in the black mulch.

It dawns on me what the red powder must be – the

307

egg casings from hatched maggots. Maggots who've spent years in that dark tin turning into flies, mating with other flies and breeding more maggots who've fed off the remains of the bird and the bodies of each other as they died and rotted in the blind and endless dark, being born and dying again and feeding their future maggot babies on themselves.

My stomach's lurching, but I force myself to pick up the tin again, slip the lid back on and carry it carefully to the edge of the trees. I launch the tin and all its contents as far as I can into the air, out from the place where me and my three best friends used to play, towards the landfill site.

Then I'm running, away from the copse, down from the heath, towards Johnny's house and the promise of people.

I don't even wait to see the tin land.

Once I'm close to Johnny's, back under streetlights and breathing easier, I check my phone. Fifteen messages and a couple of missed calls, all asking where I am, or where Mark is.

There's a message from half an hour ago saying Mark's arrived. Then nothing.

Maybe they've given me up for dead? Especially now they've found precious Mark!

Johnny's house shows none of the signs that there's a party on. It's properly dark by the time I arrive, and the downstairs windows are all curtained, just little rims of orange light showing around the edges. And it's quiet.

I go round the back. The side gate's open, and I step through it into the yellow glow from the fake Victorian streetlamp that Johnny's mum had put in the garden. It's pretty tacky if you ask me, casting everything in an odd, gassy light.

There are signs of life coming from the kitchen, the dull blur of voices through the closed back door like they're underwater. But there's no music.

As I open the door, I realise why it's so quiet. I have to squint against the smoke. There are about twenty people in the room. A few are passing an e-cigarette between them that adds to the weather system over their heads: a think-cloud of gently roiling smoke. Everyone else seems to have a joint, which they're smoking, studiedly. Some kids are coughing, their eyes watering. In the middle of the kitchen, on the breakfast bar, is a wide bowl, almost full of green. When they're not blinking away tears from the smoke, or from coughing, everyone's eyes are drawn back to that bowl, as if it holds some kind of dark secret. The weird atmosphere seems to emanate from there. Hardly anyone is talking above a low murmur. All the thin lines of smoke look, for a second, like strings, as if all these people are puppets, controlled by that big thunderhead above them.

I can't see Mark, Luc or Johnny though.

Anna comes into the kitchen, reeling like I did at the fug. She shuts the door quickly behind her, and it looks like someone's stuffed tea towels or something around the edge of it to make a seal. Anna wedges a few of these back in place. The double doors to the lounge have been shut and sealed, too, and a couple of dining room chairs put in front of them to stop anyone trying to get through.

She spots me through the gauzy air. 'Matt! You're here! Everyone was worried about you!'

She picks her way across the room, her eyes not quite focussing as she throws her arms around me. I can smell the alcohol on her breath. Cider, maybe. But sweeter. Maybe she's mixing it with Comeup.

'Grab a smoke. There's loads. Johnny gave Mark the rest of our 'fending for ourselves' money. It's on the house!' She does a woozy impression of an American hostess and attempts a curtsy.

I catch her as she almost tips over, hold her around the waist. Then she laughs, throwing her head back. 'Oooh! We're dancing!' She takes a few clumsy steps, throws an arm up towards the ceiling in a final flourish. 'Ta-daaa!'

'Can I let go now?' I try to smile as I speak, aware that I'm at a party. No one wants to be the overly concerned prude who arrived late and puts a downer on everyone else's good time.

Anna nods, and I let go. She puts both hands flat against my chest, her head at about my shoulder height. I remember when she used to be taller than me. Than all of us. This last year or so we've all switched around. 'Oh, little Matthew,' she coos. 'My baby brother's gay friend.'

'Er… OK?'

'I wish…' and she tails off, shaking her head. 'No, nonono.'

'Wish what?'

She beckons me to lean down a bit, stands on tiptoes to stage-whisper into my ear. 'I wish it was you who'd walked into the kitchen. Not Luc.'

I look at her slightly sideways. 'Anna, I *did* just walk into the kitchen. I've got no idea what you're talking about.'

Her look shifts then, and she seems to notice the cloud of smoke over our heads. She winces, wafting away a particularly offensive tendril. 'God, can't these people open a window or something? Anyway, they're all in the snug. Mark, too.' She tries to bop me on the nose at this last titbit of information, misses, and pokes me in the eye instead.

'Alright. Thanks.'

Anna puts her American hostess voice back on. 'Now, get out of the way of the fridge, honey. Mamma needs her medicine.'

I leave Anna to it and try to remember which room 'the snug' is. Before I go, I lean past one hunched form at the table and take a joint from the bowl, slipping it behind my ear. Maybe I'll feel like it later.

Moving deeper into the house, it's a relief to be out of the smoky kitchen. The tea towels and the shut door are doing their job though, and in the hallway there's only a faint echo of the smell. But that could just be what I carried out on my clothes.

The kitchen sofa has been moved into the hallway, probably to keep it from sponging up smoke. Facing it, on the little hallway table, are two orange buckets, both half full of water and a few last slivers of ice. In one, a couple of cans of Comeup are floating belly up, like dead fish. A couple of bottle tops in the other attest that it used to hold beer. I pick up a can, flick as much of the water off as possible, and open it. I could do with the energy. I sit down on the sofa, tip my head back and drink deep. But I get a sudden, vivid flashback to the flies, for some reason feeling like they're inside this can, crawling down my mouth.

I stop drinking, close my eyes, put my head between my legs.

When I open them, I spot a half-empty bottle of vodka that's rolled under the sideboard. I force myself to down about half of the Comeup, then refill the can with vodka until the mixture starts to bleed through the mouth hole, the familiar orangey-red colour and that over-sweet, chemically warm smell spilling out, cut with the shock of the vodka. I take a few quick gulps, shuddering the liquid down my throat.

Low voices are coming from the hallway's slightly open doors. The intense, concentrated mood doesn't seem unique to the kitchen. There's some music playing in one of the rooms, but it's on low. It's as if I've stumbled into a nuclear-fallout bunker or something, and everyone's trying to stay quiet and hidden.

The Comeup goes through me quickly and I get a sudden urge to urinate, so head for the door that I think is the downstairs toilet. It's slightly ajar but, as I push the door open, I hear the flush go, instantly turning on my heels. 'Sorry,' I shout to whoever I've disturbed. 'Fucking … shut the door though?'

'The fuck did you say?' It's Luc's voice. 'Oh. It's you.'

We stand in the doorway for a second. Luc's not wearing the full sling anymore, just a kind of rubbery, neoprene strap that keeps his right arm against his chest.

'You alright?' he says. 'Bit late, aren't you?'

'Yeah, stuff to do. Sorry.'

'What you saying sorry for?'

'Dunno. Sorry.'

'Stop saying sorry, man.' He gives me a light punch on the chest with his good arm. 'Get out my way, then. We're in there.' He points across the hall.

'Ah, *that's* the snug.'

'Yeah, I never know which one's which either. You seen Anna, by the way?'

'Just now in the kitchen, why?'

'Nothing. Heard she was looking for me.'

'Actually, she did say something about you walking into the kitchen one day, yeah.'

'She what?' Luc's eyes flash dark again, his brow knitting slightly.

'She's pretty far gone though, almost going left, I'd say.'

Luc does a small laugh in his throat.

'What?'

'Nothing, man. It's just, when you say things like that, it kind of sounds like an adult's saying it. Like it doesn't fit you. Know what I mean?'

'Kind of, yeah.' I smile. I keep smiling for longer than feels comfortable. 'Anyway, can I go for a piss now?'

''Course, mate.'

We swap places awkwardly in the doorway. I'm about to close the door when Luc speaks again.

'Hey. Sorry, man.'

'About what?'

'That day in the gym. Changing rooms. When you…'

'Oh, *that*? Don't worry about it, mate. All forgotten.' I wave him away, wonder if that also sounded like an adult was saying it, too. It certainly didn't sound like me.

'See you in a bit, mate.' Luc turns, heading for the snug.

I shut the door, lean back against it and take a deep drink from the can before putting it on top of the cistern and unzipping.

I'm mid flow when the door opens behind me.

'Sorry, I'm nearly done.'

'No bother. I'll wait. Lock the fucking door though, yeah?'

'What did you…? Oh, it's you.'

315

MARK

I've sold more green for tonight than I ever have before. In total, I reckon. It's mind blowing.

Johnny's been on PR for his party, and I've been getting messages all week, people putting in orders. I found my old phone, my old old phone, and it's not been quiet all week. I've memorised all the orders, costed them up, then deleted the messages, though. Just in case.

Good job I did, because that policeman was back this week. Got called out of History. I was kind of enjoying the lesson actually, about trade and business in Elizabethan England or something, colouring in maps with different colour arrows about where all the stuff was coming from and going to – and there he was again in Mrs Clarke's office. Mum, too.

The policeman said he'd been round to the house, been through all my stuff and found money.

Was it illegal, I asked him, to have money?

He said it was quite a lot of money, that my mum didn't know where it had come from. He must have found a stash I'd forgotten about.

I said it depends on how much you define as 'a lot'.

He asked what I'd been getting it for.

I said I'd been using it to buy the shopping. Mum nodded.

He said that wasn't answering the question, and I said that it was.

Then he took me into the other room and did another search and went through my bag. He asked if he was going to find anything in my bag that shouldn't be in there.

I said no. And he didn't. Again.

Did he think I'd be stupid enough to bring it into school? I'd taken the black bag straight up to the copse as soon as The Guy had left, hid it under one of the round blobs that were up there. Someone had come back and painted them silver, and the two house-shaped blobs and the giant blob were yellow. Bright yellow. I didn't have time to work out what they were, or what they were for, but they looked pretty awesome.

I'd checked the contents of the bag. Loads of green, a few bags of the orange ones, and something else: a couple of very small bags of creamy-white powder that I'd seen people use a few times, when I was out on the road. I'd never taken it myself. At least, I don't think I have.

So I'd clocked how much was there, made a mental list, then stashed the bag and gone home. The policeman had no chance. He was a low-level miniboss; I was untouchable again. He'd given me my school bag back and looked a bit disappointed. Upset, almost. He said if there was anything I needed to tell him, I could do that now.

I said there wasn't.

Anyway, a few more days and it will all be over.

Back in Mrs Clarke's office, the police officer said he'd give Mum the money back. Mrs Clarke had said something about being innocent until proven guilty and keeping a close eye on me. Mum agreed to do the same. But she had to work again tonight, so...

This evening, before the party, I went back and got the stash. I took Mum's old kitchen scales and divided it all up and worked out I still had some stock leftover. I was definitely well up on what The Guy said I owed him. I'll pay him in the morning, crisis averted, everyone happy. Minds blown.

I even started to feel pretty good again – excited about seeing my friends. About seeing Matt.

I popped half an orange one on the way down the hill to Johnny's. To celebrate, I guess.

I got here early and filled the bowl up with joints, sat rolling them at the table with Johnny. He'd seen the powder, too, and asked what it was and could he buy some. I said maybe later. See how it goes. But I won't mention it again. I don't want to see anyone on that stuff. Not here.

Anna got the buckets sorted and set some drinks out. She was worrying about how much people would bring, and about the smell, so I had the idea to seal off the kitchen – and if we carried the kitchen sofa into the hall, I'd said, there'd be no soft furniture in the kitchen, so the smell wouldn't last as long. Genius, they'd both said. Brendon used to do that with his bedroom. I'd know not to disturb him if his duvet was on the landing, and he'd time his airings between Mum's laundry missions. He didn't always get it right, but if Johnny and Anna's parents are going to be gone for another week, and if the doors and windows are left open until they come home, they won't know a thing. Genius.

So we filled the bowl with joints, then me and Johnny smoked one just before everyone else arrived.

And when they did, it was like Christmas had come early. I stood in the hall, handing everyone their orders as they arrived, attracting cash like a magnet or something. Tens, twenties, big bunches of fives. Some kid from Anna's year asked if they could do a bank transfer. Idiot. I sent them to the cashpoint at the garage down the road. They came back all apologies, crisp new notes in their hand.

I started to remember why I liked doing this in the first place.

So now, with the green all gone, I've moved onto shifting the orange ones. There must be a hundred people here, and on average they've all given me a tenner, I'd say. But a few of them I don't recognise from school – Anna's other friends, maybe? who knows – so I set about trying to find them, upsell the benefits of the orange ones: the high, the euphoria, the buzz that comes on quick.

Johnny's already done two, and is locked into the Xbox in the snug, his fingers flying over the controller. He's got one of those gaming chairs with the speakers built in, and it's like he's in a little cocoon in there, knocking back all challengers like he's one with the machine.

After doing one round of the whole party, I settle in the snug for bit, watch Johnny run amok on whatever shooter he's playing now, thrashing Luc who says he needs a piss. I wonder aloud where Matt is, but the other two don't hear me. Then I start my rounds again, passing Anna on her way down the stairs for more drinks: she's taken half an orange already and is having a great time. There are people in all the bedrooms upstairs, except Johnny's parents' room, obviously, and I swear that everyone takes a big breath in when I put my head round the door. It sounds like distant applause. Everyone's loving it. And even those people who haven't bought yet, they're watching their friends to see how they come on, to check it's OK before they buy, their little faces all lit up with wonder.

And I'm the wonder man. Bringing the joy.

LUC

Mark's on one. He's all twitchy and keeps getting up and walking around the place, trying to do his businessman thing. And that little black bag he won't put down, stuck to him like glue. He's wearing it on his chest and looks like a prick.

Not that I can talk.

I slip my arm out of the sling and rest it on my lap while I'm playing Johnny on the Xbox. It feels comfortable enough, but I can't move it much without it hurting, which is why Johnny keeps beating me. He's completely in the zone though. I don't know how much Mark's sold him but he'll go left in a bit and end up a mess on the floor, like he always does.

I keep offering him water and Cokes and stuff. But he'll only drink Comeup. After he's gone through a can and a half, I move the coffee table a bit further away from him so he can't reach it. I don't know if it would be a problem, mixing Comeup and the oranges, but part of me thinks it's best to be on the safe side.

I'm not really feeling this party yet. Alice is here, and Amy, but I haven't said hello. They're in the big sitting room with the music. It needs to be louder, though. They're singing along – I can hear through the wall – and I really don't want to go in there, but I will, later, when I get in the mood, and the music improves. Then I'll go and say hello.

I go for a piss and have an awkward conversation with Matt, who's just arrived and smells like an art classroom. Even though he tries to come into the toilet while I'm in there, I breathe through the flash of red and try to be kind. When I say I'm sorry about the other week, and he waves it off, I get this weird feeling of lightness for a moment, like something I didn't realise I was carrying has slipped off my shoulders.

Matt said it wasn't a problem, but he's lying. I can smell his lie, even through the paint and the whatever else smell. There are a few flecks of yellow on his t-shirt, too. Kid isn't even making an effort. I thought gay guys were supposed to take some pride in their appearance, at least. But maybe he's lying to make me feel better.

Either way, I want to say thank you to him. But I don't, just watch him go into the toilet then head back into the snug.

Mark's on his way down the stairs, pushing another couple of notes into his little black bag.

'Was that Matt?'

'He's having a piss, yeah. You coming back for more? Reckon Johnny's gotta drop that winning streak soon.'

'Yeah, in a bit.'

I leave him in the hallway.

MATT

'You're late.' Mark shuts the door behind him. I hear the lock click.

'Yeah, something I had to do.'

He stays there, leaning against the door while I finish. I can feel his eyes on me.

I pick up my drink, take another deep gulp, and turn. Mark's gaze shifts away from me a split second too late. I drink again, smile into the can. 'So. Hey.'

'Hey. You alright?'

'Yeah. Fine… Did you need to…' I gesture at the toilet.

'No, I'm fine. Just thought I'd come and say hi.'

'Well, you're saying it.' I want to add a 'for a change'. But I don't.

He's brimming with something. His eyes land on me for the occasional moment then fly off again, looking everywhere around the room but at me. It's electric in here. 'So I took an orange one…'

So that's what it is. 'And…?'

'And do you want one?'

'You gonna charge me this time?'

He steps closer, shaking his head. 'My treat.'

I'm trying so very hard to play it cool, but surely

he can hear the rushing in my ears, the swirling in my stomach.

'Do you remember what happened last time?' His voice is thick and honeyed.

I take a step towards him, vodka and Comeup and courage rising up through me like a fountain. 'Kind of, yeah. Did it go a bit like this?' And I take his head in my hands and push my mouth against his. He's sweet, like the drink, but there's an earthy warmness, too. He puts his hand on the small of my back, pulls me closer.

Then he pushes me away again. His finger is on the edge of my lips, and I feel him tip something into my mouth.

He breathes into my ear. 'Let's wait until later, when you're up, yeah?'

I swallow, my muscles twittering with anxiety and apprehension and excitement. 'OK.' My hand finds his and our knuckles link together. We both squeeze.

Playdough.

We kiss again, long and deep. Then Mark turns and opens the door.

'Do you think you could lose this, though?' I twang the strap of his bag. He's wearing it on his chest, across his heart. 'Looks a bit … y'know? Shit?'

Mark laughs. Gods' tongues are moving everywhere.

MARK

I could do anything right now, go anywhere, but when I heard Matt was here, that was where I wanted to be. With him. I'm not saying it saved me, that video of him looking at me, but it definitely kept me from drowning a few times. But after tomorrow, I won't need it anymore. There'll be nothing left to drown in.

Just Matt, looking at me for real.

He follows me out of the toilet and into the big sitting room, and it's amazing having this huge ball of energy trailing after me, like he's roped himself onto my back or something, just from looking at me. Like I'm a speedboat and he's water-skiing behind me, and his look is connecting us. And I think maybe this is the orange talking but I don't care.

In the big sitting room, there are about thirty people all lounging on sofas or on the floor. There's a fuggy, greenish smell, probably creeping in from the kitchen. And it's dark, the spill of yellow from the garden streetlamp the only light. Everyone's chill, but it's a weird vibe, and not the vibe I'm on, so I call out 'Up Up Up' and everyone's getting slowly to their feet, following me.

Someone's already synced up a few speakers and I turn up the volume, the bass starting to seep into the floor and the lyrics fuzzing up, but I don't care because I'm throwing my head around and the room is struggling to keep up with me and Matt's putting his can to my mouth and I take a long drink from it, my eyes locked onto his. He unclips the black bag from my chest and his hands are like sparks inside my ribs so I let him, watching where he throws it, down the side of one of the armchairs. Tomorrow, it won't matter where it is because it'll all be over, but for now I go and check it, just to see where it is. Then Matt's pulling me back across the room, back into him, and everyone's dancing, dancing, dancing.

LUC

When the volume picks up next door, Johnny doesn't really register it, just keeps locked on the screen, the controller clicking and bouncing in his hands. I gave up a few minutes ago, lost all my lives, so he's completed the last few levels on his own and shows no sign of slowing down. We're the only ones in the room.

'We need to talk about your dad.' It comes out of nowhere. To be honest, I thought he'd lost the power to speak.

'What?'

'Your dad. He's not very kind. Do you need help?'

'Fuck off, Johnny.'

The words 'Continue? Y/N' appear on the screen where Johnny's hit pause. I look away.

'Just checking in, mate. Making sure you're OK.'

'I'm fine.' I knock back the rest of my drink, swallowing hard.

'And your shoulder. Was that him?'

'No. Fuck, Johnny. No. I told you.'

'Yeah, you did. Some guy called Dell. Ex-professional or whatever. But you know what I mean.'

'No, I don't.' There's a few seconds of silence. 'Just keep playing, Johnny. I'm going to get another drink.'

I walk out of the snug, shoulders drawn back and aching with tension, particularly the right one. I bring my left hand up to rub it; consciously tell myself to unclench my fist.

I walk into the big room, the music breaking on me as I open the door. It's dark, but I spot Mark and Matt in the middle of the room, having a moment or something. I can't see Amy or Alice. Fuck that, too.

Stepping back into the hallway, I see Anna heading up the stairs. She almost trips at one point, and she giggles.

So I follow.

MATT

The orange comes on strong. I've never taken a whole one before and the room is flashing and spinning, the background blurring and washing and twisting and every nerve in my body is firing. I feel each individual hair standing up on the back of my neck and on my arms as Mark traces his fingers over them and my fingertips can feel each individual hair on the back of Mark's neck, and I know his fingers can feel mine, and it's all almost too much but also I want more.

'I'm up,' I shout into his ear, pulling his head in close to mine. I can almost taste the sweat on his forehead.

He smiles at me, nodding, pulls my waist towards him.

There's that pounding deep in my gut again. The wonderful terror and excitement, like I'm about to jump off something really high.

Mark's leading me by the wrist through the throng. There must be fifty people in here now and it's getting hot. We pass Johnny on the way out but he doesn't seem to see us. He's sitting on the armchair, Mark's black bag in his lap. But Mark doesn't notice. He's leading me out of the room. He's the leader and I'm following him, again, up the stairs.

MARK

It's a game at first, Matt putting his hands on me, trying to find my skin, me knocking him away, moving and writhing on the bed – Johnny's, I think – as he, lying on top of me, tries to move closer. Then his hand's under my shirt and it's not a game anymore.

Through the open window, a roar rises up from downstairs as the patio doors from the big lounge open and the party floods out onto the lawn. The music that was rising through the floor, through the bed, through our bodies, is now coming through the window, too. It feels like we're inside it, the music, my heart beating along with it.

I can hear Johnny's voice, slippery and warm through the window. He's running circles around the garden. It's like an ambulance siren, his voice going away and coming back, up and down, in and out of the music.

Matt hears it too, the weird patterns in the sound. Our eyes open at the same moment, fix on each other. He's above me, his head framed against the window, the yellow light from the ugly old lamppost giving him a strange halo.

'Should we shut the curtains?'

'No. I want to see you.'

LUC

'Bitches must have gone downstairs while I was getting drinks,' Anna says, standing in her empty room. She drops eight cans of cider on her bed. 'I only stayed for a joint. I wasn't long.' She seems to be speaking to the ceiling.

I step through the door. 'You alright?'

She spins around, her body tightening. 'Luc? What do you want?'

I stay in the doorway, trying to read Anna. I tell myself to wait for a sign that I can come in. But I don't know what I'm looking for. 'I was calling you. Thought you wanted to talk to me.'

'Why would I want to do that?' Her hands are fiddling with the hair at the back of her neck, drawing it into a knot, sliding on a hairband.

'Matt said.'

'Matt? No. Don't think so. But you might as well have one of these, as you're here. Come in.' She picks up a can of cider, throws it at me. I catch the can and step into the room, surprised the sign was so clear. I was expecting some girly flutter of the eyelids; something difficult. But she'd actually just said it.

I open the cider, sit at her desk on the other side of the room. 'So...' I start.

'So indeed,' she smiles, opening a can of her own and sitting on the bed.

'You alright?'

'You already asked that.'

'You didn't answer.'

There's a noise from downstairs, voices in the garden and the music rising in volume again. Anna looks a little startled as Johnny's voice blares through the window. I go over and look out across the garden.

'They've all gone out the back. Johnny's doing laps.'

'Oh God. The neighbours are going to go mad.' She comes to join me, pulls back the curtains and we watch as Johnny is chased by what seems to be the rest of the party around and around the garden, ducking tackles and arms all over the place. It's started raining very lightly, and there's a slippery sheen to the grass. After two laps he takes his shirt off, spinning it around his head as he runs, hollering halfway between wolf and foghorn.

'My fucking brother. What is he on? And what's that dangling around his waist?'

'Dunno. Looks like that crappy little bag that Mark was carrying earlier.'

MATT

Maybe it's the noise outside, but suddenly I feel like I'm underwater and I need to breathe.

I push Mark away. He thinks it's part of the game at first, until I shout out and he rises to his knees on the bed, a strange look on his face.

A few droplets of water have collected along the outside of the window frame, and they hold the pale, yellow glow from the streetlamp in the garden. They throb in my eyes like overripe fruit. I lean out underneath them, feeling the coolness of the light rain against my face. I close my eyes, and they seem to turn around and swim inside me for a bit, up to the top of my head.

Mark comes up behind me, his arms closing around my stomach, his hot breath at the back of my neck. 'What the fuck is Johnny doing?' He smiles into my ear.

'Who knows?' I smile too, my eyes still closed.

'Shit, is that my bag he's got?'

Mark's out of the room in a second, pulling his shirt back on. I look out of the window, through the milky yellow air, the smoke from the kitchen billowing out where that door's been opened, too. It mixes with the light and the rain, making a yolky mist.

I watch Johnny. There's something trailing behind him. It looks like a comet's tail, a ghost of white powder, tracing the places where he's just been.

MARK

I bring Johnny down at the second attempt, unclip the bag from his waist as he lies on his bare back against the grass, laughing. Going straight for the front pocket, which is still zipped up, I do a quick check and see that none of the cash has gone.

But the middle pocket's wide open. There are a couple of packs of orange ones left, not as many as there were when I put the bag down ... how long ago? I can't tell.

And half of the powder is gone.

I look back at Johnny, his face gleaming with sweat or rain or both. His eyes are closed, and his chest is going up and down really quickly. I can almost see his heart pushing against his ribs with each huge beat, and his pulse racing around his body, the veins in his jaw bulbing.

Then I see the powder.

There are bits of it around his nose, on his upper lip. There's a cluster on the bit between his nostrils and even some in his hair.

'How much did you take, Johnny?' My voice falters a bit, suddenly sober and dry in my throat.

'You shouldn't be here,' says Johnny, his eyes still

closed. New beads of sweat are forming on Johnny's face and chest as he speaks. 'You should be up there.'

He points behind me, to the open window where Matt's still standing, looking down.

'Johnny, how much did you take?' I think about phoning an ambulance. I saw this once, at a club I was sent to. Some bouncers had a guy in a little room – a guy who looked like this, sweating and full of too much blood. They'd shut the door as I walked past but I saw it again and again in my dreams.

'It's where you're supposed to be, Mark. Where you fit, you know? Where the map says you're supposed to be.'

'What are you on about? Can you sit up?'

'I can see it, Mark. All of it. How it all fits. The lines between everything and the threads and the wires and how it's all one big map, one big game plan. And you're supposed to be up there.' He's almost shouting now, words erupting from him with no space in between for letting a breath in.

Then Johnny's eyes are open, but it doesn't look like Johnny.

LUC

'At least if the neighbours really complain, your mum might not go on holiday so much anymore,' I say to Anna as we watch Mark try to catch Johnny. Johnny slips through his fingers once, twice.

'True. I'll drink to that.' She lifts her can and we clink. 'Ooh, he's got him.' She opens the window, leans out. 'Be careful with my brother, Mark!' she shouts. There's a buzz of laughter from the crowd gathering around Mark and Johnny where they're stopped on the grass.

Mark's sitting on the ground, going through his bag. I never knew a guy more obsessed about his stuff. I'm about to shout something at Mark, tell him the bag looks crap anyway, when Johnny starts shouting.

When Johnny gets back to his feet, I turn to Anna, the drama over. But her face has changed again, not happy anymore, but concerned. She's stepped back slightly from the window, her arms folded across her chest. I put an arm out to her. 'Are you OK?'

'Oh God,' she says, almost to herself.

Then I look back out of the window, see what she's seeing.

Johnny's at the bottom of the streetlamp. He starts climbing.

MATT

He's saying something like 'I'll show you'. I can't hear properly because the rest of the party have started cheering him on as Johnny goes hand over hand up the streetlamp, the whole thing wobbling violently.

It only takes him a second to get to head height. A few people raise their arms to help push him up. And then he's beyond their reach.

I spot Mark, standing at the back, his eyes flicking between me and Johnny, who's about fifteen feet in the air now, halfway to the top. Mark's clutching his bag to his chest, and there's a look in his eyes I don't recognise.

Johnny's at twenty feet – about the height of my window – and still going strong when I hear a voice from the window next to me.

'Johnny, get down!' It's Anna. 'Get down, Johnny!' She's stern, sounding like a parent. Then she adds, quieter. 'Please, Johnny.'

Then another voice – Luc's, from the sound of it – strong and deep. 'Johnny! Stop!'

Johnny hears this one, looks towards his sister. He stops climbing. And smiles.

But then he's off again, reaching up to the top of the streetlamp where there's a kind of rod that runs straight across just under the lantern itself. Below him, the crowd's cheer rises again.

In the room next door, Anna screams.

MARK

I take a few steps back as other people push past me, keen to be as close as they can as Johnny dangles just below the top of the streetlight. Anna's in her bedroom window, Luc's one good arm on her shoulder like he's trying to stop her from climbing out. In the other window, Matt is fixed to the spot, watching.

Johnny gets his legs over the bar, pulls himself up so he's hugging the glass lantern at the top of the pole. He must be almost as high as the roof. As he moves across the lamp, the whole garden is suddenly dark, a huge Johnny-shaped shadow falling across everything.

Then it goes light again.

Johnny is on his feet, standing on the top of the lantern. There's a feeling in my stomach like that first time in the copse, just before he brought the den crashing down.

But this time, it's not a game.

LUC

As Johnny pulls himself up and stands on the top of the streetlamp, Anna's clawing at the window slows, then stops.

Below us is a sea of faces, all looking up, all lit by the same yellow glow. Slowly, I ease my arm away from Anna, her body rigid and trembling. I step gently to the window.

Could I reach him from here?

I think, maybe, I could.

For a second after Johnny slips – and it was a slip, wasn't it? – he looks like he's going to stay there, held in the air by some miracle. I reach out to him, lean as far out of the window as I can.

Below, all the people breathe in at once, with a sound just like a can makes when you open it. And, for a split second, Johnny's right there, suspended in the air, just beyond my outstretched fingers.

But then gravity gets hold of him, and he starts to fall.

MATT

And I remember the yellow air around Johnny like he was underwater, and the barely audible pop, like a bubble bursting, as his trainer slipped. Then silence.

For that half a second, it was like the silence was keeping him there. As if all those people, faces tipped to the light, believed that the combined power of their looking could hold him up, could stop him falling.

But they couldn't.

I don't remember him landing because I didn't see it. I closed my eyes against it, closed my eyes to the possibility of it, against the inevitability of him landing.

Which, of course, he had to.

But I didn't see it. So when I close my eyes at night, there's still the possibility in my head that he's still falling.

Even after all the sirens and flashing lights and questions and tears that followed, in my head there's a world in which Johnny hasn't landed yet. He's still falling.

No. Not falling.

Flying.

JOHNNY

I had a lot of time to think while I was falling.

It might not seem like it, because every moment is as tiny as the tip of a pen – no, thinner, a needle – scratching itself into the endless map of everything that has ever happened.

But what I discovered when I was falling, wondering where all this time was coming from, is that above the needle is a huge upside-down pyramid-shaped thing which is *all* time, not just the stuff that we see and feel, but all of it, together. Time with a capital T. And that's all pushing down into each single moment. So inside every moment, or above it, is Time: everything that happened before it and everything that could possibly happen after it.

And that's quite a lot of Time to wander around in, isn't it?

So I did.

When you think of a pyramid, picture one in your head, it has smooth sides, doesn't it? Four, smooth, triangular sides that are all the same. That's what Time looked like, at first, while I was looking up at it and getting used to the falling. But actually, the more I looked at it, the more I realised that the Time pyramid is dusty and sandy and ancient, just like the actual pyramids at Giza. But upside down and balancing on the tip of a needle. Obviously.

Mum and Giles visited them once, the Great Pyramids, on one of their trips to Sharm El-Sheikh to finish their scuba-diving certificates. Mum sent me some pictures. They were amazing. I had to pretend Mum wasn't in them to look at them properly, but that was easy because she was just this little speck at the bottom of the picture. Behind her, each stone block was the size of a room, and there were thousands and thousands of them. What was really amazing was that actually the blocks are all square, so each side of the pyramid is actually shaped like a gigantic staircase. It's not smooth at all.

So to make something that square and blocky look like it's smooth, you have to stand a really long way away, and it's hard to stand a long way away from something that's so big because you need lots of space to stand a long way away *in*, right?

And there was me, looking at the upside-down pyramid of Time, and the edges looked really smooth, which must mean I was a *long* way off. A long way outside of Time. Too far away to get back from.

And that made me sad for a bit.

And then I remembered about the whole 'the present moment is a needle at the tip of a pyramid' thing and I realised that I am – or that a part of me is –

already inside all the moments that ever happened anyway, and as those moments are still happening and will always be happening, because they're inside all the other moments, I *did* stay. *Am* staying. In a way.

I'm inside the pyramid, inside Time, pushing down on the present. Always.

That made me feel better.

Another thing I love about pyramids – the real Egyptian ones I mean, not the ones made out of Time – is the booby traps. They're just stories, really, but it's fun to imagine that, if you go into a pyramid, and find your way to the middle where the important stuff is, the stuff that no one's supposed to be able to get to, then the whole thing might collapse on you because of the way it was built. In reality people stole stuff from pyramids all the time. There weren't really any traps like you get in films and games and stuff. But it's good to think about. I used to spend hours as a kid, planning out booby traps, and how to make rooms collapse or fill with sand or whatever. I'd make them out of Lego.

Then I met Mark, and we started building dens. And we booby trapped them, so they collapsed.

If you look around at anything that anyone's ever built, you know that at some point it won't be there anymore. It might last for thousands of years, but eventually it will all disintegrate to nothing. Even the Great Pyramids – the real ones – will be sand again, eventually. And think about sand for a minute. Millions of years ago, sand used to be animals and shells and life and a whole bunch of other stuff. It was a whole *sea*, at one point. Even *oceans* aren't safe. Maybe there's a whole other pyramid thing for 'stuff, I don't know about that. Just Time. On a long enough timeline, everything collapses and turns into everything else.

But if you know exactly when something's going to collapse, you're in control.

When we did that, built those dens knowing that we were going to destroy them, it's like we owned the future.

But, of course, we didn't.

It's a game, really. You play with control, with power. Sometimes you know you don't have it, and you pretend that you do. And sometimes, when you know that you do have it, you make believe what would happen if you didn't. Sometimes it feels good to lose control, but only when you know you had it in the first place, and you know that you'll get it back again.

Some people like to play with other people's sense of control, too. But that's another matter.

Too much talk. Something needs to happen, now. I could go on like this for ages – I've got ages, huge upside-down pyramids' worth of ages – but nothing's happening.

For you, I mean.

So let's do something.

Imagine me stood way outside of everything – let's

say I'm in a huge desert – and I'm looking back at this smooth-looking, upside-down pyramid that's balancing on the tip of a needle. I can't really see the top of the pyramid – the widest part disappears into some milky, slightly yellow clouds. And I can't see the needle, either. But I know it's there.

And now imagine me running back towards the pyramid, towards that needle-point moment where I'm falling through a very small bit of air between the top of an ugly garden streetlamp and the ground. I'm running really fast, the desert floor a blur under my feet. Maybe imagine I'm flying, Superman-fast, just above the sandy surface.

I'm getting closer, the pyramid looming larger and larger in front of me, and I'm under its shadow now. I look up and see the crumbly edges, all that jagged rocky stuff above me, each block like a room. Some of the edges flake off, big cracks appearing as I watch, and lumps of Time peel away, falling into the space around me. As I run on, they land behind me. Except they don't land. The desert that I've run across isn't there anymore, just a big black expanse that the old bits of Time fall into and keep falling, away from everything.

The sharp point of the needle is still a long way away, but I change direction, flying upwards towards the middle of the pyramid.

I can do that here.

I'm travelling almost straight up now, the opposite

of falling, heading straight into the blocks, the passageways and possibilities of everything that has happened and might happen. I slow down, passing each block. And I see that each block isn't just *like* a room, it *is* a room.

So I go into a few.

Here's Mark, who ran from my house as soon as his legs would let him, burying his little black bag on the heath. Sniffer dogs will find it, but it will be empty and clean of his fingers, and of Matt's touch on the strap, too.

In the next room, Mark sits at his kitchen table with his mum and two police officers. They are kind, really, and made uncomfortable by Mark's tears. Mark's brother watches from the hallway. He can't remember the name of the friend he brought over, who played with his brother at the kitchen table and gave him money. Now the table isn't a kitchen table but a colder table in a police interview room. There are more people around it, and papers, and pictures of faces that Mark points to and then turns away from, crying into his mum, who cries into him. In another room there are maps on a wall, with pins and string and the pictures of the faces that Mark pointed to, and then the wall of that room is in a courtroom and Mark's voice is there too, but not Mark, he is elsewhere: just his voice in the room, saying what happened as he remembers it, right from the start. And people listen to him.

And another room is the back of a blue van, a pile of ropes and straps in a corner, the smell of oil, an unrememberable face staring down at him, and I watch as Mark tries to hold himself to the floor as the van rounds a corner, his fingernails tightening into the dust on the wooden boards. The van door opens and he is thrown out of it but Mark lands back in the van again, this moment replaying itself, again and again, and somewhere inside all the other rooms of Mark's life this moment is always replaying – in a corner, or under a chair.

In one room, the echoes of this moment are very loud. In this room of the pyramid, the kind police officers were not able to help Mark as much as they wanted to. This room is a small, pale room, with a metal grill across its one, small window. There is a single bed, and above it Mark has stuck photographs and pictures from magazines – those pictures he is allowed to put up. There is a desk with a few books on it and a small wardrobe with the same clothes as everyone else here wears.

Further inside the pyramid are rooms where Mark is older. In one he is going to work with his mum: his first day. In another, he wears a suit, sits at a small desk and taps away at a keyboard. In another, the suit is more finely cut, the car he drives is bigger, and the desk he sits at is in a room on its own. He makes phone calls, buys things, sells things. He blows minds.

Mark leaves this room and drives to another. It is well furnished, bright and full of air. In this place, he has a room which he calls 'the snug', and it always makes him smile. But in a sad way.

There are a couple of rooms with Mark and Matt in them together, but many, many more rooms in which they are not. In the rooms that they share, they often talk about me, and about what happened. It brings them closer, makes these rooms stronger, somehow. But in the rooms where they are alone, perhaps they look happier. Here's a room where Mark comes home to his airy house, and in the snug is someone else, and there is a child, too, running to meet Mark at the door. In some of the other rooms, Mark lives there alone.

In many rooms there are old Marks. He looks after his mum. Or he doesn't. He hasn't seen his brother for years. Or they're as close as can be, living next door to each other, uncles to each other's children, great uncles to their grandchildren. There are rooms all around the world, in cities looking out over the blinking lights of skyscrapers and ant-like traffic far below, rooms in countrysides with views of fields. In each room he speaks, confidently, surely, about his life, how to impress people, about what people want. In each of these rooms, he brings the same advice. Never make yourself untouchable.

Luc is not old in any of the rooms in the pyramid. He leaves it in his late thirties: a car accident. Or loses control of his motorbike at twenty-eight. Or is caught in a natural disaster a long way from home, trying to save a young family.

He is a paramedic, a car dealer, a mechanic in some rooms. In other rooms, the owner of a gym, or a chain of gyms. A few times, a leisure-centre worker. Once, the manager. And, for a short spell, a PE teacher. Before Time takes him.

He is, by degrees, kind or unkind, wearing his scars closer to the surface, or deeper, so that when they bubble up it's as if from nowhere, bursting out in displays that surprise and disgust any number of possible wives, girlfriends, or something-in-betweens.

In some ways, he is always like his father. In others, he is his complete opposite. Only the ways change.

For a while, Luc is kind to Anna. That strong arm, the arm that he put around her shoulder as they watched me fall, stays there. She leans into it, my brilliant sister, hides behind it and the arm keeps the world out for a while. Long enough. It is her rock, and Luc likes being that for her. She stands behind him, sheltering when she needs to. He is a safe harbour, which is good for them both.

They part when she leaves school. She comes home rarely, staying at university, losing touch with her mother – our mother – and everything she did or didn't do. In the rooms where there are children, she always names them after me.

Luc watches her go. Grows from it. His shoulder heals, the joint in the bone fading to a ripple, only there when he touches it. In some rooms of the pyramid it breaks again. Sometimes it's the other side, sometimes an arm or a small bone in the foot. Once, it's a whole leg in a cast from ankle to thigh after a skiing accident and pushing himself too far, too fast. But pain is always useful for Luc. Instructive. If only to show him where he can't go. And even then, sometimes he ignores it.

But there is no pain for Luc in the rest of that whole pyramid quite like the pain he experiences at my funeral, standing with Mark and Matt, with everyone he knows, almost. No pain like that creature crawling through his stomach, aching in his veins. He feels he could have caught me. Should have pushed himself harder. I want to tell him that he couldn't. But after that stuffy church, Luc decides he will never again lose in that way, never again feel that kind of loss. He builds himself a shell around the parts of him that can be hurt like that.

There are no alternatives, in all of Time, to that room full of people wearing black, crying silently into the vaulted ceiling, the occasional sob echoing up into the rafters then fading out like candle smoke.

Mark, Luc and Matt sit in the front row. At the start.

Then Matt moves to sit between his parents, the small protection of their love around him. That's his shell.

Matt never gets to place the sculptures that he made. Never gets to enlist the help of his three friends as he thought he would, to carry them stealthily by night across the fence line, into the landfill site. To see, as he'd imagined, the photographs in the news the next day of his deflated, yellow face buried in rubbish. The Throwing Away of Happiness, the Ephemeral Nature of Joy Beneath the Burden of Late-Stage Capitalism. He had lots of titles for it. But they, and his first major artworks, go unseen.

Unlike the rest.

From that point onwards, Matt's futures are endless. He has more rooms in the pyramid than even I, here in this moment, could ever explore. But I do know that all of them are filled with pictures and painting and sculpture and beautiful colour and life because I'm allowed to know that kind of thing in this place. There will be rooms full of people who come to look at Matt's work, to draw from its colour, to imagine themselves inside it.

A few weeks after my funeral, something draws the three of them back to the copse as winter begins to tighten over the heath. And the sculptures are there, too. Of course they are. The playhouses, the crushed cans, the punctured emoji. And, Matt thinks, perhaps they're better off here. More honest. The way a gravestone is honest.

I stay in this room, this moment, for a long time,

sitting in the corner of the copse with my three friends – the entrepreneur, the athlete and the artist. I watch them all wonder to themselves what could have happened, if it could have been any different. No, I tell them. That's not possible.

It's only the future that you can change.

Unless…

What if…?

Let's play a game. One last time.

Imagine me flying again, back out of that moment, back through the pyramid and down, down towards the needle, the very point of it, where it scratches its place into the endless map of everything that ever happened. Here it is, so small you can barely see it, but you know it's there.

Now, imagine me pushing it. Imagine me pushing with all my strength against that single, teeny-tiny and immovable point in time. All my weight and my power charging into that atom-spec with everything above weighing down on it so heavily.

And think about how the gap between 'nowhere' and 'now here' is really small, but that it counts for everything. A tiny, inconsiderable little gap, teeming with possibility. And think about the gap between two bones that magically fills with something completely new, made from the two ends that insist on joining back together.

Imagine the needle again.

Imagine it starting to move.

Just a teeny bit. That's all we need. As much as that gap where one word becomes two; just as much as that little space on a page or a tiny crack in a bone. And above me, Time is crumbling, rearranging itself as vast chunks of the pyramid peel off and fall forever past me, past the needle on the map of everything. And I'm pushing so hard my vision starts to blur. So hard that everything around me starts to shift and flow over itself, yawning in and out of focus like it's all made of thick fluid, all bubbling and roiling and twisting around itself until it goes black.

And then it's not black anymore. Not completely.

There are small pinpricks of light behind my eyelids. And a faint smell of burning. And of something else, too. And is that laughter I can hear, trailing out into space? It has a colour. It colours the light.

Brighter and brighter, little orange flares are sparking out of the nothingness that surrounds them, like the briefest of stars.

Everyone's setting their socks on fire.

ACKNOWLEDGEMENTS

Making a book is an ensemble effort and I am deeply grateful to everyone that's helped bring this one into the world. To Jane, my agent. To Penny, for being as enthusiastic about these characters as I was and for being generous with your insights. To Anne for capturing the book so brilliantly on the cover. To Karen and Graeme for holding my hand through the promotional side of things and to all the team at Firefly for being amazing to work with in all ways. Huge thanks to Katherine and Caleb for early reads and suggestions. And to my family, always.

Mostly I'd like to thank all the boys I've ever met. Within these pages are the boys I grew up with, boys I have been at one stage or another, and many, many boys that I've had the privilege of teaching in my sixteen years in the classroom. You have all, through your grace and humour and sheer brilliance, given me the power to get through some difficult times and for that I'm deeply grateful. You are all distilled into these pages, and I hope that readers take you to heart in the way I took you to mine; awkwardly sometimes, and in spite of your faults. Because even when the world looked bleak and hopeless, I knew that at least one of you would find a way to make me want to play again.

Also by Luke Palmer, Grow (Firefly, 2021)

Shortlisted for the Branford Boase First Novel Award and longlised for the Yoto Carnegie Medal

Read the opening pages here:

There won't be any explosions in this book.

Sorry if that's going to be a problem. And, while we're at it, there won't be any chasing around at night, or encounters with the undead, or werewolves, or vampires or anything of that kind either.

Sorry.

A few years ago, I loved those kinds of books. I'd imagine myself in a world where all the adults were dead, or gone, or both. I think I'd have been OK. Maybe not the leader of one of the rebel gangs that stalked through the abandoned streets, shouting orders that various underlings followed with glee. It wouldn't have been me that was surrounded by hard-faced kids in ragged clothes. But I'd definitely be surviving, a sharpened stick in one hand, straddling a bike kitted out like a tank, ready to dash back to my stash of pilfered tins in the belly of an old barge down on the canal. I used to love imagining myself in those situations.

But I grew out of them.

I don't know why I liked them, really. It's pretty grim stuff, imagining your parents are dead. And enjoying it. This book won't be like those books.

It will be real.

It won't be about the future, or the past, or a world where the superpowers have gone crazy and bombed everyone back to the stone age.

You don't need all that to create terror.

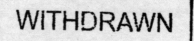

WITHDRAWN